# JESUS SWEPT

Praise for *JESUS SWEPT*...

"Chock-a-block with local color and cosmic lunacy, James Alexander Protzman's first novel is the opposite of a Chinese meal: the prose is lean and the style spare, but this tasty text continues to satisfy long after the last page is turned."
—James Morrow, *The Last Witchfinder, The Philosopher's Apprentice*

"Lean, mean, irreverent, and perverse only begin to describe this comic and outrageous satire on Southern archetypes. You could say, Harry Crews meets Christopher Moore in a head-butt! Redneck druggies, false prophet tweakers, a racist Marine, and an a university fund-raiser turned telepathic are spiritually entwined in their search for the concise meaning of life. Is it "Do good. Be nice, Have fun." "Do. Be. Have." "Do behave." or "Doobie have."? The answer will come to you through James Protzman's clever, fast-paced, and imaginative prose."
—Vicki Hendricks, *Cruel Poetry, Iguana Love, Sky Blues, Voluntary Madness*

"James Protzman is the George Carlin of the literary world, skewering with brilliant characterization and storyline the veil of religious mythology that threatens to suffocate our society. But Protzman also understands and respects our longing for answers in life. *Jesus Swept* embraces the mad chase in all its futility, humor, and hope."
—John Manuel, *The Canoeist*

"James Protzman's *Jesus Swept* is a rare accomplishment: the satire is sharp as an Exacto blade, yet the characters become real and lovable. The voices are irreverent, yet the plot leads to sweet redemption. The eye is critical; the philosophy, uplifting. This novel is funny and full of growing suspense, dry wit and wild imagination. What a combo! I highly recommend it."
—Peggy Payne, *Sister India, Revelation*

# JESUS SWEPT

James Alexander Protzman

Kitsune Books
*Quality books for eclectic readers*

*Jesus Swept*

Kitsune Books
P.O. Box 1154
Crawfordville, FL 32326-1154

www.kitsunebooks.com
contact@kitsunebooks.com

Printed in USA
First printing  2008

ISBN:  978-0-9792700-7-9

Library of Congress Control Number:  2008929351

Cover Design: Scott Buzik
Back cover portrait: Lissa Gotwals

*Jesus Swept* is a work of fiction. Names, characters, places, and
incidents are the products of the author's imagination or are
used fictitiously. Any resemblance to actual events, locales, or
persons, living or dead, is entirely coincidental.

For Jane

*Never take an old broom*

*into a new house.*

# 1

Two hundred miles east of the southern part of heaven, the disciple named Luke paces in the dark outside the Airstream he calls home, his black skin glistening in the wash of a single streetlight. He lifts up his glasses and squints through the drizzle at a scene that matches his mood. A crumbling cinderblock bathhouse. Busted plastic chairs. A row of worn-out trailers. And still no sign of Jesus and Mark.

"Luuuuuuuuukkke."

He startles at his name brushing by on the wind and spins toward the sound. Some body ducks behind a dumpster, the hint of a halo trailing in the night. Luke turns again and finds Jesus himself, his five-foot frame shivering cold beneath a flimsy purple poncho.

"You s-scared the dickens outta me," says Luke.

"I didn't mean to."

"Did s-so."

"Did not." Jesus wrestles with his plastic wrap. "Help me out of this thing?"

He smiles, raises his cool gray eyes to heaven, mumbling something that might be a prayer. Luke feels the quiet pressure.

"Thank you," whispers Jesus. "You're always there."

"I wouldn't count on always." At six-three and two hundred pounds, Luke towers over the little savior like a dark mountain. "Where's that pizza you promised?"

"I have food to eat that you know nothing about," says Jesus.

"Do not."

That's when Mark pulls up in the Jeep with a large pepperoni pizza.

"Do so," says Jesus.

Mark climbs from the car, pulling a fat roll of bills from his jeans pocket.

"Twenty-eight smackeroos," he says. Mark's been sweeping sidewalks at the strip mall all day, guilting shop owners into paying for his work.

Jesus does the Macarena in a tight little circle. "Woohoo!"

For most fundraising professionals, twenty-eight bucks wouldn't warrant a fancy dance, but this would be their best haul in weeks. The young men have been working their way up the Carolina coast since July, sweeping almost anything for anyone who'd pay. They even got hired to sweep the Hooters parking lot at Myrtle Beach.

Late one night, though, as they worked out back, a six-pack of Harleys swarmed in around them. With visions of lynch mobs, Luke quieted his broom. But Jesus and Mark just kept on pushing.

"What're you faggots doing?" said the man with the most chains.

"We're sweeping. I'm Jesus."

Mr. Chains had dealt with plenty of punks in his biker career, but the Jesus thing threw him off.

"Jesus, my ass," said another biker.

"No. Jesus, my lord." Good old Mark.

That biker got in Mark's face. "Jesus. My. Ass." The words were a threat, but Mark didn't care. He puckered up his Latin lips and smooched, which is all it took to land him in the emergency room with a broken collarbone.

Figuring they'd had enough of South Carolina sin, Jesus and his two disciples followed a trail of trash north to Wilmington, then on to Sunrise Island, where things really fell apart. It was last Saturday, a quiet day at the beach, with low waves, clear skies, and no wind. Mark was hanging around the pier, hitting up tourists for small change. Luke had waded into the surf with Jesus on his shoulders, when a big wave came out of nowhere, a speeding wall of cold green water that flipped them in a tumbling crush. Luke grabbed for Jesus, but couldn't get a hold. All he caught was the thick silver bracelet Jesus had worn since the day they'd met that summer. And then he dropped it, just like that.

They dove for the bracelet again and again till they ran out of breath and hope. It was gone.

Jesus slogged out of the surf and found Mark sitting in the sand.

"I cannot fucking believe this," said Mark.

Jesus shook water from his tangled hair, his eyes on Luke still diving in the waves. "Blessed are they who don't say fucking all the time."

"Blessed are they who don't lose the only thing they have that's worth a goddamn."

Jesus blew a long sad sigh. "I know."

This sweet Jesus tumbled into life nineteen years ago in a doublewide outside Conway, South Carolina. A week after his premature birthday, his mother abandoned him on the steps of a tidy Pentecostal church, whose congregation took less than twenty-four hours to push him straight into the harsh hands of Gus Gray and his wife Glenda Kay.

A full-time drunk and part-time snake-handler, Gus mostly wanted another slave to go along with the one he was married to, and that's exactly what he got in the boy he named Gary. Young Mr. Gray went from crying to crawling in their four-room shack, and soon became his daddy's second personal servant, shining his shoes, cooking his meals, and taking his belt without complaint.

If Kay worried about little Gary's safety, she didn't show it. In fact, she welcomed the boy's interference, steering clear of her husband by working in the Airstream trailer out back, where she handcrafted brooms.

Gary was five when his mother got swept up in the gentle art of broom-making on a visit to the South Carolina state fair. Over the next ten years, her own rare talent emerged as she married gnarled wisteria branches to handsome cornstraw heads. Twisted Kays, she called them. Collectible country chic.

Business was good for awhile. But then Kay got greedy and things went to hell. She'd been watching a preacher on TV as he read from the Gospel of John, chapter eleven, verse thirty-five. The preacher said "Jesus wept" but Kay heard "Jesus swept," and a marketing plan was born. She soon created a dozen magnificent brooms with polished dogwood handles and fancy hang tags, each inspired sweeper named after one of the twelve apostles.

Little Gary loved the happy play on words, but his daddy saw only sacrilege. Gus ripped the tag from the broom named Simon and threw it on Kay's workbench like a gauntlet. Cheap bourbon sharpened the edge in his voice, but Kay wasn't backing down this time. She smiled sweet, tucked the tag in her apron pocket, and headed for the door. Which was exactly the wrong thing to do. He accused her of being a shitty wife, and she answered with a bank statement showing a two thousand dollar balance. In honor of her financial success, he stomped the fingers of her right hand to mush with his steel-toed Timberjack boots. Glenda Kay Gray would never make another broom.

The winter after high school graduation, Gary watched as his family home burned to the ground with his dangerous daddy and depressed mama sleeping inside. When the ashes settled, he inherited a Jeep Laredo and a vintage Airstream trailer filled with a dozen unsold brooms. He hauled the trailer to Myrtle Beach, where he landed a job sweeping at K-Mart. Over the next couple of years, he settled into an easy routine, working days, chatting online at night, and trying to soothe his not-quite guilty conscience.

The truth is, Gary Gray hadn't meant to start that fire. He was just cleaning the stove when his dishtowel puffed into a bright ball of orange flames. Before he knew what happened, the kitchen curtains caught, and then the wallpaper. He imagined the black wall of smoke rushing into the cramped room where his keepers slept. What would Jesus do? He left through the back door.

On Sunday mornings Gary scoured North Myrtle Beach for treasures with his Holy Grail metal detector, walking for hours, mining the bad luck of others. He loved the static crackling in his super-sensitive headphones and the rush of real signals beeping through the white noise. Last Memorial Day, the pickings were especially good. Sun-burned drunks honoring dead soldiers can lose lots of stuff in a hurry, and Gary had nearly filled the pocket of his shop apron with detected metal. He made one last sweep down the beach. The silver was singing.

*These are the threads of life fully filled.*

The silky string of words slipped through his skull like a brain freeze, stopping him cold in his low-tide tracks. He wavered and wobbled, swinging his detector back and forth, zeroing in on the song beneath the sand.

Gary had heard plenty of strangeness growing up in a Pentecostal church, but this was the first time he'd ever come across buried music. He dug and sifted the clumpy sand, his blood pulsing faster the deeper he went.

Then he felt the quiet clink that treasure hunters die for.

The bracelet was his.

Later that night he polished the thick silver to a gleaming glow, discovering enough strange engravings to qualify for latter-day sainthood. Like Moses on the mountain with his magical commandments, like old Joe Smith and his wondrous golden tablets, little Gary Gray took the symbols for a sign. The bracelet's whispery voices made him Jesus overnight.

Lucas and Markos jumped on the Jesus bandwagon a few days later in front of Ripley's Believe It or Not, where they had been looking for summer work. The new Jesus showed them the bracelet and said follow me, which is all the boys needed to take the ride. Neither could resist the silvery pull.

Plus Jesus had wheels.

# 2

When a back-sliding Baptist sees a sign from god wash up on the beach in front of her, she should know enough to worry. But with her passport to paradise having long since expired, this Sunday stroller wouldn't know a sign from god if it bit her on the butt. Which explains why she doesn't so much as flinch when the cold Atlantic brine crashes hard around her ankles. Doesn't see the troubled twins who watch her from the dunes. Doesn't stop to think. Doesn't think to pray. Moving fast to break a sweat, moving slow to comb for shells, she tracks the scalloped driftline with abandon. She angles past a willet standing one-legged in the sand, its head tucked onto its back like a spoon. The whisk of her walking springs the bird to life. It skitters away with her thoughts.

She spies a gleaming glimmer in a swirling tidal pool. She stops and stoops and reaches. She falls face first in the foam.

In the time they can say, "Holy shit, that lady's in trouble," the twins rush down to save her from the surf. Smelling of shrimp and pot and booze and beer after a rough night on the beach, they collect the fallen woman, her bag and her baseball hat, and the heavy silver bracelet lying by her side. They drag her over the storm-carved scarp and dump her on a prickly bed of broken shells and seaweed.

The twin named Hook struggles as the glow of too much hooch leaks from her eyes like acid from a battery. She settles on her knees to check the woman for signs of life. Wipes a crust of sand from the woman's languid lips. Tries on the woman's hat. It fits.

She rifles through the woman's bag. Washed-up Twinkie wrappers. A tangle of fishing line. Broken sand dollars. An iPod.

*Score.* Hook drops the bracelet in the bag and sits back on her happy heels, taking in the woman like a breath she can't quite hold. Big eyes. Big bones. Big boobs. Short skirt. No make up. No shoes.

The woman's not so lucky with her second savior though, Hook's twin brother Sinker, who's set on sneaking a peek up under that skirt.

He cracks his knuckles. The woman's mind restarts with sharp alarm. He slides his eager fingers through the gap between her knees. The woman's strong right hand slams across the side of his head, ripping out his fourteen-carat gold earring, and knocking him senseless to the sand beside her.

"God damn, lady. What you done to Sinker?" Hook scrambles to resurrect her brother, but not before the woman finds balance on her shaky legs, grabs her bag and her senses, and leaves the startled twins beside themselves.

"That's the last time I'll save some old lady from drowning," says Sinker.

"You didn't save shit." Hook stifles a yawn with the back of a tattooed hand, her inked-in angels stir the morning air.

*Old lady my ass*, thinks the woman. Elizabeth Lena Forsythe. Assistant director of development at Duke University. Nobody's mother. Nobody's daughter. Nobody's fool.

Her size-twelve feet perforate the sand in long urgent stitches. Past the Slip-n-Dip Water Slide, past the house with the heated saltwater pool, past the RV park, to the Blue Heaven Villas, where she left her husband an hour ago, quiet as a corpse beneath their quilted queen-sized comforter. Frank Hunter Forsythe. She'd tried to coax him into walking, but he wouldn't budge.

"I wish you'd come with me," she'd whispered. Her gravelly voice sounded more like sex than usual.

He'd turned away. After twenty quiet years together, she knew what he was hiding. A gaunt face. Tired eyes. A stuffy nose. A morning hard-on. He smoothed the sheets to keep her at bay.

"It's too early to walk," he said.

"Wanna fuck instead?"

And they did fuck, wishing that their pre-dawn sex could count as exercise, as a speed walk down the beach.

She climbs twenty weathered steps to the crest of the dune and stops to catch her breath. She scans the deserted beach for the man who might have molested her. His missingness alarms her.

"You awright, Mizz Forsythe?"

Grayed and worn as driftwood, Bill Beak, the Blue Heaven maintenance man materializes beside her. She startles, then steadies herself against a railing. She runs a hand through her short blonde hair, feeling for something to say.

"I must have fainted."

Bill Beak's old face fixes in a skeptical scrunch.

"Down on the beach."

Nothing.

"A man attacked me."

Bill Beak blinks, the undertone of oceanfront drama agitating his primitive brain.

"There was a woman, too," says Liz. "With tattoos." She touches her own arms, feeling for angels.

Bill Beak scuffs his feet, looks sideways at the ground. He slides his tongue around the edge of his lipless mouth. He glances at her face, then down. Past her broad forehead. Past her sturdy neck and shoulders. Down to the pushy nipples straining through her chartreuse cotton blouse.

Liz watches him try and fail to drag his stare from her chest. It feels so familiar, she almost lets it pass. She crosses her arms instead, nails him with her blank blue eyes, and brushes past him toward her building.

Bill Beak squawks. "Yaforgotcherstuff." He holds out her bag like a peace offering, like a promise to behave.

She turns, angry, takes her possession. He ducks his head and slinks away.

In the vacuum the old man leaves behind, Liz's brain begins to shimmer and shake. Her mother was done in by a stroke ten years ago, and Liz can't help fearing the worst. Good thing she'd made that living will.

"Just don't let me go veggie," Liz said last fall when she and Frank were in a Chapel Hill law office, working out the rules of dying. "I want to go in peace. No heroic crap. No Terry Schiavo. Put that in my will." She laughed and fretted, as she always does, when sickness, lawyers, and official documents are involved. This legal business pulled all three nemeses into one sorry session.

Liz has had a thing about morbid paperwork since the day her daughter was born dead twenty years ago. Her name was Francis. They would have called her Frannie. She would have slept in a yellow crib.

*Inhale. Back straight. Shoulders down. Collarbones out.*
*Exhale. Chest relax.*
*Inhale. Lift the spine.*
*Exhale. Chest relax.*

On the next breath Liz looks up to see three brown pelicans gliding over the crest of the dune, sailing above the grasses that hold the sand in place. They slip past silent, nearly in her reach. The last pelican, she is sure, winks at her with a sad and ancient eye.

*What's wrong?* she almost thinks.

*You cannot hold the threads.*

*Why not?* she almost asks.

The pelican does not answer. It has said too much already.

# 3

Plopped on a boggy slice of Atlantic oceanfront, the Sunrise Beach Holiday Travel Park claims fifty RV hook-ups and a dozen singlewides, but only three year-round residents. Hook, Sinker, and Eddie Junior.

Eddie Junior, the park manager, lives in the tidy Coachman Classic near the front gate. Hook and Sinker own the Roadliner on lot fifteen.

The twins inherited the decrepit trailer from their daddy, the same half-wit who gave them their nicknames a dozen years ago. He'd parked the piece of junk for what would prove to be the last time, downed six shots of Jim Beam, and started a list of unflattering descriptors for his two children. With no mother to soften the abuse, the kids grabbed hold of their Hook and Sinker labels and tried to stay afloat.

"Quit your damn whining," says Hook. She's tending Sinker's ear in their mess of a kitchen. Despite a five-star hangover, her hands are mostly steady. The scratchy buzz of a fluorescent light over the sink grates on her brain, putting her on edge. "You don't want this getting infected. You still don't got insurance, you know."

"And I still don't need no lecture from no shit-ass cashier." Sinker sprawls in a folding chair, glassy-eyed and hangdog, blood gooing in a thick red rope down his neck. He drags on a Salem and blows smoke in Hook's face.

Still not having insurance is a sore point with Sinker, who covets his sister's glamorous job stocking shelves at Bobby's Fishing Superstore in Jacksonville. The store provides her with something resembling health coverage, plus the chance to see what's hot in saltwater fishing gear. But Hook pays for her benefits. As the only woman on the payroll with a Barbie-doll body, she swallows a daily dose of harassment from all the men who work there, including the pervert who owns the store. Old Bobby Beak, brother of Bill, just can't seem to keep his mouth shut about Hook's tits and tattoos.

"Least I don't work in no stupid sign shop." She mashes a square of gauze on Sinker's ear, feeling the outline of pain herself. Hook's more like her brother than she'd want to admit. At five ten, she's three inches shorter, but they both have clear green eyes, thick black hair, and a smoldering drift toward self-destruction. "And I told you I ain't no cashier."

"Stop that shit," says Sinker.

"It's not my fault you got hurt. I'da smacked you, too." She chooses a needle from a red tomato pin cushion, the only useful thing her mother left behind. "Or maybe I'da just stuck you."

Hook's simple threat is the upshot of too many wretched family relationships. Starting with a mama who left when she was four. Continuing with a daddy, who treated her like a boy until he began treating her like a sex object. And then with Sinker. When the brother tried his hand on her, she ripped a five-inch-long Water Devil shark hook through his left bicep. Now she carries the hook on a retractable keychain wherever she goes – with a spare in her glove compartment.

"Gonna start sewing," says Hook. "Be still."

"This ain't no damn quilting bee. Just gimme a stitch and leave me the fuck alone."

Hook goes quiet as dead fish. She screws the top on the rubbing alcohol and wipes her hands on her faded black jeans. She heads for the door, grabbing the baseball hat she took from the woman on the beach.

"Where you going?" says Sinker.

She doesn't look back. "None a your business."

"What about my ear?"

She turns in the door with enough calm to worry him. "What about it?"

As soon as Hook saves two hundred dollars for a deposit, she'll rent her own trailer and move out. Sinker knows she's good as gone.

"Come on, Hook. We gotta stick together."

"*We* don't gotta do nothing. *You* gotta get your stupid ear fixed. And *I* ain't gonna have shit to do with it."

Hook slams the door on Sinker's sniveling and stops on the porch to make a plan. The rain has moved on and she's thinking about a nap in the dunes.

"Hey there, Hookster." It's Eddie Junior, checking on things, wasting time. Eddie Junior doesn't take work too seriously, partly because his daddy owns the RV park, and partly because he's usually stoned. He's never hit on Hook, which is the main thing she likes about him. Plus he's cute. He has his momma's round face and curly brown hair, his daddy's broad shoulders, and his own golden tan. She gives him a lazy look and bats her stubby lashes.

"You holding, Eddie Junior?"

"Not on me." He pulls his pants pockets inside out to make sure. A clump of fuzz slips through his fingers and tumbleweeds in the wind.

"What good are you?" Hook kicks at a plastic pelican planter and thunks it down the steps. Her Ked flies into the yard.

"What'd you do that for?"

Hook cocks her hip. "Get me my durn shoe." She stomps her bare foot to make the point, sending a groan through the sun-bleached planks.

"I need that rent," says Eddie Junior, throwing her the sneaker.

"Sinker hadn't paid?"

Eddie Junior studies his fingernails.

"That son of a bitch."

Eddie Junior backs away a couple of steps.

"I can't do nothing about it right now," says Hook. She slumps off the porch and opens the door of her beat-up Ford Ranger. Pokes around in the ashtray for something to smoke and finds it. Lights up the raggedy roach and tokes it down to nothing.

She takes a second to watch Eddie Junior chewing on his thumbnail, then grabs a blanket from the seat, knees the door shut, and heads toward the beach, flashing back to the woman from this morning and her bag of trashy junk. She guesses they haven't seen the last of each other, and her guesses about such things are usually right.

Hook's friend Layla says that's because Hook has ESP. The subject came up again last spring while Layla was putting the final touches on Hook's latest tattoo. Layla owns Holes over on Oak Avenue, where Hook gets all her body art done. The ooze of blues and greens and blood on Hook's forearm would soon heal into her eleventh guardian angel.

"You and that Zeke," said Hook. "Ya'll just can't let it go."

Zeke is one of the few full-time psychics around these parts, and an old boyfriend of Layla's. They both think Hook's the real deal when it comes to paranormal ability.

"I don't need no Zeke to tell me what's true," said Layla.

ESP. Mediums. Channeling. Whatever. Hook figures half of it's bullshit, she's just not sure which half. But she talks to her angels every day, and they usually steer her straight.

"Yeah, well. Maybe you should stop pestering me and answer that phone." Hook winked and forced a smile. The phone rang two minutes later, almost in time to qualify for a real premonition.

# 4

The sweepers wake early that morning with breakfast on their brains. It takes them no time to tidy up the Airstream, load their brooms and head for Jacksonville, twenty minutes away. They park near Camp Lejeune's main gate and start their morning ritual, walking the strip of porn shops and bars that borders the base, sweeping up crud like nobody's business.

Scanning the littered path, Jesus smiles with the certainty they'll always have work. When he stoops to collect a bloated Pampers from the side of the road, a wave of dizzy spins him to the ground.

"Are you okay?" says Luke, pulling him up by a hand.

"Something's happened."

Luke straightens his glasses to study the situation. "What is it? Terrorist attack? Flu pandemic?"

The savior stumbles toward a dumpster, ignoring Luke's questions. He slides open the door and drops the diaper, breathing in the sour of so much human waste. Luke catches up and grabs him by the arm.

"You're s-scaring me."

Jesus coughs from the stench. "Be not afraid."

"Are you s-sick?"

"Someone found our bracelet."

Markos jumps into the conversation with wide eyes. "Are you sure?"

Jesus goes blank. "Am I sure?"

"Are. You. Sure." Marks parses the words like he's talking to a first-grader.

"Now are we sure that thou knowest all things, and needest not that any man should ask thee," says Luke. "By this we believe

that thou camest forth from god."
"Knock off the crap," says Mark.
Jesus slams the dumpster shut. "Yes. I. Am. Sure."
"Well?"
"Well what?"
"Who has the damn thing?"
"I don't know."
"You have to know," scowls Mark. "You're Jesus."

The boys work their way toward the Waffle Shop, sweeping past Zeke's, where the old hippy's out front shilling for his fortune-telling business. Though Sunday morning isn't the best time for new customers, Zeke's still hoping to connect with some wandering souls.

"Excuse us, sir," says Mark. He dusts up a little pile of nothing around Zeke's feet, then folds his hands and bows. "Don't you agree that Jesus should be all-knowing?"

Zeke's too stoned to make sense of the situation. He eases down onto the ladder-back chair he keeps outside the door, studying the scene through deep-fried eyes.

The colored guy looks like a big baby who's bound for college. Preppy and rumpled. Fancy new glasses. Khaki pants with a pale blue button-down shirt and worn Topsiders. Dark chocolate skin. He carries a broom with a long crooked handle and bright red strapping stitched into the graceful straw head.

The talker has a foreign flavor, maybe Mexican. Black eyes. Black hair. Black beard. Black shirt. Black jeans. Black running shoes. His body tight and compact, his broom a short little stump with a thick head wrapped in braided yellow cords.

The last guy looks like a miniature version of Zeke himself. Skinny, with wild tangled hair that's pretty much on its own. Worried gray eyes with a hint of blue. Loose jeans, shredded flip flops, and a t-shirt with the word *Jesus* faded beyond belief. His broom is a slender, wispy brush, the kind an old-time chimney sweeper would carry.

Jesus steps forward, straightening his shirt so the name shows better. He clears his throat. "All-knowing?" he says. "What would be the point?"

"Okay, Mr. Jesus," says Zeke. "What exactly *is* the point?"
Jesus takes a determined breath and plants his feet. He swirls

his broom in a ninja flourish, stopping with the tip of the handle aimed straight at Zeke's heart.

"The point is sharp," says Jesus, glowing with the grace of truth.

The boys leave Zeke in a daze and pile into the Waffle Shop, where they stack their brooms in a corner and wait for a greasy booth to clear. The place is filled with camouflaged Marines and hostile stares.

"The point is sh-sharp?" says Luke. "What the heck was that about?"

"The point *is* sharp," says Jesus. He looks to Mark for help, but Mark's not looking back.

"Why didn't you tell him about the threads?" says Luke.

"No one wants to hear about the goddamn threads," says Mark. "It's nothing but a crock of shit."

Luke gasps, caught off-guard by the blasphemy. "Don't you dare s-say that."

"F-f-fuck you," smirks Mark.

"Fuck you back," says Luke.

"F-f-fuck you twice."

Coffee shows up, interrupting the fuck-you frenzy, and the boys slip into their Sunday caffeine rituals. Luke takes his black. Jesus goes for Splenda. Mark pours three little buckets of half-and-half into his cup before he lays an exaggerated sigh out on the table. Jesus reaches across to touch Mark's hand, but Marines in the next booth take notice. Mark jerks away, remembering his run-in with the Hell's Angels at Myrtle Beach.

"Don't worry," says Jesus. He fishes an ice tube from his water and slips it on his pinky. "We are the frozen ones."

"This isn't funny," says Luke, a hot tear leaking down his cheek. That always happens when Mark makes fun of his stuttering.

Jesus settles his gaze on his big black friend. "What would make you happy?"

But it's Mark who answers. "Tell me who found our bracelet."

"I said I don't know."

Mark meets the savior's eyes for a long, hard look. "Then I want to be Jesus for awhile. " He says the name in Spanish. Haysoose.

# 5

Back at the Blue Heaven Villas, Frank's scrubbing mildew in the bathroom, holding his breath to escape the bleachy fumes. He starts to see stars and wonders if his eyes are on the blink again.

A few years ago during a routine physical, he'd told Dr. Sarah Stern about the swirling patterns that creep into his peripheral vision whenever he's stressed. "Pale green triangles with yellow serrated edges," he'd said. "And stars. Floating in circles. Like ceiling fans."

Sarah turned off the overheads and shined her light through his anxious pupils.

"You're not having headaches, are you?"

"Not today."

"Sounds like ocular migraine."

With her parted lips just inches from his, Frank had given up worrying about his kaleidoscope eyes in favor of worrying about what was happening beneath his crinkly paper gown. Sarah Stern is a big-busted, red-headed knock-out, which didn't make things any easier. He was relieved when she told him to roll onto his side, relieved again when her aggressive prostate probing put an end to his half-baked hard-on.

"Looks pretty good," she laughed over the pop of a powdered latex glove. "For an old man."

"I'm not an old man," he'd said, looking at himself in the mirror behind her. His pale, thin features seemed to age as he stared, his ear lobes drooping longer and lower, his hairline receding like a dried-up lake. "I'm forty-seven."

"Whatever. Just don't go getting sick on me. You promised."

Frank had agreed to see Sarah after two years of nagging from

Liz. His wife and his doctor are best friends, a cozy relationship that partly explains his reluctance to tell Sarah about his sketchy memory and troublesome tremors. His memory for names has never been good, but lately it has also not been good for parking places and grocery shopping. His last few trips to the store have netted thirteen cans of crushed tomatoes and ten packages of frozen lasagna. Frank's hands are another story. Lately they've started shaking so much he can't read his own writing. But his absent mind does not want to know more. Frank is trembling in denial.

He steps out to the balcony and sees Liz standing on the walkway over the dunes. She looks to the east, tracking three brown pelicans sailing past her perch. He blows her a kiss. It soars high in the breeze and drops, looping toward her like a falling kite, missing her lips by a foot. He's scrubbing the toilet when she comes in behind him a few minutes later. "What'd you do, walk all the way to Wilmington?" He turns to find her big body standing stiff in the doorway. She doesn't answer his question. She says she needs a shower.

Frank takes the hint and leaves, carrying her bag to the kitchen to dump her load of trash. Ever since she watched a *National Geographic Special* about sea turtles choking on plastic bags, Liz scours the beach for litter whenever she walks. This morning's collection contains a mess of Twinkie wrappers, a burned-out Roman candle, some fishing line, and a Tanya Tucker cassette. It all suggests a party Frank wishes he'd been invited to, not that he would have gone.

Near the bottom by her iPod, he finds a heavy metal bracelet covered with wild engravings. It's a strip of silver one inch wide, curved to form a tight, round C – carved inside and out with a jumble of letterish symbols. As he rinses off the sand, the tang of precious metal seeps like a song into his wobbly fingers.

Pipes clang in the bathroom, breaking the silvery spell, signaling the end of Liz's shower. He sets the bracelet on the counter and goes to start the laundry.

He notices a syrupy dribble on the Tide bottle and wipes it with a towel. He finds smudges on the dryer door and polishes them away with his sleeve. He eyes a herd of dust bunnies trembling in the corner. He turns on the washer and leaves.

# 6

Hook's paranormal talents are hit and miss, but when they hit, they hit big. Like last spring when she helped the police find a drowned boy. She'd heard about the kid one morning on the beach when a cop pulled his Honda four-wheeler up to where she was surf-fishing. Clumps of foam and seaweed littered the beach from a storm the night before.

"There's a boy missing, Hook. You seen any kids around?"

Hook doesn't like the law as a matter of principle, so she didn't volunteer anything.

"He's ten," said the cop.

She stared at the horizon.

"Hook?"

She squeezed her eyes shut and wrapped her head with her arms, listening for songs from her angels.

"You okay?"

She pulled at the skin on her neck. Her breathing turned fast and shallow. She opened her eyes to the sky. Her brain hurt.

The cop scratched his head.

Hook swallowed her dizziness and found her voice. "In the sound, just east of the marina. There's a skiff." She turned back to fishing. "Better get a move on."

The cop sped away, talking on the radio. They found the drowned boy twenty minutes later, right where Hook said he'd be. The police tried to keep her contribution secret, but word got out like it always does. Zeke was the first to track her down. He knocked on her trailer door and walked right in.

Hook had just come home from work and was already chatting online. Aside from smoking dope, Internet journaling is the main way she escapes getting bored to death. Zeke's interruption pissed her off.

"What're you doing, Zeke? This ain't your damn house."

"Heard you done some re-mote viewing for the cops." Zeke settled on the sofa and put his feet on the coffee table. "You looking at porn?"

"No. I ain't my stupid brother. And get your damn shoes off my furniture."

Hook started dabbling in the not-so-real world of Internet journaling a few years ago after a kid in high school told her about a website called Emisphor.

"M is for madness. You'll fit right in. Just give yourself a fancy screen name and off you go. You can be anybody you want. Even make up a whole new person."

"What's the point of that?" Hook figured she had enough trouble being the person she already was.

"No one knows it's you. You can say anything."

"Gee golly. Sounds like a real fun time," said Hook.

Until then, most of her experience with the Internet involved her brother watching fuck flicks. That's why they have a high-speed connection in the first place, and a clunky old laptop Sinker stole from a car at the shopping center.

"You should try it," said the kid. "You'll get tons of friends if you post about Sinker."

"What's posting?"

"Posting's when you write stuff like 'my brother's a moron' and then people comment," The kid looked at his own arms. "Lotsa cutters there, too."

Hook had a few of her own cuts to chronicle, so she logged onto Emisphor one night and set up *Hook's Journal*. Within minutes, four anonymous friends had welcomed her to the fringy online community.

"What're you doing on that computer then?" Zeke spread his arms and smiled his greenish teeth. "Looking for a spiritual ad-visor?"

"I'd sooner be dead." Hook slammed the laptop shut.

"You really see that kid in the sound?" Zeke watched her fiddle with the Water Devil hanging from her belt. "Cause if you did, me and you oughta be in business."

Hook stopped to think. She remembered the dead boy swirling through her brain like a riptide, pulling her down into the cold wet dark of knowing too much. She shivered the thought away. "Get the hell outta here, Zeke."

# 7

Mark's request to be Jesus throws the boys off until they have a chance to think things through. Luke comes up with the answer while they're sweeping up Freedom Fries at the Semper Fi Grill. It's like he's back in philosophy class at Clemson, back before a summer fling with acid hooked him up with the latest son of god.

He clears his throat and waits for Jesus and Mark to pay attention, holding his broom like American Gothic.

"After s-serious deliberation and careful analysis of the request from Brother Markos, I hereby conclude that Jesus must, in fact, be relative."

"Ha," says Jesus. "I knowed you wuz my cuz." He bobbles his head and earns a smack from Mark, who's in a better mood after breakfast.

"He's yo' mama," says Mark.

Mark and Jesus swagger like rappers, a ghetto duet with Luke caught in the middle.

"Hold on," says Luke. "There's more. S-since Jesus is, in fact, relative, I have no objection to Mark taking over." He pauses for a beat. "And then I get a turn. We rotate. Gary. Mark. Me. Gary. Mark. Me."

Jesus starts dancing and singing. "Duck, duck, goose. Duck, duck ..." Then he jumps behind Luke and squirms against his butt. "Goose!"

"Dang it," yells Luke. "It's no wonder we need a new Jesus."

"Speaking of which, when do I start?" says Mark.

"How about now?" says Jesus, offering up his throne with one clean sweep.

"Really?"

"I appoint unto you a king dumb as my father has pointed to me." He tips to his toes and kisses Mark on the lips. "It's all yours."

# 8

Cool October days are Hook's favorite. You can still swim, but the tourists are gone, and there's room to be alone with the ocean. Today the sky's clear and cool, perfect sleeping weather. She heads for her secret spot in the gap between two shifting dunes, following the ziggy tracks of ghost crabs. She spreads her blanket on the sand and lies back tired. "Shit." The angry word flies past her like a spear. She edges round a clump of grass for a peek.

"That you, Eddie Junior?" He's been stalking her lately, though she can't say she minds.

"Goddamn sand spurs."

Hook laughs over her annoyance, watching him pick at the spiny stickers velcroed to his ankles. "What're you doing on my dune?"

"Someone broke in the bathhouse. I'm patrolling."

"You patrolling? Will blunders never stop ceasing."

Eddie Junior doesn't know what to do when Hook gets sassy, so he mostly just ignores her. "We gotta talk about that rent," he says.

"I told you I can't do nothing about it, Eddie Junior. Now leave me alone."

She ducks back into her hiding place full of worry. The strain of not enough money has plagued Hook for years, ever since her daddy tried to turn her body into cash back in the eighth grade. He'd picked her up from middle school and stopped for a drink at Tall Paul's. Before she knew it, she was in a booth with a horny staff sergeant, and daddy was counting a stack of dirty money. Tall Paul himself interrupted the sleazy transaction by popping her old man in the face, slinging a splurt of blood across the table. Hook can still see the flash of dragons tattooed on her savior's arms.

Hook huddles against the press of a rising offshore wind. Sea oats sway, etching creases in the sand. A solitary pelican dives just beyond the breakers. It doesn't come up for the longest time. She remembers the woman's iPod and wonders how she let it get away. The silver bracelet too. She tugs the woman's baseball hat down low over her eyes. It smells like some other body.

# 9

Liz stands at the bedroom window wrapped in a Duke beach towel, the snarky grin of the Blue Devil mascot spread across her chest. She looks out to the lawn where Bill Beak's talking to Doug Dipper, the condo's swimming pool guy. Bill's skinny arms poke the air like a traffic cop, pointing from her building to the beach and back. She guesses he's telling Doug what little he knows of her story.

Doug Dipper works all the pools on Sunrise Beach and is every pool owner's best friend. He keeps their pumps pumping and their filters filtering during the high summer season and does routine maintenance in the fall and spring. He's great at getting homeowners to replace their perfectly fine sand filters three years earlier than necessary. Selling premature filters is Doug Dipper's springtime cash bonanza.

"If it was me, I'd be putting in one of them StarClear sand filters right about now." That's how he always opens his spiel. "I'm not saying you absolutely need it, but you sure don't want that thing failing on you in the middle of the summer. Leastwise I wouldn't." Three out of ten of his contract customers fall for the seasonal pitch.

Doug is also a hit with the ladies. He gossips freely and is said to have a dick the size of Delaware.

Like long-haul truck drivers peddling clap up and down I-95, he spreads wild rumors without restraint. As he himself often says with a wink, Doug Dipper is totally plugged in. Once when a bale of marijuana washed up near Eddie's Pier, Doug was there three minutes before the police showed up to claim it.

But whether Doug's dong truly rivals the state of Delaware depends on who's talking. The women down at JJ's Diner all smile and swear it's a monster. Liz first heard the story while waiting for takeout last summer.

"I bet it ain't no bigger'n a Vi-enna sausage," a man told the sun-dried woman on his arm. The two were drinking beer and eating boiled peanuts at the bar. "It's just another one of his bullshit stories and you're a fool to believe it."

"Now why would a grown man lie about his own pee-pee?" purred the woman.

"We ain't talking about no grown nothing. We're talking about Doug D. Dipper." The man slid his sweat-stained hat back on his mottled head. "That sumbitch could just about get away with murder."

# 10

The boys sweep a clean course from Piney Green Road to Gum Branch and halfway back, earning a few bucks here and there. They even pick up some inside work at the Head and Boulders adult video store, though Luke refuses to step inside. When Gary and the new Jesus come out grinning fifteen minutes later, Luke growls and scowls and stomps away.

"Dude," says the new Jesus. "We're just having fun."

"S-screw you, Markos," says Luke.

"The name is Jesus."

"For he who is least among you all will be great." says Gary. "Porn shops need cleaning too."

"Did not he that made that which is without make that which is within also?" says Luke.

"What we *made* is ten dollars," says the new Jesus.

"That's all you think about, Mark?"

"I said, the name is Jesus."

"And I s-said, s-screw you."

Gary steps in to fend off the fight. "Blessed are the fleece makers," he whispers. "For they shall inherit the wind."

Luke and the new Jesus try to keep their snarls, but Gary pulls them into a broom-bristling hug. "All is well," he says. "You'll see."

"Yeah," says the new Jesus. "We have like two hundred dollars saved up."

"Dang money," says Luke.

"It just s-so happens I've been praying about our dang money," says the new Jesus, imitating Luke perfectly. "And god told me it's time to spend some of it on our very own church."

"God's not talking to you," says Luke, hoping he was. What

Luke wants most is their very own house of the lord. And the chance to do some baptizing.

"Tell him, Gary," says the new Jesus.

Gary doesn't hear his old name. He'd gotten used to being Jesus and the switch back isn't going so well.

Luke knocks him on the shoulder. "Maybe we'll s-start calling you Matthew. Or Peter."

"Let it be," says the new Jesus. "Gary *es muy bueno*."

# 11

Liz collapses onto to the bed, hugging a pillow to her chest.

"I went all the way to the inlet," she says. "It was gorgeous. Low tide. Hard sand. Even you would have liked it." She releases her breath one molecule at a time. "Down past the water slide, I bent over to pick something up and – I don't know what happened. I must have passed out." She rolls to her side and props up her head. At six feet one, her big body fills the bed. Frank sits beside her, on the edge.

"Next thing I know I'm on my back in the sand and this guy's pawing me. I punched him." Her shoulders tighten in reflex from years of karate. "There was a woman with him. She had tattoos."

Liz bites her thumbnail, reliving the rough hand between her thighs. She shakes her rage away, centers with a sigh, and presses ahead with the brightest smile she can muster. "There were these pelicans, Frank. I know it sounds weird, but I think one of them winked at me."

As the director of planned giving in Duke University's development office, Liz Forsythe has all the smiles of an undertaker. Her work involves getting rich alumni to contemplate death and will the school their fortunes. It takes a certain charm. Her current hot prospect, Mrs. Catherine Cross, of Cross Casualty and Life, is almost onboard for twenty million. She and Liz had brunch in Catherine's Watergate apartment three weeks ago.

"Sometimes I feel like an ambulance chaser," joked Liz.

"You should." Catherine's laugh came hard. "Which of your other prospects are planning to die in the next three months?"

That's how the well-heeled old woman announced her cancer prognosis.

"I'm so sorry." Liz dragged out a sympathetic smile.

"Am I your best bet?"

Liz leaned forward and met Catherine's eyes. "You are," she said. "This is an amazing gift you're considering."

"Gift? I thought twenty million from a dead person was called a bequest. What'll you do if I don't come through?"

Business smile. "Same as if you do come through. Make my phone calls. Have my lunches. Sweet talk, flatter, nag and beg. You know how it works."

"Not that I fall for any of it." Catherine coughed. "Well. Maybe the begging."

Frank sits with his chin in his hands and stares at the floor. An uneven carpet seam jumps onto his to-do list, along with a speckle of mildew on the wall. He sifts through other tasks. Something about bunnies. He checks his hands for evidence of wobbling and finds it. He remembers the silver bracelet, singing through his fingers.

"A pelican winked at you?" He tries to mask the sarcasm, but it bleeds through all the same.

"Never mind," says Liz.

"Come on." He reaches toward her, trying to make nice.

She pulls away. "I said never mind."

"Is this one of those times when you just want me to listen, or do you actually want to know what I think?"

This is one of those times when Liz wants him to already know what she wants, and she hates that he doesn't have a clue.

"Forget it," she whispers. "Let's just go get breakfast."

Frank finishes cleaning the bathroom while Liz rifles through the closet for something to wear. Blessed with passable beauty, clear skin, and good posture, this middle-aged woman has given up the time-consuming rituals of personal paint and polish. From her squarish jaw to her boldly veined feet, she lives in her body with almost no cosmetic intervention. She settles on navy Capris, a lime green cotton sweater, and turquoise flip flops – and is ready to go in minutes. Frank triple checks to make sure windows are locked and faucets aren't dripping and toilets aren't running. He finds Liz standing on the balcony, the bracelet circling loose around her wrist.

"Where'd you get that?" he says.

"It was on the counter."

"It was in with your beach trash."

"In my bag?" Liz chews at her thumb, slicing loose an invisible sliver of cuticle, spitting it over the banister.

Frank winces.

She looks out along the coast, the graceful crescent of Sunrise Beach stretching to the horizon like a postcard. "I shouldn't have hit that man." She presses the bracelet up toward her elbow, tight into her skin.

He gives her half a hug. "Everything's okay."

"Everything's not okay," she says. "I lost my good luck hat."

# 12

Hook wakes chilled and achy to a parade of black ants filling her close-up view of the sand. She imagines she's one of them, slogging through the desert of her life on an invisible trail to nowhere worth going. She has to pee. She pulls down her jeans and squats, laughing when the ants scatter. She makes up a poem to post on Emisphor.

> *scared some antsies when my pantsies*
> *slipped down off my butt*
> *yellow raindrops wished and washed them.*
> *pissed them off.*
> *so what?*

By the time she gets back to the Roadliner, Hook's jittery. She finds Sinker poking around the grill out front, a slew of cleaned bluefish piled on the porch. A tinge of blood seeps through the clunky bandage on his ear. Eddie Junior's lounging in a canvas chair, his butt dragging the sandy ground. He's taken his shirt off, and doesn't look half bad.

"You need you more lightning fluid," says Eddie Junior.

Sinker rummages through a storage shed beside the porch and drags out a beat-up metal gas can. "Hot damn. This here's got two-cycle mixed in. Perfecto."

Hook watches the comedy from behind her truck. Sinker's about to blow himself up, but she knows it won't be serious. When he sprinkles gas over the grill, the unleaded stream explodes back in his face. The grass catches fire and Eddie Junior stomps on it. Hook grabs a jumbled garden hose and douses the side of the trailer before she turns the hose on Sinker.

The nozzle feels like a gun in her hand.

# 13

On the way back to the Jeep, the sweepers pass the expansive main entrance to the Camp Lejeune Marine Corp Base, a manicured stretch of heaven between two halves of hell. Outside the gate lies a red-necked world of doublewides, strip malls and yellow ribbons. Inside, forty thousand wild-eyed grunts fighting to save the world through brute force. And in the middle, a no man's land with the greenest grass and whitest curbs and cleanest gutters and tightest guards you'd ever want to see.

Back before America made itself the target of choice for terrorists worldwide, visitors to Camp Lejeune had free rein. You could get a pass just by asking a sentry who'd call you sir or ma'am no matter what. Back then you could come and go as you pleased, strolling around the tanks and firing ranges like tourists at Disneyworld.

Nowadays you're liable to get shot if you get too close, which is exactly the risk Gary, Luke and the new Jesus are running when they stop to rest on the fresh-cut Marine Corps fescue, less than a hundred yards from a guardhouse full of trigger-happy sentries. Lying on their backs with brooms in hand, they start to plan their church.

"God told me we should keep things simple," says the new Jesus. "And do lots of baptizing."

"Now you're talking," says Luke.

"You can be our John," says Gary.

"Where's the church going to be?" says Luke.

"It shall be built on Sunrise Beach." The new Jesus tries to sound like god, but it comes out squeaky.

"But everyone who hears these sayings of mine, and does not do them, will be like a foolish man who built his house on the sand." Luke loves scriptures. It's the only time he doesn't stutter.

"Yeah," says Gary. "You sure god said Sunrise Beach?"

"Duh. Of course I'm sure." The new Jesus sits up, brushing off more questions. "Looks like we have company!'

Two Marines in pressed utilities are heading their way. Both carry M-16s.

"This is not good," says Luke.

"Let's do Sweep for America," says Gary. "They'll like that."

"Sweep for America!' says the new Jesus. "Hit it."

With the guards still thirty yards away, the boys start humming the *Star Spangled Banner* and move into their favorite synchronized sweep. Luke stands back until the rockets red glare, then joins in the swirling. If you watched from above, you'd see them tracing wild stars and stripes in a choreographed frenzy that only a god could appreciate.

"What're you people doing here?" barks the guard named Stone, a tall, thick man with close-set eyes, a shaved head, and teeny tiny ears. A sour cloud of sweat laced with Old Spice hangs in the air around him.

The new Jesus raises a finger and stops their performance. "We're sweeping for America, sir," he says, smiling as he bows. "Doing our part to keep this great country clean and safe."

Stone turns to the other guard, Rodriguez, and nods. They lift their weapons.

"Easy there, captain," says the new Jesus. "Is something wrong?"

Stone stretches himself taller and harder. "What's wrong is that you are not using this Marine's proper fucking rank, which for your fucking information is sergeant. What's wrong is that you and your terrorist friends have brung your sorry asses onto my United States Marine Corps base without my fucking permission."

"But we aren't on your fucking base, sir," says the new Jesus, waving a hand in the direction of Jacksonville. "And we aren't fucking terrorists. We're Christian soldiers, here to spread the word."

"And sir?" adds Gary. "Blessed are they who don't say fucking all the time."

"Looks like we got us some crazies, Corporal Rodriguez," says Stone.

"Come on, guys," says Luke, backing away, holding his broom like a shield. "Let's get out of here."

"You should listen to your friend," says Corporal Rodriguez. He's looking straight at the new Jesus, tethered somehow by a shred of Hispanic heritage.

The new Jesus presses for advantage. "We're not going to hurt anyone."

Rodriguez blinks twice and eases his weapon up until it grazes the hairs on the new Jesus' chin. "But we might, amigo," he says. "You and your friends should go."

# 14

The four-hour journeys between Sunrise Beach and Chapel Hill are some of Liz's favorite times. With Frank captive behind the wheel, the trips present rare opportunities for extended conversations. As they pass through Jacksonville, Liz wants to make sense of her morning.

"There's more to my pelican story," she says. "It's kind of weird."

"As weird as that?" he says, pointing toward a scuffle near the entrance to Camp Lejeune. Liz sees a Marine grabbing a broom from a black man. Another guy, a tiny soul in a faded t-shirt, turns and stares at her for the longest time.

Frank speeds up, leaving the shakedown behind.

They pass through Jacksonville fifteen silent minutes later, and Liz brings up the pelican again. Frank pretends not to hear. He checks the rearview mirror instead, and pulls around a truck emblazoned with the Mackey Family Farms logo. The hogs of the Mackey Corporation grace the state of North Carolina with sixty million tons of shit every year, some of which was flying out of the truck, splattering their windshield.

"Why would a pelican wink at me?" Liz persists.

"Why would a pelican wink at anyone?"

"It winked at *me* Frank."

"A pelican didn't wink at you, Liz. That's crazy. And if it *did* happen to wink at you, you shouldn't even think about asking why."

"Don't start."

Too late. Frank's already on a roll.

"No one knows why anything happens, Liz. You know that. Just like with Phil killing himself. Any explanation is just a likely story."

Frank's older brother committed suicide two years ago, and Frank still isn't over it. The absence of a note had left everyone guessing, further fueling Frank's cynical fires.

"I know why he did it," said their sister. It was Christmas dinner at her house, a month after Phil's funeral. "He was depressed. Just like Mama. Our whole damn family's depressed. Phil just did something about it."

"The lord has his reasons," said Deacon Duncan, who helped manage the flock at the sister's church. He'd dropped by the holiday gathering for some free food. Phil, who didn't have a church, would have told the old man to go fuck himself.

Liz stifles a sigh that Frank can't help but notice.

"Oh come on," he says, shifting in his seat, unsure which way to lean. "You really think it was trying to tell you something?"

"Why do I bother talking to you?" She twists the bracelet on her arm. "You don't believe anything."

"What's *that* supposed to mean?"

Liz glances at the speedometer. He's pushing seventy-five. He's pushing too hard.

"Slow down," she whispers, refusing to share what she heard the pelican say.

Her mind escapes to the fields speeding by outside the window. Chopped brown stalks and scraggly wisps of uncollected cotton. Fast food trash. A tiny graveyard with a wrought-iron fence. Her spirit sags, then sinks.

# 15

After their little blow up, Eddie Junior takes Sinker over to his place to grill the fish. As soon as they're gone, Hook grabs the laptop and logs on to Emisphor. She tries to remember the shape of her ant poem, but the words won't come. This isn't Hook's first try at a poem. She's written dozens in her online journal, with a ranting debut last Memorial Day weekend that earned her an instant online fan club.

*stinky smelly stubbly faces pushing at me cold*
*stop it or i'll rip your heart out shark bait bastard*
*not as good as dead*

She figured it was more interesting than most of the poems she'd seen at Emisphor, but she was still nervous when she posted that first one. Five minutes stuttered by. Her heart was going hot. No one was commenting. She clicked refresh. Her mood swung. They hated it. They were laughing at her. She shouldn't have put it out there. She hit refresh again. And again. A little blue square popped up by her name. Boom boom ear drums. She clicked the square and opened a comment from an unfamiliar name. Grayson.

Grayson: you sure are one pissed off hook
Hook: i know I am but what are you
Grayson: broom boy
Hook: whys that?
Grayson: i sweep
Hook: what?

Grayson: moitle beach
Hook: you sweep myrtle beach?
Grayson: finders bleepers losers sleepers
Hook: huh?
Grayson: bounty hunger
Hook: your weird
Grayson: found my treasure
Hook: yeah?
Grayson: sliver circle
Hook: huh?
Grayson: time to shine
Hook: silver?
Grayson: gotta go
Hook: bye
Grayson: buy
Hook: nice to meet ya
Grayson: rice to eat ya
Hook: : )
Grayson: ice to sleet ya
Hook: wacko
Grayson: back hoe
Hook: stop
Grayson: you get used to it
Hook: doubt that
Grayson: grout splat
Hook: snout rat
Grayson: yay for hook!
Hook: trout flat
Hook: pout pat
Hook: stout cat
Hook: route bat
Hook: out fat
Hook: you gone?

# 16

It's mid-afternoon when the boys get back to the Jeep. They escaped the Marines mostly unscathed, though Sergeant Stone threatened to shove a broom handle up somebody's black ass. Luke climbs into the backseat, settling in somewhere between seething and scared. Twenty mad minutes later on Sunrise Beach, he can barely stop himself from strangling the new Jesus, who has just run the only stop light on the island.

"What's the matter with you, Markos?" screams Luke. "Are you trying to get us killed?"

"Don't call me that." The reckless new savior presses harder on the accelerator. "Okay," snarks Luke, leaning into the front seat to yell in the new Jesus' ear. "How about I call you s-stupid?"

The new Jesus slams on the brakes, fishtailing off Ocean Drive onto the grassy lot in front of Doug Dipper's Pool Palace. After the Jeep slides to a stop just inches from the custom-built above-ground vinyl display pool, the new Jesus throws open the door and stomps away.

"Damn it. Will you two please stop all this arguing?" Gary rarely swears, and the damn-it pulls them all up short.

"Only if you take over being Jesus again."

"You screamed in my ear," yells the new Jesus.

"You ran a red light."

"Both of you say you're sorry," says Gary. "Jesus?"

"Luke has to go first."

Gary sighs with the weight of the world. "You're Jesus. Blessed are they who apologize first."

But before the new Jesus can answer, Doug Dipper rumbles up in his black Dodge van on the way home from the Blue Heaven Villas.

"What're you boys doing here?" Doug says, hopping from the driver's seat.

The new Jesus picks up the question, winking at Gary.

"We were wondering, sir, if we might be able to rent your pool. Sunday after next would be good."

"What the hell for?" says Doug. He inspects the scene for damage, his hand sliding down his beer belly on its way to tug at his crotch.

The new Jesus winks again. "We're planning a baptism."

Luke looks surprised, but Gary grins.

"You some kinda preacher?" Doug eyes the new Jesus, resting his gaze a beat too long on the bulge in the young man's jeans. "You don't look like no preacher."

The new Jesus reaches into his pocket and pulls out a fat wad of bills.

"We can pay."

# 17

Four hours west of Sunrise Beach, the life of Elizabeth Lena Forsythe takes a hard right turn. On a misty Monday morning commute to work, her three-year-old Honda Accord slides off a slick ribbon of asphalt, tumbles down a hill, and crashes into a tree.

Liz had taken uncharacteristic offense at Frank's smartass comments on the way from the beach and they spoke sparingly for the rest of their trip. At home, he'd slipped into unpacking, while she settled with the dog-sitter. He watered the plants, she picked up the mail. Circling on parallel tracks, the couple had little cause to connect, and didn't.

When it was time for bed, Liz gave Frank a cold shoulder and spent a fitful night puffing and pouting. She watched 12:34 flicker into existence on the digital clock. She remembered why she didn't like going to sleep mad. The next morning, she left for work before Frank dreamed of waking. She was still upset. She was driving too fast.

When the sheriff's phone call rouses him from bed, Frank goes wild with worry. He arrives fifteen minutes later at the scene of the accident, a drizzly daze made surreal by the flashing lights of an ambulance and two patrol cars. He parks on the shoulder beside a growing knot of traffic and hurries through the exhausted air. Thirty yards away, paramedics in yellow slickers carry his wife on a stretcher, her head immobilized in a brace, her face covered with blood.

By the time Frank catches up, they're angling her into the ambulance. It's all he can do to say he's her husband and ask if he can ride with them. They say no. They say he should follow them to the hospital.

As the ambulance pulls away, Frank sneezes and loses his footing on the slippery bank. He lands on his butt in the mud, stars swirling wild in his eyes.

"Frank?"

He looks up to see the thick tilting body of his friend Oscar Ornstein in a shapeless raincoat, squinting through fogged-up glasses. Oscar's permanent backward slouch makes it look like his feet are moving too fast for his body, even when he's standing still.

"Oscar? What are you doing here."

"I was on my way to school. I saw your truck."

Oscar stops to pray at accidents whenever he gets the chance. He says being around dying people brings him closer to understanding god.

"Liz had a wreck." Frank can't think of what else to say. It scares him that Oscar's here.

Oscar pulls him to his feet and guides him toward the road. "She's going to one of the best hospitals in the world," he says. "She's Duke's top fundraiser. They'll take extra good care of her." He tries a smile, but it doesn't stick.

When he's not wandering around car wrecks, Oscar attends Duke University Divinity School. To say he's religious, though, is to misinterpret his inclinations by a wide margin. Oscar Abram Ornstein studies religion, he doesn't practice it.

"It would be difficult to overstate how little confidence I have in organized religion," he told Liz and Frank when they met a few years ago. It was the fifty-fifth birthday party of Rachel Rose, Duke University's director of development, Liz's boss.

"I don't mean to be nosy," said Liz, "but don't you have to believe in god to go to divinity school?"

"I did. In fact, I still do on occasion. But honestly, they couldn't resist me. The son of an Iron Duke?"

Liz whistled. No wonder Rachel had invited the young man. His daddy's a big donor.

"Two years ago I spent Thursday afternoons reading the *Book of Mormon* for one of my classes. I'm afraid it did me in."

"You don't approve of the latter day saints?"

"Delusions of a paranoid schizophrenic."

"Sounds like most religions to me," said Frank.

"My point exactly."

The three had kept up the patter until the party collapsed, and then carried their conversation to a late-night breakfast at the Hillsborough Street Pancake House. Over plates of pecan waffles with whipped cream and strawberries, they pondered the question of omnipotence.

"If god's not in charge of everything, what's the point of having him in the first place?" said Frank.

"Or her," said Liz.

"People need someone to talk to," said Oscar.

"Does she talk back?" said Frank.

"Only when you're listening,'" said Oscar, forking a syrupy clump of waffles into his mouth.

# 18

Had Hook been born into a halfway normal family, her decent looks might have been a ticket to some kind of happiness. But the one-two punch of a missing mother and a feral father knocked her over an edge that rattled her developing brain. By the time she entered high school, she'd begun defacing her body with cigarette burns, cuts and piercings, recreating herself as a sliced-up shrine with each new instance of bodily harm.

Over the past few years, she's had eleven angels scabbed into her skin, and nearly sealed her vagina shut with titanium bead rings. Her current project, another angel, is just about ready for blood. It's late Monday afternoon and she's waiting for Layla in the quiet back room at Holes.

A hundred yards north of Ocean Drive on the dead-end part of Oak Avenue, Holes Tattoo & Piercing occupies the ground floor of a sunny two-story cinderblock cottage. Layla, who lives upstairs, has run the body shop for a dozen years, and is known on the Carolina coast for her sterile equipment and affordable prices. She does any piece of tattoo flash for whoever comes around, and has recently tapped into a piercing craze that's doubled her annual sales. She goes out of her way to make sure clients know what they're getting into, with a strict policy against face tattoos, branding, and working on drunks.

Hook slides onto the bodywork chair and scans the familiar space for something to pass the time. She picks up a fortune-telling eight ball from the clutter on a table and rolls it in her sweaty hands. An answer floats up in the inky sphere. *Ask again later.*

"Stupid ball."

Layla drifts into the room. "I don't know, girlfriend." She

settles on a rolling stool, holding an illustration of an angel wing in one hand and a cup of peppermint tea in the other. "You might need you a vacation."

"Got a bad headache. Like someone smashed me in the face with a brick." She sets the eight ball down, takes off her hat, and peels out of her long-sleeved sweater. She stretches back in the chair and stares at the ceiling.

Layla thinks headaches are caused by psychic disturbances and wants to raise the subject, but Hook doesn't seem ready for a paranormal discussion. Layla settles for small talk.

"I didn't know you was no Duke fan."

"I ain't."

"You got their hat."

"That D means Duke?"

"Or maybe in your case, duh."

Hook looks away, but can't hide the hurt.

"I'm just kidding, hon," says Layla. "There ain't no reason you should know anything about Duke." She takes a centering breath. "Now what do we got here?" She holds the drawing up to Hook's bare chest and surveys the scene. Spiked black hair. Translucent twitching eyelids. A splash of acne on each cheek. The hint of a gap between her two front teeth. A long, slender neck. Full breasts, with a silver cross hanging from a loop through the left nipple. Dark-skinned arms crawling with angels. Farmer's tan.

Layla takes a good long look, then lifts the art away. "You sure you want that angel wing going all the way up your neck?" She sips her tea. "I don't much like that idea."

Hook grabs the little cross and stretches her nipple like a thick rubber band. "You didn't like this one neither."

Layla ignores the drama. "Holes ain't permanent."

# 19

With his income winding down for the season, Doug Dipper figured he might as well grab some cash from his roadside display. He told the boys they could rent the pool for a hundred bucks, half up front. They tried to talk him down, but Doug held firm, agreeing only to heat the pool and let them put up a sign.

The whole deal has Luke worried. He's sitting with Gary in the Airstream, watching him doodle on scrap paper at the collapsible Formica kitchenette table. The new Jesus is nowhere to be found.

"We need s-something catchy on the s-sign," says Luke. He leans over Gary's shoulder to look at his drawings. "Dunk & Go Nuts? You can't be s-serious."

Gary scrunches a pencil between his nose and lip and crosses his eyes. "Of course I can't be serious."

Luke grabs the pencil and scribbles for a few seconds. "How about this? Get S-s-saved Or You Will Burn In Hell."

Gary turns into Jesus and flashes a quiet smile. "You know I don't believe that."

"It's right there in *John*. He that believeth not is condemned already."

"John was full of baloney."

"John was the Baptist," says Luke.

"Then he was full of wet baloney."

Gary and Luke have this argument at least once a week. Luke throws out a couple of verses about hell, and Gary laughs them off. "I know what's in the Bible," says Gary. "But those old guys got it wrong. God's not that much of an asshole."

Luke surrenders, like he always does, and settles in to watch Gary fill a page with familiar engravings from the bracelet. None of the sweepers has any idea what those strange inscriptions mean, but that hasn't slowed them down one bit. The bracelet told Gary he held the threads of life fully filled, and that's all they needed to know.

"I don't get how you can s-s-sit back and let Mark take over everything," says Luke.

"Your turn's coming."

"I don't want a turn. You found the bracelet. Not Mark. You're the one."

Beyond the allure of the silver band, it was Gary's gentle ways that won Luke over in the first place. He wants his old Jesus back.

"But I'm the one who lost it, too," says Gary. "Besides, does it really matter who's Jesus?"

# 20

Oscar manages to collect only an old silver bracelet from the floorboard of Liz's smashed car before a state trooper noses in. When the officer asks what he found, Oscar slips into silent prayer without skipping a beat. He closes his eyes and thanks god for giving him such a dependable way to escape the crush of uniformed authority.

When he arrives at the hospital a few hours later, Oscar finds Frank in a swivet, bouncing from nurse to doctor to orderly to receptionist, ever more frustrated with each paltry response. He's just cornered a harried neurologist outside the emergency room.

"It's okay, Frank," says Oscar. "Let's just sit here for a minute." He wraps an arm around Frank's shoulders, praying him down from his panic.

Sixty seconds on the molded plastic furniture is all it takes for Frank to report everything he knows about the condition of Liz. She's stable. She's breathing. She has a cut on her head and a crack in her skull. She's unconscious. She's not dead.

By late afternoon, doctors tell Frank to go home, but he won't. It's all Oscar can do to drag him down to the Commons, a posh Duke eatery that taps into the hospital's vein of anxious visitors.

"I found this in the car," says Oscar, sliding the bracelet across the table.

Frank knows he's seen it before, but he's not quite sure where. Before his wobbling mind can focus, the smallest waitress in the world appears at their table. Her tight black pants and tight white blouse and tight orange hair and tight red smile are stunning in their cumulative effect, made stranger by the oversized silver ring hanging lavishly from her navel. Frank imagines slipping his finger through the seductive circle. Instead he wraps his hand around the bracelet and slides it into his pocket.

The miniature woman bounces on her heels. "You want some drink?"

Frank's eyes jump to see her tap-tap-tapping a blue Bic pen against the shiny white teeth that line her mouth, before slipping down again to the silver ring, down farther to the woman's vulva parted by the satiny seam of her poured-on pants.

Oscar coughs and jolts Frank back to business.

"Right. I guess I'll have a margarita." Frank regains some of his footing, but none of his dignity. "You want one, Oscar?"

"No thanks. I'll be the responsible adult."

The waitress leaves.

"I know your wife's in a coma, Frank, but jeez."

"Hey, I'm not the one with a size three body in size one pants. Why would she do that if she doesn't want men looking at her?"

"Let's see. Could it be to get old geezers like you to buy more drinks and leave bigger tips?"

"Well, it's working."

Encouraged by Oscar's chitty chatter, Frank quaffs his drink. As he licks the salt from the rim of his glass, his shoulders shudder, finally, with the fear of unthinkable loss.

"Time to go home, old boy," says Oscar. He takes the cash Frank offers, leaving a ten dollar bill under the empty salsa bowl.

# 21

Layla drags her feet on starting Hook's tattoo for so long that Hook gives up in frustration.

"Tell you what," says Layla. "I'll buy you supper at JJ's as a consolation prize."

"I ain't no charity case," says Hook. She stretches her arms, flexing her angels in a muscular dance.

"I know that, hon. I just like your company. Besides. You're good for business."

Hook slips back into her sweater. "Won't nobody be there besides us."

It's a nice evening, so the women walk the eight blocks to the restaurant. Hook gets nervous along the way. "I think I was wrong," she says. "We ain't gonna be the only ones out tonight."

Layla pulls her close. "We'll have us a good time then."

For a seafood restaurant that doubles as a dance hall, JJ's isn't half bad. Locals come around for cheap coffee, big breakfasts, and fried shrimp dinners that keep the register ringing year round. The greasy spoon features ten tables, four booths, a tiny dance floor, and the best oldies jukebox on the island.

Layla is only half surprised to find her old boyfriend Zeke hanging around the parking lot. There's an open bottle of Budweiser stuck in his front pants pocket and half a grilled cheese sandwich hanging from his mouth. His long graying beard and hair are in the early stages of dreadlocks, and his Hawaiian shirt's unbuttoned enough to show the yin-yang symbol Layla tattooed on his skinny chest ten years ago. It's the first job she ever did for a paying customer.

Zeke goes after Hook the second he sees her. "Got me a

rocket in my pocket for you, Hookster." He pumps his pelvis in her direction, sloshing beer down the front of his khakis. Hook busts out laughing.

"You're still a moron, ain't you Zeke," says Layla. "I figured them ghosts you talk to all day woulda straightened you out by now. Can't they find somebody smarter'n you to channel through?"

"Smart don't matter. Hell, even Hook could do it."

Layla gets in his face. "What're you doing here, Ezekiel? I thought Monday was when you got your beauty rest. Lord knows you need it."

"It's my fortieth birthday. I'm waiting for the party to show up."

"Forty again?" says Layla.

"Just like Jack Benny." Zeke takes a show business bow.

"Jack Benny stopped at thirty-nine, dip shit. Forty's a stupid birthday to keep having."

Layla and Zeke smart aleck back and forth like this all the time. Hook thinks it's because they're still in love, and says so.

"No way, Jose." Zeke fakes a seizure, rolling his eyes back in his head so only the whites are showing. "I read her mind once. She comes from a long line of witches."

"Speaking of spooky, you need you some breath mints." Layla laughs and pushes past Zeke through the restaurant door.

It's a thin crowd. A clump of loud women drinking wine coolers have commandeered the bar, but only a few tables are taken. Stale fried grease fills the air, with traces of beer, cigarette smoke, and a hint of perfume rounding things out. Hook and Layla settle in the blue vinyl booth by the jukebox, the same one Liz and Frank sat in for breakfast the day before. *Proud Mary* rocks through the Wurlitzer speakers.

"Something wrong, sweetie?" says Layla. "You seem kind of fidgety."

It takes Hook a few seconds to notice the question. She grabs the Duke baseball hat from her head and throws it on the seat. She rubs her fingers deep in her eye sockets till she's seeing stars and black holes.

"You'd be fidgety too if your whole damn life was screwed up as mine. And this stupid headache won't go away."

"Zeke can help. He may be a sleaze ball, but he does know

how to get rid of headaches." Layla slips two fingers between her lips and catches Zeke's attention with a sharp whistle. He's hustling the ladies over at the bar. "Come here," she yells.

Hook winces at the loudness. *Beast of Burden* starts up on the jukebox and Zeke dances to their booth, leaning in low over the table.

"What can I do you for?" he says to Layla. "Wanna take me home and fuck my brains out, your hineyness?"

"Watch your damn language," says Layla. "Hook here's got a headache."

Zeke scoots in next to Hook. She inches away.

"Hands off," warns Layla.

Zeke answers by shaking his head and blanking his face. Layla's seen enough of his bullshit to know something's up.

He lets his words out carefully. "I got a feeling your mama might be visiting."

"Don't mess with me, Zeke," says Hook. She looks around the diner. There's no sign of anyone who might qualify as her mother.

"I'd love to mess with you, darling, but I ain't. I mean just what I said. Your mama's here. Floating right beside my shoulder."

Hook covers her ears, the angels on her arms whispering soft and crazy.

"She seems kind of upset," says Zeke.

"She should be upset," says Layla. "She's channeling through a goddamn idiot."

"This ain't funny, Zeke." Hook's voice is five years old.

"All we wanted was help with a damn headache," says Layla. "We didn't request no frickin' séance."

Zeke lowers his eyelids. He stretches his shoulders back and points his chin up high like he's sniffing for smoke. He shakes his wooly head. "I don't know if she's still here."

"Is she dead?" Hook whispers without meaning to.

"She might be headed that way."

"This is such bullshit." Layla rearranges condiments on the table in a huff. She picks up a bottle of Texas Pete and aims it at Zeke, who sits up alert.

"Damn it, Layla. You scared her off."

"Ain't that a surprise." Layla's moved past having fun into being pissed. She tells Zeke to leave them alone, and he does.

When a basket of hot hush puppies lands on the table, Hook catches Layla's eye. "What the heck're you looking at?"

Layla studies her friend. "You think your mama was really here?"

'Zeke didn't do nothing special."

"I know, sweetie," says Layla. "It's just his standard pitch."

"You don't think it was her neither?"

Layla unwraps the napkin from her knife and fork. "I didn't say that."

That night Hook smokes a joint and settles down with Sinker's laptop. She checks to see who's online and finds a rant unfolding about stupid men. She conjures up a new poem on the spot.

*brains and tongues like slinky lizards*
*looking for the heat of skin and moans*

Her virtual friends pile on.

Solitude: hookkkkkksssss hottttttt
Justagrl: stop it soli. this is serious. hahahaha
Hook: its a stupid poem
James: haiku
Justagrl: screw you
James: you're pretty angry about men
Hook: and you sure got a way with words
James: *hangs head in shame*
Hook: *bangs head in game*
Justagrl: stop being a jerk james
Hook: the only decent man i know is eddie juniors daddy
James: the ONLY one?
Hook: eddie juniors okay too I guess
James: your boyfriend?
Solitude: fuck you james
Justagrl: duck shoe games
Hook: suck screw dames

# 22

The new Jesus spends the week haunted by hopes of finding the silver bracelet, and his worry is contagious. Especially with Luke, who's in a snit about their big baptism service. It's coming up fast and they're nowhere near ready.

For one thing, the new Jesus can't decide what to wear. He's thinking Mexican, but Luke wants to play things straight. Being the only black person in a rising storm of white Christians, he's nervous enough without adding Latino to the mix. And Gary, the only one who really knows anything about the full immersion method, is having second thoughts. He's been born again twice, but his memories are mostly grim. He was eight years old the first time it happened.

"I still think he's too young," Glenda Kay whispered as they pulled up to their little country church one Sunday morning. She pushed open the passenger door, letting Gary out, struggling with the reality of being a prisoner in her own life. A dozen years ago, she'd been on her way to a teaching degree when Gus popped her cherry and whisked her away under the threat of a ruined reputation. In the years that followed, she learned to speak softly or get smacked. Gus always knew she was smarter than he was, and didn't like it one bit.

"God told me it's time," he said. "Now get yourself straight and stop your goddamn whining. People are watching."

And watching they were.

A dozen eager souls hung outside the open doors of the shabby church, looking to see whether crazy Gus had brought a rattler along for the big celebration. He had.

Any young sheep joining the flock is a big deal for Conway

Pentecostals, but a baptism service for the son of a snake-handler raises extra high expectations. The possibility of Gus Gray meeting a tortured death on the church's linoleum floor brought visitors from as far away as West Virginia, filling the sanctuary with the potential for high drama.

Little Gary's baptism turned out to be a predictable sideshow to his old man's circus. No sooner had the son stepped into the church's pool, than the father started his snake tricks, taking a sharp rattler strike on the arm. That scared some Pentecostals into speaking in tongues, including the preacher himself, who rushed through the baptism in record time. But Gus didn't die. He'd long since removed the snake's poison glands. And though some in the congregation suspected as much, that's not the kind of thing you'd ever say to Gus Gray in person.

"Maybe I'll find us some choir robes," says the new Jesus. It's late afternoon, and he's planning a trip to the thrift store for supplies. Gary had snagged a left-behind three-meat pizza from their connection at Domino's, and the boys are picnicking under one of the creaky live oaks that line the RV park.

"How many people you expecting for this baptizing?" says Luke.

"No idea," says the new Jesus. He tosses a crust of pizza on the ground, triggering a scramble of gulls from out of nowhere.

"I thought Jesus was all-knowing," says Gary. He smiles to blunt the impact of his words, but the question is on the table. And the new Jesus is pissed.

"Damn it, Gary. I didn't say shit like that when you were Jesus."

"As a matter of fact, you did," says Gary.

In the face of more fighting, Luke goes darker than usual. Gary notices the worry and backs down. "I'm sorry, guys," he says. "I don't know what got into me."

"Those by the wayside are the ones who hear, then the devil comes and takes away the word out of their hearts," says Luke. "All this money business. It's evil. It's s-setting us against each other."

"Damn devil," says the new Jesus, letting his anger pass. "He's working overtime to screw up our plans."

# 23

Three days after her accident, Liz awakens with a tangle of threads buzzing bright inside her brain. They've been on a transcranial tear since her crashing in the car, and though she couldn't feel her fingers or toes or lips or nose, the threads have shifted into high gear, scrambling to give meaning to the dizzying daze behind her. Slipping and tumbling together in their own slow-motion calamity, they are pulling her off course, pushing her out onto the fragile thin ice of hope.

Her eyes crack open, cringing at the stark white light in her hospital room. Dr. Sarah Stern is futzing with her bandages, checking the tubes and wires snaked around her body.

The two women have known each other since their senior year at William and Mary, when Sarah helped Liz through a disastrous pregnancy. She had been bravely on her way to becoming a single mom until doctors discovered the child growing inside her was fatally malformed. When she decided to have an abortion instead of a still birth, all hell broke loose in her Southern Baptist family. That was one more rung in her steady climb away from god.

After graduation, the two women moved to Chapel Hill where Liz studied sociology and Sarah started medical school.

"I'm okay, you know." Liz's voice comes out husky and weak at the same time. If the words catch Sarah by surprise, she doesn't show it.

"You mean except for that little crack in your skull? And the fact that you've been unconscious for three days?" She walks to the foot of the bed for a straight-on view. The steady thrum of monitoring machines says there's no need for immediate action. "What happened?"

"You had a wreck on Erwin Road."

"Where's Frank?" Worried voice.

"He was here all night. I made him go home and get cleaned up."

Liz goes beyond pale into panicked. "I have to talk to him." She stretches for the bedside phone and punches in her home number.

Sarah's relieved she remembers it.

Fifteen miles away, Frank's eating SpaghettiOs out of the can with a plastic spoon. He picks up the phone and muffles hello through the pasty circles.

"It's me," says Liz.

He swallows. "Oh god. You're back."

No response.

"Liz?"

"I had that bracelet, Frank. In the car." Her voice strains across the space between them.

It does not occur to the husband at that moment to wonder why his woozy wife, after seventy hours in a coma, is worried about the bracelet. He's been living with it for the past three days, and though he couldn't begin to explain why, not in any words you'd understand, he is not surprised she wants it.

"I have it, Liz. I'm on the way."

# 24

A mile up the coast on Eddie's Pier, Hook and Sinker have their hands full with a screaming seagull tangled in Sinker's fishing line.

"About time you caught something," says Hook. "Reel that sucker in and we'll have it for dinner."

"You can't eat a damn seagull."

"You sure can. Bring it on up here."

"Gonna have to cut the line."

Hook'll do just about anything to avoid losing a rig to a seagull, so she tries to help. With Sinker waving the tip of his rod back and forth, she grabs the line over the railing and eventually shakes the bird loose.

"Well lookie who's here. If it ain't Jack and Jill." It's Doug Dipper, leaning against the railing three feet away, clapping at Sinker's disappearing bird act. "Done caught you a damn CGU-11." Doug spent a few years as a Marine at nearby Camp Lejeune, and is always spouting military nonsense.

"We ain't caught nothing." Sinker's never quite sure when the Dipper's pulling his leg, though Hook always feels the tug.

"It's a joke," says Hook. "C.G.U. Eleven? It's Marine for seagull. Get it?"

Sinker doesn't get it. "Who gives a shit anyway. Make yourself useful and get us some Mountain Dews."

"I ain't your errand boy." She takes his three crumpled bills. "You want some, Doug?"

"Nah."

Hook heads toward the pier entrance, talking over her shoulder. "Try not to catch no more birds while I'm gone."

Doug and Sinker got acquainted a few years ago in the back

of Doug's Dodge van outside the local Piggly Wiggly. It was graduation night for Sinker, who was hell-bent on scoring a six-pack of Miller High Life to celebrate his escape from two years in the twelfth grade. Doug Dipper was trolling for trouble in the grocery store parking lot, when he ran into Sinker hanging around the drive-thru cash machine. He agreed to buy the boy's beer for a blow job.

"How's it hanging?" says Sinker.

"Low and loose. Like always." Doug rearranges his notorious tool with a wink. "But that ain't what I come for."

"Yeah? What's up?"

"I heard you and Hook was hassling some old lady on the beach last Sunday."

"Where'd you hear that bullshit?"

"Bill Beak."

"That guy don't know jack."

"What guy?" Hook returns with two bottles of cold green caffeine. She takes off her Duke hat and rolls one of them against her forehead.

"Shut up," says Sinker.

"Heard you was fucking with some lady on the beach the other day."

"It won't nothing," says Hook.

"We saved that bitch," says Sinker. "Dragged her ass outta the ocean."

Doug eyes the delicate wings wrapping Hook's forearms before he throws out his lie. "More like tempted rape is what I heard. Plus some girl was there, too. A girl with tattoos."

"I told you to shut your mouth," says Sinker.

"You're the one tried to feel her up," says Hook.

Sinker whips a knife from his belt and pushes a thin curved blade up under Hook's long neck. Though he's prone to outbursts, he's never before threatened to cut his sister's throat. She eases her hand down to the five-inch shark hook dangling from her belt and presses the point up into his crotch. Sinker's eyes get shiftier than usual.

"You best put that knife away, little brother."

Doug steps back a safe distance. "Leave Hook be, Sinker. I'm the only one knows it was you."

Sinker lowers his knife. "I didn't do nothing."

"Whatever," says Doug. "I gotta go to work. You girls get on back to your bird fishing." He turns to leave, stops and looks back. "Going to the baptizing at my pool on Sunday? Three crazies putting on a show."

"I gotta work," says Hook.

"Well, maybe your idiot brother'll show up." Doug's talking like Sinker's not even there. "He could use the bath."

# 25

With two hundred churches inside its city limits, Jacksonville, North Carolina, gets wild on Sunday mornings. Armies of Christians in grumbling trucks clog the streets with fat tires, shiny wheels, and enough red, white and blue to start a revolution. And near the center of it all sits the New Gate of Heaven Baptist Church, the promise of certain salvation, wrapped in a thirty-foot star-spangled flag.

With their own plans still in limbo, the new Jesus figured they should check out the competition and pick up some baptizing pointers. So on this particular Sunday, here they are, lured through the New Gate by the lighted sign out front.

*Jesus swept so you can come clean.*

"I don't know about this place," says Luke. He swallows his words when a hulking man and his tight-faced wife glare from the cab of a passing Toyota Tundra covered with Confederate flag decals.

Gary waves at the gawkers like they're old friends. "Hey ya'll," he sings. "Coming to church today?"

As if on cue, a waltzy rendition of *The Old Rugged Cross* spills from the open church doors.

*On a hill far away stood an old rugged cross,*
*The emblem of suffering and shame;*
*And I love that old cross where the dearest and best*
*For a world of lost sinners was slain.*

That song has given Gary the creeps since the first time he heard it as a kid. He could never understand people going gaga over a bloody old cross, especially since his daddy burned the sacred symbol in public at least twice a year.

Gary's first and last experience with a gathering of the Klan was a hard hour of angry white men with Bibles in one hand and guns in the other, hell-bent on driving the coloreds out of Conway. The meeting took place a mile from Gary's high school, where a celebration was scheduled to honor their football team. Gus Gray couldn't stomach so many darkies getting awards, so he made Gary skip the pep rally to take in the hate. In the bright light of a burning cross, the old man prayed for God to drive the football niggers back to Africa. Gary still grimaces when he sees a cross hanging from a rearview mirror. Good thing they didn't kill that old Jesus in an electric chair.

"They won't bother us," says the new Jesus. He's moving toward the church entrance, full of good-morning's and how-are-you's.

"It's not *us* I'm worried about," says Luke. "Did you s-see all those rebel s-s-stars and bars?"

The organist cranks up *By the Waters* and Gary brightens. "Come on, sweet bear. They're playing your favorite song," he says, coaxing Luke into line.

# 26

It's been twenty years since Liz has done time in a hospital. She was nine months pregnant and had come in for the routine delivery of Frances Hunter Forsythe. Twelve hours later, everything went wrong. She had an emergency C-section and a daughter who didn't live to be born. After that, Liz took a leave of absence from work, drank too much, and blew her days away. When things skidded too close to the edge, her sister Faye moved in for six weeks. She and Frank nursed Liz back to something just short of normal.

Today Liz is thirsty for outside air. She's packed and pacing, ready to check out. As soon as the doctors give her one more once over, she'll be gone. Her thoughts wander through the week behind her. Three days of that week are missing, the other four are fuzzy.

She hears a sharp knock.

"Mizz Forsythe?"

A bald head with a black combover pops around the door. "I was hoping I might visit with you for a few minutes." The man's bright pink shirt and lime green tie give Liz the creeps.

"Joe Peters."

She hedges. "I'm just about to check out."

He extends his right hand, followed by an elbow-grabbing left that lingers longer than a handshake should.

"Glad I caught you then."

She waits.

"I'm here at the suggestion of our friend. Rachel Rose. She made me promise to get in here to see you. How are you doing, dear? I know. You been through a lot."

"You know?"

"Rachel and I enjoyed dinner together last night. I'm the pastor at Calvary Mission. In Rougemont."

Liz wrestles with the idea of a dinner shared between the Calvary man and her promiscuous partner in fundraising. After two breast implants, a facelift, and a surgically tightened vagina, Rachel Rose may be the most fuckable old lady in the development business.

Joe Peters pokes around her room like he's been here before.

"So this is how you spend Sunday afternoons?" Liz asks.

"Deed I do," he says. "Keeps us in touch with the Lord."

"Funny. I have a friend who stops at car wrecks for the same reason."

"That Ornstein boy. Rachel said ya'll were friends."

Liz thinks it's weird that this guy knows about Oscar's penchant for accidental praying, but lets it go.

"What's that you got there?" says Joe, pointing to her bracelet. She's tracing the smooth engravings with an absent-minded finger. The question stops her, raises her guard a notch.

"Just something I found at the beach."

He reaches, expecting her to give. She holds back. He moves in closer, the day-old scent of Rachel still hanging on his clothes. He takes Liz's hand and presses it to his chest.

"Tell me dear." He closes his eyes. "Are you right with Jesus?" He wraps around her wrist, his clammy fingers flitting too close to the bracelet. Her skin goes hot and pale.

"Excuse me?"

"I feel the Holy Spirit coursing through you like a storm." He presses between her tendons, like he's taking her pulse.

Joe's smarmy touch is more than Liz can stomach. Literally. She gushes out a stream of watery puke flecked with green peas from lunch, flooding the preacher's polyester pants in a stinky stew.

He's aghast, she's annoyed. He grabs a sheet and wipes his clothes. She pushes the bracelet up tight around her arm, says good-bye. She runs into Frank coming out of the elevator.

"Checked out already?" he says, cheered by the thought.

"No," she grumps. "But I'm leaving anyway. A creepy preacher came to see me. A friend of Rachel's."

Frank furrows his brow. "What'd did he want?"

"He told me he felt the . . ."

The words to finish the sentence refuse to form on the lips of Liz.

"He felt what?"

"Can we talk about this later? I just want to get out of here." She searches his face for evidence of understanding and finds it.

Frank waits, more jittery than he'd want to admit, while Liz presses the elevator button a dozen times. The doors open and they escape.

They walk evenly through the hospital hallways, like Bonnie Parker and Clyde Barrow slipping through the lobby of an east Texas bank. A fog of odors shrouds their escape. The metallic smell of too many x-rays. The tang of fresh-cured casts. The after-taste of vomit. Too much floor wax.

A security guard at the front door slides his sunglasses down his nose, tilting his head to take a closer look at the woman who is getting away. But he doesn't choose to stop them. He doesn't want to see their papers.

# 27

Hook spends Sunday morning doing inventory at the fishing superstore with her boss, Bobby Beak. She had fun Saturday night journaling about her job, and her online friends said she should ask for a raise. That's her plan, but old Bobby has other things on his mind.

"When you gonna let me see them titties of yours, missy?" It's the third time he's asked today. "Tell you what," he says. "I'll give you that raise and the afternoon off for a little peek."

Hook's backed up against a spool of anchor chain. There's no way out except to squeeze by her lecherous boss. "I ain't no whore."

"Course you ain't no whore." Bobby pushes his slid-down bifocals up his bulbous nose. Unlike his older brother Bill, Bobby leans toward the chunky side of the family. "I never said you was. I just wanna see them tits." He pushes closer.

"You seen tits before, Mr. Beak. And you know they ain't worth all this trouble." Her hand eases to the shark hook on her belt.

Bobby backs off a few rickety steps. His puny left leg has slowed him down ever since polio introduced him to limping at the age of seven.

"You know what, missy? You ain't the most cooperative damn employee I ever had. Maybe you oughta think about working somewheres else."

Hook's tempted to drag her Water Devil through Bobby's butt on her way out the door, but even a half-assed raise would make her transition to independence smoother.

"How about this. You write me a letter about the raise and all, something official, and I'll show 'em to you."

"Don't seem like you trust me too much." Bobby looks from her steel hook to her green eyes and back.

"It ain't about trust, Mr. Beak. I gotta take care now that I'm moving out on my own. You understand that."

"About time you left that shithead brother of yours. Heard he tried to rape some lady down the beach. That right?"

"Nah. He was just looking. Got his head smashed for it, though." Hook's hint of a smile brushes Bobby back a few more steps. He parks himself on a carton of fishing line, picking at his ear with a gnarly fisherman's finger. She drops the Water Devil. It joggles on its chain like a just-hanged man. Bobby's relieved to see the hook swing free.

"What kinda raise you got in mind?"

"Dollar an hour."

His whistle echoes through the stockroom. "Pretty damn rich."

"Suit yourself." Hook starts for the door.

"Hold on now." Bobby struggles to his feet.

"I'm the best damn worker you ever had around here. And you don't pay me nothing like them others."

Bobby nods his oversized head. "Fair enough, missy." He looks her over, licks his lips. "You just keep up the inventorying till I get back."

When Bobby leaves to write up the offer, Hook second-guesses her decision more times than she can count. Sinker happily sells his body for beer and booze, but Hook's steered clear of whoring so far. She says as much when Bobby hobbles back into the stockroom.

"We made us a deal." Bobby's voice takes an edge as he sets a folded piece of paper on the spool in front of Hook. "Signed and all."

Hook picks up the letter and reads aloud.

"In recognition of your service and dedication to Bobby's Fishing Superstore, you are hereby granted a raise to $8.75 per hour, effective immediately." Hook grins big. "Damn, Mr. Beak. I didn't know you could write so good."

"I did them citations that goes with medals," he says. "Purple Hearts was the only ones worth a shit." He takes off his glasses and smears them with a handkerchief. "Let's see them nice titties now, missy. We still got us a shitload of work to do."

Hook stands her ground. "You said you'd give me the afternoon off."

"I might and I might not," says Bobby. "It depends on what you got under that shirt."

# 28

The first thing visitors notice about the New Gate of Heaven Baptist Church is the steel. Thick engineered beams diving to the ground like spider legs covered with slick corrugated skin. In the belly of the beast, rows of cushioned pews lead to a stage covered with fluffy white carpet, the blue aisles cordoned off for the choir, the red ones for the multitudes.

Before you get to those soft seats, though, you have to pass the greeters, a tight platoon of bull-necked men stuffed into black suits, with starched white shirts and American flag ties. The Gatekeepers. A few good men, dressed to shill for the Sunday morning crunch. And the biggest Gatekeeper of all is Sergeant Stone from Camp Lejeune.

Gary sees Stone's little bug ears over the crowd. "Our friend in freedom! Praise bees!"

Stone blinks slow, like a lizard. He can't believe the bums he almost shot are here in his very own church. He makes his fists and slits his eyes and looks around for help.

"*Cómo estás?*" says the new Jesus. He tangos up to Sergeant Stone and gives the big grunt a hug. His arms don't quite reach around Stone's barrel chest, but he squeezes like his life depends on it.

"Hey, Stone," says another Gatekeeper. "Didn't know you had you a boyfriend."

Despite its steel trappings, the service doesn't deliver much in terms of cash donations or souls saved this day. Sitting in the back row, the boys get a good look at the piddly offering when a brass plate passes their pew.

But the real surprise is the big zero in the redemption

department. No little kid or old lady or anybody in between bothers to stroll down the aisle at the end of the hell-raising service. The preacher preaches himself hoarse, calling on sinners to repent. The organ blasts *Just As I Am* through a dozen loud speakers. And two Gatekeepers open thick velvet curtains behind the stage to reveal a shiny aluminum cross flanked by the American flag on one side and the Marine Corps flag on the other.

But not a soul steps forward to be born again.

# 29

The back roads between Duke and Chapel Hill run through packed subdivisions bordering Duke Forest and the Eno River. With its thirty miles of tidy trails, Duke Forest is one laudable legacy of a tobacco industry that created unimaginable wealth for a few families and unimaginable misery for millions more.

When they pass their favorite spot near the river, Liz asks Frank to stop. It's raining again, and the white noise of the rushing river fills the air outside.

"We need to talk," she says. "Just for a minute."

He bites his tongue and pulls off the road.

After twenty years of marriage, Liz still can't predict how Frank will handle any particular conversation. She complained about it to her friend Sarah Stern a few months after they'd gotten married.

"Who cares what he thinks?" said Sarah, who wasn't sure she liked Frank anyway. "Besides, sometimes he's just full of crap. Remember when we drove to the mountains and he was going on about those cable boxes on telephone poles? The Frankster had no idea what he was talking about. My brother was a cable guy. I know."

Afterwards, Liz confronted Frank.

"They weren't cable boxes?" he said.

"That's not the point."

"What is the point?"

"The point is you go around behaving like you know what you're talking about, and half the time you don't."

"Not half the time. Just every now and then."

"And how am I supposed to know when it's now and when it's then?" said Liz.

"Dearest, you don't pay attention to what I say anyway. Especially about telephone poles."

"That's not the point either."

"What is the damn point?"

"The point is, you're lying. That's the damn point."

He hadn't considered that his loose interpretations of the physical world might qualify as lying, and the accusation slammed him into a binge of truth-telling. Oscar was especially troubled by the newfound honesty.

"I don't like this. You used to know things." Oscar wanted Frank to explain the exact cause of thunder. "Come on. Tell me some tales."

But Frank Forsythe had stopped prevaricating. He could no longer tell a lie.

Frank cranks his seat back, almost lying down. Liz often complains that if you give Frank five minutes, he'll find a way to get horizontal. But today she's glad to have him settling in to listen. She studies the wrinkled skin of his neck and chin, the spots he missed shaving. She wonders when he began to look so old.

"Something weird's going on," she says. The rain picks up, hammering the roof. Even in the small cab of the truck, Liz has to speak up to be heard. She wishes she could whisper. "It's about that pelican, Frank."

He waits.

"It didn't just wink. It said something, too.

He waits again.

"It said you cannot hold the threads."

Frank's mind slips like a failing clutch. "It said you cannot hold the threads?"

"Or maybe I just sensed it. I'm not sure."

"You mean telepathy?"

"I don't know."

He's staring through the windshield, watching rain pool into snakes on the glass. "That's it?"

"Isn't that enough?" She takes a deep breath, relieved to have it out.

"You're serious about this?"

"Of course I'm serious."

He almost scoffs. She draws away. "This isn't funny," she says, thinking it might be.

# 30

Hook was more shocked than she should have been to see old Bobby Beak reach inside his droopy pants and feel around for his dick. She bolted out of the stockroom in search of penance, heading straight for Layla and Holes. Another spike through her outer labia is what she had in mind. Layla has a long history of handling client emergencies on her day off, and Hook's pale face at her kitchen door has all the makings of a crisis. She draws the belt around her faded yellow robe and lets Hook in.

"You don't look so good, sweetie."

"That's cause I ain't." Hook's not one for drama, so Layla figures this is serious. "I hoped maybe you could do me another bead ring."

Layla turns to a pineapple on a cutting board. She wouldn't mind doing a little tattoo touch up on her day off, but not pussy piercing. The thwack of her knife nails the awkward silence.

"Fixing me a smoothie. Want some?"

Hook backs against the door and slides down till she's straight-legged on the floor.

"Suit yourself." Layla tosses peach, banana, and pineapple slices into a blender with yogurt and orange juice. She flips the switch and buzzes the room with a high-pitched whir. She fills two Tupperware tumblers and sits beside Hook. "Now tell me what happened."

Hook takes a gulp and wipes her mouth with an angel wing on the back of her hand. "What happened is I fucked up. Bobby said he'd give me a raise if I showed him my tits, so I did. God, I'm so stupid."

# 31

Most Baptist preachers let you out by lunchtime, but the service at New Gate that Sunday turns out to be a two-hour marathon. When no one comes forward at the end of the sermon, the preacher gets perturbed. So instead of a serene "Go in peace" at noon, the congregation gets treated to a breathless rant that could easily be mistaken for hell itself. With more eternal fires and bloody lambs than the sweepers can stomach, the whole business scares them silly. The Gatekeepers are watching, though, and they can't get away.

Before the rant is over, the preacher's will is done. None other than Sergeant Stone himself comes forward to confess his great unworthiness and rededicate his life to Christ.

At a year under thirty, John Paul Stone is a hard-ass airborne Marine, not the kind of man you'd expect to see crying on his knees with a preacher hugging his fresh-shaved head. But that's what happens, just like they rehearsed it, right there in front of the new Jesus, Gary, Luke, and a hundred other witnesses.

"Holy smoke," whispers the new Jesus when the preacher calls Stone's name in his booming Bible voice. "Sergeant Stone is named John."

"Shhhh," says Gary. The sign of the fish catches his eye behind the pulpit. "We're witnessing a mackerel."

Even Luke laughs at that.

"Maybe he'll join us," says the new Jesus. "We need a John. Let's ask him when we lay on hands."

"We don't need a John," grumps Luke. "I can do the baptizing.

If you've never had the pleasure of laying-on hands, you haven't missed much. Anyone who wants to can touch the convert's bowed head, mumble something prayerish, and move along. The ritual can take forever when the head in question is soft and fluffy, but business is brisk with the clammy skin of John Paul Stone. No one wants to finger his slick skull a second longer than necessary. Except for the new Jesus. When he gets to the front of the line, he embraces Stone's cue-ball head and prays for a full thirty seconds, sputtering a stream of nonsense that only Gary recognizes as their own brand of Pig Latin.

"Okie-yay achy-kay," says Gary. "Oovie-may itty-yay."

Luke comes next, offering only a token touch. Then Gary, spouting Beatitudes and cuddling the sergeant's little ears.

"Blessed are the poor in spirit, for theirs is the kingdom of heaven. Blessed are the meek, for they shall inherit the earth. Blessed are they who mourn, for they shall be comforted. Blessed are they who hunger and thirst after justice, for they shall be filled. Blessed are the merciful, for they shall obtain mercy."

"Blessed are the other people in line," whispers one of the Gatekeepers. "For they are getting pissed."

Gary turns and smiles at the waiting worshippers, then resumes his recitation.

"Blessed are the clean of heart, for they shall see God. Blessed are the peacemakers, for they shall be called the children of God. Blessed are they who suffer persecution for justice' sake, for theirs is the kingdom of heaven."

When he finishes, Gary locks eyes with Stone and whispers, "Follow me."

# 32

Tucked on the side of Morgan Mountain, a modest hill by real mountain standards, the house of Liz and Frank is a series of blocks stacked atop and beside one another. Narrow windows slit the gray walls to the north and round peepholes dot the west side. A screened porch out back offers a clear view of the Chapel Hill skyline seven miles to the south.

Liz gets out of the truck and finds Molly waiting on the front porch, her tail thwapping the door, ready for cuddling.

Anybody can tell Liz loves her little dachshund like a daughter, and the feeling seems mutual. An hour later, they're both snoozing on the living room sofa. Frank had offered a Milk-Bone to the dog, Sleepytime tea to the wife, and covered them both with a cotton throw. He's in the kitchen worrying about dinner when Oscar calls.

"I feel like I should be doing something," says Oscar. "But I can't figure out what. Need any help?"

"Only if you know something about pelicans. One's been talking to Liz."

"What?"

"She says she heard a pelican talk. At the beach." Frank can't believe he's having this conversation.

"That's crazy."

"I know."

Oscar thinks it through. "Wait a minute. There was a professor in Divinity who had this thing about pelicans. Gloria Grace. Strange old gal. She retired, but I think she's still around."

While Oscar chatters, Frank gets to his laptop and Googles *Gloria Grace*.

"We're in luck," he says. "She lives in Chapel Hill."

"You don't believe in luck."

Frank looks at Liz sleeping on the porch and reconsiders his cynical view of fortune.

"Maybe I'm changing my mind."

# 33

After her stockroom misadventure, Hook figured her escape from Sinker was in jeopardy, and Layla offered little relief. So with nothing to lose but her job, she returns to the superstore for business as usual on Tuesday.

Old man Beak is climbing out of his black Chevy Suburban when Hook pulls into the parking lot. His gimpy leg is acting up, so it takes him awhile to get to the door. He turns and stares at her for a good three seconds.

"Never figgered you for no tit-and-run driver," he says through tight lips.

Hook isn't sure she heard him right.

"Get it?" Bobby's slash of a mouth spreads to a grisly grin. "Tit-and-run?"

Hook dips her head with a swallow. "You ain't mad?"

"I'm mad alright." He glances over her shoulder at a car turning into the lot. "But a deal's a deal, missy. I got my look, and you got your damn raise. Now get your ass to work. Customers'll be here soon."

Hook heads for the stockroom feeling better than she knows she should. She risks a smile as she strolls the orderly aisles, weaving her way through the best inventory of saltwater fishing gear on the North Carolina coast. Despite Bobby Beak's unwelcome advances, she loves her job and its promise of independence.

When she reaches her locker in the stockroom, a hand-drawn sign taped to the door steals the happiness from her face. It's a crude drawing of a naked woman with black hair and a little cross hanging from her nipple. A Styrofoam coffee cup is taped under the picture and the words *We Appreciate Your Tits* scrawled in black marker.

Hook's heart cranks up. She grabs her Water Devil and slashes the cup with two wicked swipes. She hears a snorting snicker behind her and turns to find Henry, the store's skin-and-bones purchasing manager, standing cross-armed, watching from behind a stack of tackle boxes.

She walks toward him, brandishing her shark hook.

"This your work, Henry?"

"It's just a joke." Henry's voice cracks.

"Just a joke?" Hook flushes crimson. "I tell you what's a joke, Henry. You're a fucking joke."

She kicks at the boxes, triggering an avalanche of colored plastic that crashes around Henry's feet. She scrambles over the mess and slices the Water Devil through the superstore logo on Henry's shirt, grazing his skin. She pulls the little man toward her.

"You like pierced nipples, Henry?" She smiles, twisting her hook in the yellow fabric. Bobby's coming up behind her carrying a heavy tuna gaff.

"You back offa him, Hook."

She rips the Water Devil from Henry's shirt and spins to face the old man, staring him down for a second before she sees a yellow thread twisted on the steel in her hand. She takes her time to pick it off and drop it on the shiny waxed floor.

Bobby's voice comes out quiet and hard. "You need to get on outta here, Hook. Now."

She stands pat, shifting her eyes from Henry's torn shirt to Bobby's tuna gaff and back.

"You understand what I'm saying, missy?" Bobby lowers his weapon.

"You can't let her off like that," says Henry.

"Shut the fuck up, Hank. Me and Hook got us a deal that needs a little renegotiating."

"You gonna pay my last two weeks?" says Hook.

"Course I am. But that's it, missy. It don't look like you can work here no more."

Hook wonders if she hears a hint of sad in Bobby's voice. She surveys the stockroom, thinking this could be the last time she'll ever set foot in this big-box world of fishing. The thought drags hot tears from her eyes.

# 34

"That guy Stone should join us," says the new Jesus. It's another meal of pizzas on the beach, and the new Jesus finds optimism in his full stomach.

The boys had wanted to corral John Paul Stone after the Sunday service, but it didn't happen. Stone got whisked away to the preacher's house for another round of praying, which was fine by him, since praying with the preacher usually involves good bourbon. That's why he'd volunteered to do the preacher's bidding in the first place. John Paul Stone is the on-call convert when the church has visitors who might need impressing.

"He gives me the willies," says Luke, sailing the empty pizza box at seagulls diving too close to their picnic.

"Hey," yells Gary. "Those are god's screechers."

"You gotta admit. He has the right name," says the new Jesus. "Fits right with our plans."

"Plans?" says Luke. "We rented a dang s-swimming pool for a baptizing in the middle of October. You call that plans?"

The new Jesus rises slowly, without a word, and walks toward the RV park.

"Where you going?" says Gary.

"I will return into my house from whence I came out."

"And when he is come, he findeth it empty, swept, and garnished," says Luke.

"I'll meet you back at the trailer," says the new Jesus. "We'll figure it out."

Luke and Gary lounge on the beach until big splats of rain explode in the sand around them. In the three minutes it takes to run to the Airstream, they get soaked.

"Where the heck is Mark?" says Luke, peeling out of his wet clothes. The new Jesus is nowhere in sight, the Jeep's gone, and Luke is pissed.

"He'll be back," says Gary. "He's probably out sweeping."

"You can't s-sweep when it's raining," says Luke. "He's up to no good."

There's no talking to Luke when he gets suspicious, so Gary tries to change the subject. "Why don't we just go to bed?"

Ever since Luke hooked up with Gary earlier that summer, the two young men have been tight. Most nights, they sleep together on the Airstream's fold-out bed, clumped like puppies in a kennel, a big black lab and frisky terrier, snuggled in for warmth. Mark can't stand being in the same bed with anyone else, so he sleeps in the single behind the galley kitchen.

"You awake?" says Luke. His big body has been flopping like a flounder since they climbed under the covers, so there's not much chance Gary's asleep.

"I think so."

Luke responds with a shuffling of sheets.

"What's the matter?"

"I don't know," says Luke.

"You're worried about the baptizing."

"I'm jealous. You and Mark went in that porn shop and had s-s-sex, didn't you."

Gary laughs. "You know I don't have sex."

"All that giggling."

"Awww, you *are* jealous. That's sweet."

Luke stays quiet.

"We watched a video," says Gary. "That's all."

"Were there dicks?"

"A couple."

Gary reaches down and cups the crotch of Luke's jockey shorts. "None nice as yours, though." The spongy lump quickens in his hand as Luke shudders. Gary lets it drop.

"You didn't have s-s . . .?"

"I told you. I don't have sex. We beat off. That's all."

Luke takes a second to think.

"Would you do it with me?"

Gary takes even longer. He knows Luke loves him too hard, and keeping the right distance isn't always easy.

"One last time," he says, scootching his own pants down. "Let's spill some seed."

# 35

Retirement communities in Chapel Hill come in two political flavors, reactionary red and bleeding-heart blue. Among them all, the Village of Weaver Woods leans hardest to the left, making it a safe haven for old hippies, lesbians, and eccentric professors. Dr. Gloria Grace qualifies on all three counts.

On this warm fall day, Liz finds the tiny professor enduring the insults of aging on her postage-stamp porch, cutting a fleshy stalk of aloe with a worn pocket knife.

"Got to have aloe," she says to no one in particular. "Never know when an old lady might get burned." She wipes her hands on her baggy pants. "You must be Liz."

"I am. Thank you for seeing me."

"Seeing. Ha. That's a good one."

"Excuse me?"

"Going blind as a mole."

Gloria fingers the magnifying glass hanging on a chain around her neck, turns her mottled face toward the sky, soaking in the sun, tired of her own complaining. "Enough of that," she says. "Come in and let's hear about these birds of yours."

Liz sits beside Gloria on a sturdy Victorian sofa, two searching souls in a musty one-room reliquary. Morning sun floods through the window behind them, spilling across a bizarre collection of crucifixes sprinkled along one wall. Liz can't take her eyes off sequined Elvis on a plastic gold cross, *The King* engraved above his bloodied head.

"From one of my doctoral students," says Gloria. "She wrote a fascinating dissertation about Mr. Presley's passions for the Christ."

Liz imagines Frank rolling his eyes. She's glad he didn't want to come along.

"Tell me," says Gloria, "does Oscar Ornstein still spend time praying at car wrecks?"

"He does."

Gloria clucks her tongue, then pushes on. "Interesting bracelet you have there."

Resisting the temptation to talk about her own recent wreck, Liz hands Gloria the bracelet. The room shifts imperceptibly with the transfer of power, settling again when the old woman lifts the silver to her face. She takes in its magic like a breath.

"I found it at the beach," says Liz, her big-boned body tense from the telling.

Gloria studies the bracelet for a good long minute with her magnifying glass, hands steady as time. Five words whisper by, just beyond her reach.

*She cannot hold the threads.*

Liz waits, biting her thumbnail.

"You seem worried," says Gloria.

Liz looks to the wall of crosses for help, but there's none to be found. "Something strange is happening." The old woman listens, eyes closed. "A pelican spoke to me, not long after I came across the bracelet."

At the mention of pelicans, Gloria snaps to and gives the bracelet back. "Pelican. Now there's an interesting bird." She bumbles to a shelf and finds a fat book bristling with scraps of paper. She zips it open with a finger.

*People in the Middle Ages believed that female pelicans tore at their breasts, harvesting blood to feed their chicks. Males joined in the mythical sacrifice, slashing their own hearts for blood that might resurrect dead fledglings. They are the Christ, stabbed on the cross for a river of blood. "Pelican of mercy, Jesu, Lord and God, cleanse me, wretched sinner, in thy precious Blood."*

"Some sculptors carved pelicans atop their crosses," says Gloria. "A pelican in her piety." She closes the book. "You've heard of god the father, god the son, and god the holy ghost?" Gloria points to a porcelain cross with a silver pelican nesting above Jesus' head. "Well, this is god the bird."

Liz flinches.

"Don't worry, dear," says Gloria. "God doesn't mind. She likes pelicans. Besides people have been hearing animals talk forever. What did yours say?"

"It said *you cannot hold the threads.*"

"Are you certain?"

"That's what I heard."

"Let's see that bracelet again." The professor takes another close look, pointing to some squiggly marks in the silver. "See this? It's the word *threads* in Aramaic."

Liz goes pale.

"Threads," says Gloria, the hint of a twinkle in her fading gray eyes. "Something to do with the fabric of life?"

"The fabric of life." Liz almost laughs. "I have been at loose ends lately."

# 36

The back of Hook's Ford Ranger carries a beat-up camper shell covering enough gear to go fishing whenever she's in the mood, which she is right now. She pulls into the lot at Eddie's Pier, smokes a chunk of hash, and unloads her FishMate pier cart. She takes her time checking her rods and reels and lures and leaders and hooks and jigs and planers, making sure that everything's arranged for easy access.

Walking up the handicap ramp, she drags her cart through the familiar smells of piss, dead fish, and beer. She eases through the salt-sprayed glass doors to find Big Eddie, Eddie Junior's daddy, reading the newspaper behind the counter. He's wearing his regular uniform – bib overalls and a white tee shirt. Big Eddie taught Hook most of what she knows about fishing and he's always happy to see her.

"Hey, darlin'."

"What's runnin'?" Hook pulls a handful of change from her pocket and spreads the money on the counter.

"Depends who's fishin'."

"Ain't that the truth." Though she's stoned as a stump, her voice carries a trace of glum.

"You seem a little blue. Anything wrong?" Big Eddie reaches in the cooler and pulls out a Mountain Dew. He sets it with a Snickers on the counter and scoops up her coins.

"Bobby fired me." She tears a bite out of the candy bar, stuffing the rest in the pocket of her fake leather jacket. "I sorta stabbed Henry. And Bobby said I had to leave. Asshole."

"You stabbed Henry? I know he's a worthless piece of shit, but still."

"I don't want to talk about it, Big Eddie." She waits for him to nod his understanding, sliding her hat back on her head. She grabs her drink and slugs half of it down.

"Got you a new hat. Next thing you'll be a college girl."

Hook imagines herself walking across the campus she saw once during a TV basketball game. Her fantasy disintegrates into a bunch of preppy cheerleaders and drunk jocks.

She heads for the pier, settling into her favorite spot, where her name's carved on the railing. She baits up a couple of rigs and casts them out thirty feet. She unpacks her whetstone and sharpens her Water Devil. The rhythmic scrape of steel on stone lulls her into calm. She imagines slicing the hook through Henry's stupid grin. She remembers Bobby Beak grabbing at his silly dick, and almost feels sorry for the old man. In her daydream, his dick becomes a snake. She smashes it to nothing with a baseball bat.

The first fish hits, jolting Hook full of adrenaline, even after all these years. She slips out of worry without noticing. Two hours later, she's caught and cleaned a half-dozen black drum and a couple of flounder. But her high's turned low and her mood's gone sour. Time to go home.

"Set any records today?" asks Big Eddie when she comes in. Hook won top honors in Big Eddie's Tenth Annual Fishfest two years ago with a prize king mackerel.

"Just in the job losing department."

Big Eddie scratches his chin. "I made me a call. Irene says you could clean condos if you want to. One of the girls quit." Irene is Big Eddie's wife and Eddie Junior's mom. She runs Irene's Sunrise Services over on Inlet Court.

"I don't wanna be no damn maid again, Big Eddie."

"She said you could start next week. Get you a little nest egg going."

Big Eddie visits the RV park enough to know that Hook needs to get away from her brother's reach. He's tried to like Sinker over the years, but can't quite get there.

Hook stares down at the dirty gray linoleum.

"Just till you get something else."

Big Eddie dials Irene's number and hands Hook the phone.

# 37

When Gary and Luke spill out of the Airstream the next morning, they find the new Jesus sitting in the Jeep, the red glow of crank brightening his eyes a few shades past normal. Doing meth has always been the shortest path to the divine for Mark, and he's well on his way to heaven this morning.

"I got us a sign," says the new Jesus, pointing to a vinyl banner rolled up on the passenger seat.

"Hot night, huh?" Gary had never drawn a clear line with the disciples about drugs, and now that Mark's the new Jesus, there's no real point to push.

"Michael, *mi amigo*, he works at Signs by Tomorrow. He made it. No charge."

Gary gives the new Jesus a close look. "Really?"

"Didn't cost a cent."

"Let's s-see it," says Luke.

The new warns Luke away. "I want it to be a surprise."

"That's dumb," says Luke, taking off his glasses like he's ready for a fight. "Because I get to be Jesus on S-s-sunday. And as the next new Jesus . . ."

"Bullshit," says the new Jesus, his meth eyes flaring. "We never agreed to that."

"Gary s-said I could be Jesus after you."

Gary looks out to the ocean, where smoke belching from a container ship smudges dark on the horizon. "We didn't say when," he sighs. "Mark's only been Jesus for a few days."

The new Jesus blows a raspberry and sings, "I'm sti-ill Jesus," causing Luke to charge, smashing against the door of the Jeep in a rage.

"Jesus. Luke." Gary swears the names out of breath. "Stop it."

"He's high as a kite. I can s-s-smell it," says Luke.

"I'm doing the best I can."

"Well, it isn't good enough."

"You can do better? You're nothing but a chicken-shit stutter-bug faggot. You won't even go in a goddamn church."

"Jesus," warns Gary.

"Listen," says the new Jesus, climbing out of the car. "I got the fucking sign made, which is a hell of a lot more than you two have done lately."

Gary turns weary on his flip-flopped feet and walks toward the dunes.

"Blessed are they who don't say fucking all the time," he whispers. "I need to be alone."

"Come on, Jesus. He didn't mean it." Luke catches up with Gary and wraps around him. "S-stay with us?"

Gary pushes him away with a kiss on the cheek. "I'm not Jesus."

"You can have my turn," says Luke.

"You should give it a try," says Gary as he disappears into the dunes, a dreadlocked ghost in a drift of sand.

# 38

For nearly two decades, civic boosters in Durham, North Carolina, have tried to convince outsiders that their old tobacco town should be known as the City of Medicine. But with strong competition from major league crime and minor league baseball, the City of Medicine moniker has yet to stick. Despite the mild identity crisis, however, there's one way in which the Bull City is truly blessed: it holds a smorgasbord of remarkable restaurants, one of which serves as the favorite meeting place of Preacher Joseph J. Peters and Rachel Rose, Liz's boss.

On most Tuesday evenings, observant diners at the Halifax Grill will find the couple holding down a brocade booth in the backest, darkest corner of the restaurant, sometimes laughing, occasionally groaning, and frequently leaving before even glancing at their menus. On this particular Tuesday, while Liz weighs the news of mysterious inscriptions and Hook considers renewing her career in domestic engineering, Rachel and Joe gauge their chances of getting caught in a wild game of footsies under the lavender linen table cloth.

"I didn't wear no socks tonight," says Joe, nudging his nubby toes up under Rachel's short leather skirt.

"And I didn't wear no panties," says Rachel, grabbing his big toe and guiding it home.

Putting their passion on pause while a waiter freshens their water, Rachel slides off her Joan and David pumps. When the waiter leaves, Joe lifts her feet to his lap, pressing her painted toes around the pole inside his pants. "Oh my," she barely whispers, milking her mate in a two-footed tango.

What it is that attracts Rachel to Preacher Joe Peters would be a puzzle to anyone seeing the odd couple standing side by side. But beyond the confines of the Halifax Grill, such sightings are rare. As the fundraising maven of Duke University, Rachel Rose is always turned out with style and grace, and can ill afford to be seen on the arm of Joe Peters. Yet somehow they manage to hang together, bound by shared obsessions with sex and brand new Jaguars.

It was the automotive angle that spawned their affair two years ago. Joe had walked into the Carolina Jaguar showroom and found Rachel sitting in the silver XK8 he intended to buy. Five fucks later, the car was hers, a leased symbol of love from the good Preacher Joe.

Parked behind her Forest Hills home that evening, Rachel claims her just desserts in the backseat of Joe's new XJ Sport. "Don't forget to take out those silly teeth of yours, Joe. Can't have you biting my sweet pie."

Though Rachel would never tell Preacher Joe outright, his toothless gumming of her well-worn clitoris is the single treat that keeps her coming back for more from the raunchy reverend. And though Joe Peters would never tell Rachel outright, the chance to savor the smooth flesh between her surgically crafted thighs brings a thrill he can't resist.

"Tell me more about Lith." Joe says, wrapping up his back-seat feast.

"She's not your type, Reverend, though she does know how to squeeze money out of old ladies. Just like you."

"Tha'th not what I mean," says Joe, trying to keep Rachel happy.

"What do you want to know about her, Joe? I doubt she's the Calvary Mission kind."

"Ith she thaved?" Joe asked.

"Is she shaved?"

"Not thaved. Thaved. Born again."

"Put your teeth in so I can understand what you're saying. Besides, why do you care about that? I can see you asking about her bank accounts."

He digs his dentures from under Rachel's butt and slips them in his mouth.

"There's something about her. I swear. She had the glow of the Holy Spirit."

"You met her for five minutes."

"That don't change what I saw."

# 39

"S-some Jesus you turned out to be. Three days and you've already driven Gary away. Good going, Mark."

The two young men stand arguing outside the Airstream, watching Gary fade into the dunes. Luke towers over the new Jesus, who seems ready to explode from the meth crackling in his skull.

"Stop calling me Mark." He spits the words like a curse.

"I'll call you what I want."

"Fuck you."

"Blessed are they who don't . . ."

"Fuck you."

"Is that all you got?"

"Fuck you."

That last fuck-you drives Luke into a fury. He lifts the new Jesus by his arms and slams him against the trailer. "I told you," Luke says through clenched teeth. "Blessed are they who don't s-say fucking all the time."

"Fuck you."

Luke goes wilder, shaking the new Jesus like a worn-out rag, smacking his head on the trailer. It's a miracle when all the manhandling seems to have the desired effect.

"You're hurting me," says the new Jesus.

"You're dang right I am."

"For god so loved the world that he gave his only begotten son," says the new Jesus.

"Too late for that."

"That whosoever believeth in him."

"Sh-shut up."

"Shall not perish."

Luke releases his grip.

"But have everlasting life."

Luke slumps.

"It's time to build our church," whispers the new Jesus, sensing a come-from-behind victory. He spins a quiet tale of glory about the church they'll build right there on Sunrise Beach. How it will be so easy. How god will provide. How they'll be on TV. How they'll spread the gospel and share the light. How they'll baptize the multitudes.

'Upon this rock I will build my church," he says. "And the gates of hell shall not prevail against it."

After living with Mark for four months, Luke knows enough to be leery of impromptu scripture-quoting.

"You're up to no good," says Luke.

"I am not," says the new Jesus, his eyes flitting to the banner still on the seat.

Luke follows the flit and gets suspicious. "Maybe you'd better show me that s-sign."

The new Jesus looks around helpless, surprised to discover he's on his own. No Gary. No god. No way out.

He drops the banner on the ground, unrolling it with a few quick strokes of his broom. The words emerge one flaming letter at a time, followed by a thick red arrow. *Turn or Burn Sunday.*

Luke's smooth black skin goes darker still. "Turn or Burn S-sunday?"

The new Jesus mutters something that should have been an apology.

"TURN OR BURN S-S-SUNDAY?"

"You don't have to yell."

"What were you thinking, Mark?"

"It was Michael's idea. And my name's not Mark."

Luke kicks the vinyl sign into a jumble. "You know Gary hates all that hell business."

"Who cares what Gary hates? I'm Jesus. And I get to choose the damn sign," says the new Jesus, slipping out of his brief spell of reason.

"Can't we please just try to get a different banner?" says Luke.

"No way, Jose." The new Jesus slides into a sinister smile. "Turn or Burn Sunday. That pool's gonna rock."

# 40

Gloria asked if she could study the bracelet for a couple of days and Liz agreed. Liz had to make an emergency fundraising visit to Catherine Cross, so the timing was good. Because of her still-cracked skull, Frank insisted on coming along.

"I know I said six weeks," Catherine said when she called, "but I'm not sure I'm going to make it. Come see me, and bring the paperwork. You know the deal. Twenty million. Wire transfer. No sense changing wills at this late date. The name I want is Cross Fellows. Nice ring, don't you think?" She laughed till she coughed.

Liz left Frank in their hotel room and headed for Catherine's Watergate apartment. Her previous visits had been upbeat reunions, but death was in the air this time. Catherine sounded terrible on the phone, and looked worse when she opened the door. Her skin carried the yellow hint of too much pain and her eyes had flattened. Liz felt tears brewing.

"Don't start." Catherine faked a smile. "I've got too much to do and no time for nonsense. Let me see the papers."

Fifteen minutes later, the dying woman handed Liz the signed documents. "You should leave," she said. "You've done a good job wringing money out of this old tightwad. Now go while the getting's good."

University fundraising offices and business schools are notorious for perks, and Liz and Frank have circled the world twice on junkets over the past twenty years. So it's not surprising that on their trip home the couple slips into a familiar flying symmetry. She has the window, he's on the aisle. She's abuzz, he's asleep. He's dreaming about laundry, she's thinking about heaven.

Unlike Oscar and his passion for car wrecks, Liz engages in metaphysical mystery almost exclusively in airplanes. Speeding through the gap between the stratosphere and the ant farm below, she wrestles with things more easily ignored on earth. Frannie comes to mind and she chases the ghost away. She lets her mind fill with last night's hotel silliness.

"This bracelet business is getting weird," Frank had said. He was lying next to her on the king-sized bed during an afternoon nap. She'd just finished closing the deal with Catherine, and they had an hour before dinner.

"I know," said Liz, remembering the feel of the silver on her arm.

"I'm not kidding."

"I said . . ."

"Know what I think?" Frank tagged the question with an elbow in her ribs. His voice slipped out monotonic, like a zombie. "I think you are possessed."

Liz caught her breath as Frank read her mind.

"You think I am possessed?"

"I think you are possessed," said the zombie. He threw his thigh over her pelvis, rolling over to sit upright on her hips, staring down at her half-closed eyes.

"I think you are possessed." He slowered his hands to her breasts.

Her eyes sprang full open, wider than wide, a modern Bride of Frankenstein looking up at the sprayed-on ceiling.

"I think you are possessed," she moaned, a zombie herself, sliding a hand around his hard-on. She pulled his face in close and ground her hips and whispered, "Quit messing around and stick this thing in me."

"You don't *really* think I'm possessed, do you?" Liz finally forces the question as they fly over southern Virginia, nearing home.

"Something's going on," says Frank.

"That's ridiculous," she says, knowing it isn't.

"It's not just the pelican. Or even the bracelet. What about that preacher? He said he could feel the lord moving inside you."

"This isn't fair, Frank. You're always talking about what's-his-face's razor."

"Occam."

"And now you're . . ."

"It's just something I feel."

"Maybe you're the one who's possessed."

"Okay. Possessed probably isn't the best word. It's not like we're in the *Exorcist*. But you can't pretend nothing's happening." He stops to gauge her reaction. "And remember. That professor said *threads*."

How could she forget.

"But you're the one who said *possessed*. And as you've pointed out a thousand times, you don't say things you don't mean." She watches him fight the urge to withdraw.

"I've been wanting you to be possessed for years."

"That's silly."

"I'm serious. Our lives have gotten too normal. This would definitely liven things up."

"Duke wouldn't like it."

"Are you kidding? Between you and Rachel? You can put a hex on geriatric donors. And if that doesn't work, Rachel could put a lip lock on them. Either way, you'd get the money."

A flight attendant comes by with pretzels, distracting Frank.

"What do you mean our lives have gotten too normal?" Liz looks out her window, studying the spidery waterways carved through marshes on the edge of the Chesapeake Bay, squinting when the sun flashes bright off the tangled streams.

"I just meant we might be falling into a rut." He backpedals. "Or maybe just me." They both know he's in a rut, and it's deeper than either wants to admit.

"What does that have to do with me being possessed?"

"If you were possessed, I'd have something to do. I could be your spin doctor."

"You think you could spin me?" She doesn't mean to laugh, but it doesn't matter. He's unfazed.

"Let's say that of all the forms of possession you might have, we want to steer clear of anything to do with the devil, demons, the occult, etcetera, etcetera. Right?"

"As far as I know, it's not the kind of thing you get to choose."

"That's right. But your PR guy does get to choose what to call it. Think of it like this. You go on Geraldo and say, "Hi. I'm Liz the Witch Woman Forsythe. I'd like you to meet the evil spirits swarming in my skull.'"

"I wouldn't be the first."

"Or you say, "'Hello. I'm the Reluctant Prophet of the Silver Threads.'"

"You're nuts."

"I could have you on the cover of *Newsweek* in thirty days."

"Okay. If it turns out I really am possessed, you get to spin me. But you'll have to do it fast. You never know how long a possession might last. I could be a five-minute miracle. Or who knows? This could be part of the end times."

"That's not supposed to happen till the whole world goes to shit."

She looks out the window again. The glimmering Chesapeake has given way to the monstrous sprawl of the Norfolk Naval Shipyard. Two nuclear-powered aircraft carriers dominate the harbor.

"We're probably due then."

# 41

When Hook shows up Thursday morning at Irene's Sunrise Services, she finds the cinderblock storefront hopping. Irene has cornered the market for house-cleaning, and late October always brings a last gasp of commerce before the beach goes into hibernation. She has five maids on part-time payroll, counting Hook.

Hook did summer cleaning a few years ago, so she knows the drill, like lots of young women on the Carolina coast. She's a decent worker, and Irene's glad to have her back.

"Got you at the Blue Heaven Villas today." Irene's sitting at a desk covered with Beanie Babies and coffee cups, smacking her Big Red chewing gum rat-a-tat-tat. She has the same wide nose as her son, Eddie Junior, and a similar fondness for Hook. Irene can't understand why Hook and Eddie Junior haven't gotten together, despite her best efforts at match-making. She's pretty much given up.

The blackboard behind her desk keeps track of customers, and Hook's name is already up there in Irene's choppy cursive, along with Maria, Isabel, Ava, and Inez. The other girls are gossiping in Spanish, which annoys the hell out of Hook.

"There's a two bedroom needs the Works," says Irene. "You remember the Works?"

The Works is Irene's deluxe service option, a wall-to-wall cleaning frenzy that turns overused beach homes into antiseptic showrooms for scores of household cleaning products. Bon Ami. E-Z Off. Handi Wipes. Lysol. Orange Max. Pledge. Soft Scrub. Tilex. Windex. Irene swears by them all.

Hook sticks her hand in her jeans pocket and fingers the half-smoked joint she grabbed on her way out the door this morning. "Course I remember. You still got that checklist?"

Irene pulls the fourteen-point list from her cluttery desk drawer and hands it to Hook.

"Do we still have to clean disgusting globs of hair out of slimy drains?" asks Hook.

"Number seven," says Irene. "Disgusting globs of hair. Our trademark." She smirks at her Mexican crew. Irene's never quite sure if they understand what she's saying, but then again, neither are they.

Hook risks an easy laugh.

"The list's got shorter," says Irene. "But it's still a full day. And do a extra good job. It's a new customer."

Hook spindles the paper into a tight little tube. "Working by myself?"

"You okay with that?"

"Suits me."

"Here's the keys then. Give me a buzz before lunch and let me know how you're doing."

Hook won't clean houses unless she's stoned, so she finishes her joint on the way to the Blue Heaven Villas. She tried working straight once and almost gagged halfway through the checklist. Number six was bad – scrubbing pissy tiles behind toilets. But the goopy slime of number seven really creeped her out.

She floats out of her truck and goes to have a look at the ocean before she starts work.

It's low tide. The wide smooth strand is deserted except for a few SUVs heading to the inlet. She sits on the walkway over the dune and settles in with her buzz. Her eyes pull toward the RV park half a mile away where a lone figure walks into the surf. It's way too cold for swimming, must be some kind of crazy. Like Sinker. She smiles at the thought of her brother's ear getting infected. Serves him right.

She tugs down her hat and squints into the bright. The ocean spills like dancing diamonds all across the horizon.

Hook hears a scuffling noise and turns to find Bill Beak standing behind her. Bobby must have told him she got fired.

"What're you doing here, missy?"

"Got me a job cleaning."

"What unit?"

Hook wants to say it's none of his damn business, but she holds back. Irene won't put up with the least bit of trouble. "A dirty one."

"Don't get smart with me." Bill scratches his butt. "You already lost one job this week."

She looks at the key in her hand. She flashes on the big woman from the beach, falling like an angel. She can't quite catch her breath.

When she gets through the door of unit seventeen, Hook locks the deadbolt and marches straight to the master bedroom. She likes to know who she's working for when she starts a new job, and poking around in nightstands is the best way to find out. The sun behind the blinds throws sharp stripes over a small chest beside the bed. She slides open a drawer and finds a phone book, reading glasses, some pens and pencils, a bottle of Sudafed.

The next drawer holds a collection of grey sweaters and black jeans. She reaches under the clothes and finds a couple of old Penthouse magazines. Men are all the same.

The rattan nightstand on the other side of the bed has the girl stuff. A vanilla candle. A box of Kleenex. A plastic photo cube. When she flips the cube, her stoned heart picks up its pace. It's the woman from the beach. Standing by the ocean in her Duke ball cap. Wearing the happiest face. Holding a beer. Camera smile.

Hook stops short of getting spooked and coughs out a nervous laugh. Her eyes linger on the photograph as she pulls open the top drawer. Some paperbacks. A notepad. A roll of stamps. A stack of business cards. Elizabeth L. Forsythe. Duke University. Office of Development. She laughs again. ELF. She slips one of the cards into her pocket.

The next drawer has a bottle of Astroglide and a sleek, contoured vibrator. She turns it on and snickers, not quite a giggle. She sits on the bed, knocks off her flip flops, and slides out of her pants. She pushes the curve of the vibrator up into her crotch. Clicks it against her titanium bead ring. Switches it to high. Settles in for the ride.

Hook's been fucked by more men than she wants to remember over the past three years, all blurred now into a sweaty mess of grunting bodies with bad breath and beer bellies. Not one of them ever made her come. That's why she turned to machines.

After a minute, she feels the edge of an orgasm starting to take shape, pressure and promise, picking up speed. The hum of the vibrator turns to white noise, blanking her brain for just long enough. She tightens up low for the clench. Glances at the nightstand and sees Elizabeth Forsythe, still smiling. Closes her eyes and escapes.

Hook wakes hungry twenty minutes later. She steals a peach yogurt from the fridge and a can of SpaghettiOs from the pantry. Aside from her pants piled on the bedroom floor, the condo looks perfect. The owners must be Virgos. No dirty dishes or laundry to be done. Piece of cake.

She Lysols the toilets, Windexes the mirrors, 409s the trash cans, Pledges every horizontal surface, and arranges stuff under the bathroom sinks. Then she gets on the phone to Irene, who's happy to hear from her.

"Glad to be back in the cleaning business?"

"I would be if all my jobs turned out like this one. These folks got their own pumice stone." She knows Irene thinks pumice stone is the ninth wonder of the world, right up there with a canister vacuum.

"Well, good," says Irene. "You ready for another one?"

Hook lies without thinking. "I still got a few things to do. Beds. Blinds. Wax the kitchen. Maybe another hour or two."

Irene lets it slide. "Alright then."

"Don't worry, Irene. They'll be happy. I promise."

Hook wanders through the condo, looking for easy stuff to tidy. She leans over the table where a half-finished puzzle spreads out in a shore scene. She spots an oyster catcher's bill and plugs it into place.

Next to the puzzle is a book filled with warm and funny greetings from people who have visited. It's like Emisphor on paper, so she decides to join the chatter. When she's finished her entry, she draws a little hook for a signature and catches herself smiling in a mirror.

*happy person you. cleaning per sin me. hope good. found hat. here you. go.*

# 42

Liz and Frank arrive in the Raleigh-Durham airport terminal a few minutes after noon on Thursday. Half an hour later, they're inching like toxic snails through gridlocked traffic on Interstate 40. Liz spends hours each week in the worsening congestion around the Research Triangle Park and knows there's no easy way to get from here to anywhere. "Let's cut through Durham," she says. "Might as well go ahead and get me a new car."

Frustration with traffic is just the tip of Liz's I-hate-waiting iceberg. Waiting for movies to start, waiting for clothes to dry, waiting in dentist chairs, waiting through cute answering machine messages. Whatever the occasion, waiting distresses her. And the prospect of waiting forever in a car salesman's tiny cubicle is taking a heavy toll on her fingernails.

Like many small children, young Elizabeth was impulsively impatient. A family trip to Disneyland was the first big event ravaged by her resistance to waiting, and may have spawned her younger sister's career as a hypnotherapist. Unwilling to walk away from a much-anticipated ride on Space Mountain, little Faye entranced Liz with a steady stream of silly chatter during their tedious two-hour wait. Liz toughed it out, but it was the beginning of the end.

When she later refused to stand in lines at the Washington Monument, the Empire State Building, and the Statue of Liberty, her mother decided to give up destination travel in favor of low-key vacations at the beach.

Even as an accomplished fundraiser, Liz's impatience shows through. Once when she and Rachel had spent half an hour in a Chicago hotel lobby waiting on a donor, Liz explained her sensitivity.

"Start with the word time," said Liz. "Take the *t* and the *m*, and replace them with *l* and *f*. That changes *time* into the word *life*. And how we spend our time is exactly equal to how we spend our lives. Right now? This is how we're spending our lives, Rachel. Time is the currency of life."

Rachel was caught off guard by the philosophical outpouring. "Lucky you didn't make the *l* into a *w*. Because then *life* would be *wife* and we'd all be in trouble."

She looked around the lobby for Mr. Big, but spotted instead the entrance to a posh urban shopping center. "Let's make sure I've got this straight. How I'm spending my life right now? I'm waiting in a hotel for some jerk who thinks I have nothing better to do."

"Correct."

"And by jumbling a few letters around, I can say, 'This is not how I'm going to spend my life.'"

"Or your wife."

"Well." Rachel cleared her throat. "This is not how I'm going to spend my wife. We'll call the jerk later. Let's go shopping." Which they did, leaving the million-dollar man to wonder why Duke University wasn't lapping at his boots.

Two hours later, Liz climbs into the driver's seat of her new gas-electric Honda hybrid, complete with extended warranty. She had wavered only once during the mercifully short car-buying ordeal, sitting with Frank while their salesman copied her driver's license.

"I already wrecked one Honda this year," she said.

"Which means your odds of wrecking another one are zilch," said Frank. "It'll be fine."

# 43

When Gary crawls back into Gospel Town three days after his early morning departure, he's missing both his flip-flops and half his mind. He'd said he wanted some time alone and that's exactly what he got. Seventy hours of searing solitude, interrupted by a few quick rifts of cosmic communion. It wasn't exactly weeks in the wilderness, but it had the same effect.

His first stop had been Eddie's Pier, where he ate a stale turkey sandwich from the trash. He walked down the pier to get some water at the cleaning station, breathing in the mixture of fish guts laced with creosote. No one was catching much, though he saw one guy reel in a shark and stab it in the head.

Gary sat in a pier hut, hypnotized by the rhythm of the waves breaking below. An old woman settled in on the bench beside him like fog, her soft round face shaded by a yellow hat embroidered with *Dog Ho* in white letters. Her gray eyes wandered, no need for seeing.

"Seem kinda lost." Her voice vibrated low inside him, somewhere between thought and feeling, but real all the same. She pulled a pocket knife and a whetstone from somewhere and began sharpening the stubby blade. She slid the knife back and forth, back and forth, never stopping to test the edge.

"Might be," said Gary.

"Good thing I found you then." The scrape of steel on stone brought a calm to the day that did Gary good. "Name's Dog."

"Why's that?"

"Why not?" said Dog, putting her knife away.

They sat for an hour while pier people came and went around them. The blurry grumble of wind and surf dampened their conversation, though neither seemed to miss the words. The old woman rolled to her feet and stretched like a yogi.

"What're you gonna do now?" She bent to place her hands flat on the pier, downward facing Dog.

"Should I keep on being Jesus?" He couldn't make sense of his own words. "Or maybe he should keep on being me."

"Ha." Dog slapped a wooden plank and hooted. "That's a good one."

"You don't think I can do it?" Gary was mostly asking himself, though he didn't much trust his answers. He thought for a minute and asked the old lady why she wasn't fishing.

"*Am* fishing," she nodded in the general direction of nothing.

Gary nodded off. When he woke up, Dog was gone.

He waited around all afternoon while the wind shifted to the northeast and the air went cool, but there was no sign of her. He looked toward the RV park, hoping to see Luke running after him. The beach was deserted. He sucked down a few glogs of water from the scaly fish faucet, zipped up his windbreaker, and walked back down the pier.

"Getting chilly," said Big Eddie. "You been out there a good long while."

"You seen Dog?" said Gary.

Big Eddie gave Gary the once-over. His ratty hair and worn-out clothes crossed somewhere between comical and sad. But Big Eddie gets all kinds on his pier, and he's learned to take weirdness in stride. "Dog who?" he asked.

"This old lady with a yellow hat. I don't think she catches much."

Big Eddie sees every single person who steps on his pier and would not have missed an old lady with a yellow hat.

"You musta been dreaming."

Gary eyes a nubby O-Cedar broom in the corner. "Need any sweeping?" he said. "I'm good." He grabbed the broom and conjured up a pile of dusty dirt in front of the counter. "I'll do the whole place for a couple of hot dogs and a pint of milk."

The prospect of someone besides Big Eddie himself sweeping up after a long day had its appeal. Especially since the kid wasn't asking for cash. "Go ahead," said Big Eddie. "I'll have them hot dogs ready when you're done."

A mile past the pier, Gary came across a beachfront house under construction, wrapped and roofed and framed and wired, but nowhere near done. It's one of the monstrosities that spoil almost every North Carolina barrier island, finally taking its toll on Sunrise Beach, just in time for global warming. He dragged a shredded tarp to the top floor of the house and climbed in the fiberglass garden tub sitting unplumbed in the master bathroom. He made a nest and slipped into dreams.

It's a cool, foggy morning. He's walking at low tide, following Dog, who's just ahead, dancing twirls across the smooth wet sand.

Dog raises one hand toward the ocean and two dolphins fly from the breaking waves. She raises her other hand and a brown pelican dives deep into the water, staying under for the longest time. It flops to the surface and shakes, lifting with a bulge in its translucent pouch. The bird sails low over Dog and opens its mouth, spilling a thousand finger mullets onto the hard-packed beach. Gary runs to catch up, but Dog disappears in a fog. The flying fish become a storm of galvanized roofing nails, spiking the sand like metallic sleet.

The steel storm turned out to be real, a crude awakening for Gary, courtesy of the sheetrocker crew that showed up for work early the next morning. Pouring a bucket of galvanized tacks on top of a sleeping bum was their idea of a good time, and Gary wasn't big enough to complain. It was all he could do to scramble away from his bed of nails.

The mile back to the pier looked so unappealing, he moved off in the other direction, avoiding the glare of the morning sun. He walked for hours all the way to the skinny part of the island, scrubby land low enough to suffer regular over-washes during big storms. The few houses still standing had long since been condemned.

Gary felt light-headed. He hadn't eaten since hot dogs on Eddie's pier, and though he'd learned to live without much food, the assault of sun and thirst wore him down. Plus his foot hurt. In his hurry to escape the sheetrocker storm, he'd stepped on a nail and punctured his sole.

He crawled up a small dune and fell asleep again, waking to find Orion's studded belt hanging low in the sky.

"Well, look who's here," said Dog.

Gary leaned up on an elbow and took in the silhouette of the old woman stretched against the night.

"I thought you might show up again," he said.

Dog dropped easy to the ground, looking up, smiling at every one of the billion stars that grace the heavens.

"Milky way," said Gary.

"Snickers," said Dog.

"You're making me hungry."

"Might need a little rest." Dog sat up and patted him on the shoulder. Glittery sparkles danced around her fingers.

"I am kind of tired."

Dog waited. Gary yawned.

"How's that Jesus business going?"

"Mark's taken over."

"He doing a good job?"

"He's planning a baptism this Sunday."

"What for?"

"A baptism? It's how you get saved."

"From what?"

Gary scanned the sky for an answer. "From being sad?"

Dog seemed to think it through. "Probably worth it then," she said. "But it's gonna rain on Sunday."

Gary gets back to the RV park late the next morning. Even with aching hunger, he'd slept soundly and made the long walk without too much trouble. When he took a quick dip in the ocean to clean up, the cold salt water turned him blue.

Luke sees him first and runs across the sand for a big sloppy hug. The new Jesus joins.

"You're sh-shivering," says Luke.

"I told you, we are the frozen ones." Gary tries to laugh, but his teeth are chattering.

"I'm glad you're back. We were worried," says Luke.

The truth is, Luke hadn't been worried about Gary at all. The new Jesus said god would take care of things, and Luke needed something to believe. Plus they'd somehow made peace with the banner. *Turn or Burn Sunday.* It was what it was.

"I'm hungry," says Gary.

"Let's go get waffles," says Luke.

"Do we have enough money?"

"Jesus has been raking in the dough."

Gary whistles. "How's that baptizing shaping up?"

Luke and the new Jesus trade a sneaky glance. "Really good," says the new Jesus. "We're just about set."

"Dog said it's going to rain."

"Who's Dog?" says Luke.

"This old lady. She seemed pretty sure about it."

The new Jesus scans the sky like a weatherman. "Doesn't look like rain to me."

The next day, the new Jesus and his meteorological skills are put to the test – and fail. A dark line of low clouds moves in over the island, with the strong scent of rain hanging heavy in the air. Luke tunes in the car radio and gets the word. Cold front moving in. Showers all weekend.

# 44

When Liz's silent hybrid rolls to a stop in front of the house, Sarah comes running from the porch. She's been dog-sitting.

"Molly had a seizure," says Sarah.

Liz flies inside, fear in her eyes. Molly barely raises her head.

"Her whole body was shaking," says Sarah. "I wrapped her in a blanket and called the vet. He said to bring her in. I was just getting ready to go."

Liz picks up the dog and cuddles her. "Let's hold off on the vet," she says, remembering that Molly's last old-age diagnosis cost three hundred dollars.

Liz spent her earliest years on a farm outside Richmond, Virginia, and acquired a matter-of-factness about death that would make some people squeamish. At least that's how Frank reacted when she explained how she earned money wringing sparrows' necks.

"A nickel a neck? Your father paid you a nickel for each baby bird you killed?"

"And a penny an egg."

"That's disgusting."

"We lived on a farm, Frank. And sparrows are gross. They make a huge mess. They kill bluebirds, and they get into seed bags. What would you do, call Terminex?"

That's exactly what Frank would do. As a city boy and the son of two bookkeepers, the closest he'd ever come to killing anything warm-blooded was when he threw a rock into a flying flock of grackles, knocking one of the iridescent black birds cleanly from the sky. Seeing the ruffled body on the sidewalk at his five-year-old feet, Frank dropped to his knees and cried. When he reached for the fallen bird, it pecked his hand and flew away.

But growing up on a farm provided Liz with more than a neck-wringing income. It also gave her a practical sensibility about the shape of life itself. Her father died under a tumbling tractor when she was thirteen, leaving the mother and two daughters with a hundred acres to tend, and just enough insurance money to repair the busted John Deere. Over time, Florence Forsythe leveraged the desirable property into a cash and equity deal in the New Richmond Southside Mall, and eventually moved to a condo at Sunrise Beach – the one Liz and Frank now own.

Of all the waiting Liz has done in her fifty years of living, waiting for Molly to die is proving the most difficult. No amount of sparrow-killing has prepared her for the crush of Molly's last breath. At eight o'clock Friday morning, the dachshund's freed spirit disappears into the cheerless kitchen air. Three hours later, Liz settles Molly on a blanket in her favorite traveling basket, which Frank lowers into a well-dug grave on the hill behind their home. Working together, husband and wife fill the hole, tamp the dirt, and place a fieldstone marker.

Back in the house, the living room floods with the little dog's absence. The coffee table where Molly hid during thunderstorms. The indentation of her body on the sofa. More missingness.

Frank and Liz wander around the house, death in their hearts, while the daughter they never had fills the space between them.

Liz lies awake in bed, missing Molly, while Frank putters downstairs. The promise of sleep slips farther away with each red blink of her digital clock. Under normal circumstances, the thrum of rain on the flat-roofed house would put her away in minutes. But these, she thinks, are hardly normal circumstances. She pulls the bedspread up under her chin and searches the room for nothing that can be found. A nightlight casts a dim halo up the peach-colored bedroom wall, where a Balinese shadow puppet, Sita, hangs like a pinned butterfly. The image triggers a cloying wave of warmth that slides down Liz's neck, over her breasts and abdomen, and envelopes her thighs. A jag of lightning rips through the dark, pumping a jolt of adrenaline through her veins.

*A hot flash?*

Though she's well into menopause, Liz isn't yet used to the heat that surges through her body every few hours. This wave coats her skin with shimmering sweat. She tosses off the bedspread and flops on her side, nightgown tangled around her legs, eyes falling on the puppet, whose flat brown arms shudder, touched by an invisible breeze.

She glances at the window. It's closed.

*I know you hold the threads,* says the old puppet. *But now you must release them.*

*Now I must release them?*

Sita does not answer. She has said too much already.

Summoned by an insistent bladder, Liz rolls out of bed and walks to the bathroom, grazing the walls with her fingertips, steadying herself. She hikes up her nightgown and backs up to the toilet, the rain splashing on the roof above her, pee splashing on the porcelain below.

The wall at the foot of the bed is covered with a floor-to-ceiling mirror, courtesy of the dance enthusiast who used to own the house. Liz stands inches from the giant looking glass and peers into her own weary eyes, searching for the loose ends that have stolen her dreams. A shadow creeps over the wall behind her.

"I thought you were asleep."

Frank steps behind her and clasps her bare upper arms in his hands. She freezes. He meets her eyes in the mirror.

"You're burning up."

Lightning crashes outside the window, painting the husband and wife with a bright white brush. Thunder pounds their ears. The lights flicker. A torrent slams the windows. The electricity goes off, dropping darkness on the room like a veil. In the flat black space, Frank Hunter Forsythe is not as shocked as he should be to find his dear possessed wife almost completely aglow.

The lights come back, turning off the woman's halo in a flash.

# 45

Hook gets home from a long day of cleaning, relieved to find no trace of Sinker. No dirty dishes. No overflowing ashtrays. No crumpled beer cans. No pizza boxes. She'd done a little tidying before work and was glad he hadn't come home to trash the place.

Staying ahead of Sinker's messes would be a full time job if Hook took it to heart, but she doesn't. The Roadliner's a dump, plain and simple, and the extra effort of keeping it nice is nowhere near worth the trouble. The living room carpet alone would make you gag from fifteen years of gross ground into its matty orange fibers. The La-Z-Boy's just as bad – their daddy's favorite getting-drunk spot, with its ancient trails of crud. The only piece of furniture worth a damn is the vinyl sofa Layla gave Hook two years ago when she refurnished Holes.

Hook walks past Sinker's bedroom and a tinge of worry settles in the back of her brain. She closes the door and flashes on her brother trapped and scared. He's probably in jail again, but she decides she doesn't care. He's been arrested twice in the past year, first for peeing in public, and then for stealing a purse from a car at the shopping center. He answered the woman's cell phone when the police called an hour later and they recognized his voice. That piece of stupidity cost Sinker a week behind bars.

Comfortable that there's nothing big to worry about, Hook puts a chicken pot pie in the oven, and logs on the computer. She visits her favorite tattoo site before she checks to see who's online at Emisphor. None of her friends are there. She flips through a Bobby's Superstore catalogue and finds a big color picture of the old creep. She rips it out and burns it over the sink. Checks Emisphor again. And again. Nobody's there. She goes to her room to get her stash.

Hook's bedroom is the only one hundred square feet on earth she can call her own. Over the past few years, magazine pictures of prize fish have given way to a controlled frenzy of angel paraphernalia picked up at flea markets: nine guardian angel prints, two ceramic angel lamps, a dozen haloed figurines, and a handful of angel key chains. Her most recent find is a small wooden box with a lacquered picture of an angel protecting two children crossing a bridge. That's where she keeps her dope.

She breaks off a chunk of hash and loads her favorite pipe. Three hits later, she lies back on her bed and laughs to discover she's in the mood for sex. Her laughter turns snorty when she remembers the rush of Elizabeth Forsythe's vibrator. Then she worries. She can't remember if she washed it off.

The smell of burning food seeps into her stoned head. She hops from the bed and dances to the kitchen. The pot pie is perfect. A little burned on the edges, with bubbly drippings down the side. She wonders if her mother ever fixed her food like this and smacks herself for caring.

When she gets back in front of her screen, a couple of friends are chatting about their shitty jobs. Justagrl wants to kill some customers at her credit union, and Trixiebedlam was just laid off from a web design company in New Jersey.

Hook: least your not cleaning other peoples toy lets
Trixiebedlam: disgustible
Hook: plus washing there cummy sheets and gnarly pubes
Justagrl: you did that today?
Hook: plus played with the ladys dildo.
Trixiebedlam: *blush*
Hook: bzzzzzzzzzzz
James: well?
Hook: well what?
Justagrl: yeah . . . well what?
James: did you come?
Hook: how old are you? eleven?
James: fifty
Justagrl: liar
Trixiebedlam: well?
Hook: none a your beeswax

Trixiebedlam : tell us tell us tell us tell us

Justagrl: smell us smell us smell us

Hook: yes i did

James: was it as good for you as it was for me?

Hook: huh?

Justagrl: ignore him hook

Hook: i had to change the sheets anyway

James: interesting

Justagrl: you are such a dork sometimes

Trixiebedlam: all the time

Hook: it belongs to that lady i saved

Trixiebedlam: she owes you a big time tip

James: you don't get tips for saving people

Trixiebedlam: and just how many people have you saved?

Hook: she doesnt know it was me. long story

Justagrl: you should tell her . . . get a reward

Trixiebedlam: you grossed out her sheets???

Hook: gushed all over em : )

Justagrl: flushed tall clover stems

Hook: dork

Justagrl: pork

Hook: cork

James: torque

Hook: bork

Trixiebedlam: snork

Hook: fork

Justagrl: what's her name?

Trixiebedlam: mork

Hook: elizabeth fancy pants

James: sounds rich

Justagrl: pounds bitch

James: don't tell me you're still upset from last weekend

Justagrl: hes anal . . . constipooted

Trixiebedlam: speaking of witch, i gotsta go.

# 46

If you could look down at North Carolina from heaven tonight, you'd see a thick blanket of clouds stretching from the mountains to the coast, an unbroken mass of soggy skies spilling cold, hard rain onto the earth. And you'd see three young men worrying themselves sick in a crowded Airstream trailer.

Gary can't get his mind off the hot red lines of infection streaming up his calf from the jagged wound in his foot. He's feverish, chilled, drifting in and out of sleep. Luke has grown obsessed with the baptism and can't stop making lists of all the things they've yet to do. And the new Jesus is tripping like a circuit breaker from the mushrooms Sinker gave him earlier that day.

"I'm going to throw up," says the new Jesus, careening out the trailer door in a full run to the bathhouse. Gary startles awake and hobbles after him in the downpour.

The seedy RV park is no great shakes, but even by those low standards, the bathhouse is a dump. The twelve-by-twenty cinderblock shack features a corrugated roof, mildewed everything, a failed septic system, and a couple of rust-stained toilets that need constant plunging. The walls are covered with graffiti, featuring a smorgasbord of magic-markered tits, pussies and dicks, plus a who's-who of good-time local phone numbers.

Gary catches up with the new Jesus and hugs him through the doorway into the dark.

Storms rage through the night, hail popping on the tin bath house roof like cheap firecrackers, while the new Jesus scribbles madly with a black magic marker inside one of the stalls. Being the son of god has gone to his head, along with the psilocybin mushrooms, and he has no choice but to leave his mark.

Luke wanders in with the dimmest of flashlights and finds Gary kneeling beside the new Jesus.

"Is he okay?"

"He's talking to god."

Luke's heavy sigh disappears in the rainy clatter. "If this is what happens when you get to be Jesus, I think I'll pass." Though he whispers, he hopes someone will hear.

"Did you call me Mark?" asks the new Jesus. He's huddled next to a toilet, scrawling thick black graffiti low on the wall.

"I didn't call you anything," says Luke, sniffing the dank air. The sharp odor of permanent marker pushes past the urine and mildew. "What are you doing in there?"

"I don't know," says the new Jesus.

"You have to know," says Luke. "You're Jesus."

"I can't see."

"That doesn't matter."

"Leave him alone," says Gary.

"It's okay," says the new Jesus. "I'm almost done."

# 47

When Gloria arrives to visit Liz on Saturday afternoon, they greet each other like old friends. Frank's upstairs taking a nap, trying to fight off a cold. They let him sleep.

"Got a few things figured out," says Gloria. The two women sit in the kitchen, picking up their conversation from their phone call last night.

"That's good to hear. Heaven knows I sure don't."

Liz pours tea while Gloria unwraps the bracelet from a handkerchief and sets the silver C on the counter. It gleams, radiant in the glow of the old professor's smile.

"First off, this bracelet is old," says Gloria. "Maybe even ancient."

"Seriously? What do you mean by ancient?"

"A thousand years, give or take? The Aramaic is the real thing."

Liz whistles.

"You'll need to have it examined by someone who knows what they're doing. I have a some ideas we can talk through later."

"You're the expert."

"Not quite. But I know at least one person who is. I'll call him tomorrow."

"What else have you learned?"

Gloria drags the magnifying glass from her sweater pocket. "See this on the outside here? It says *these are the threads of life fully filled.*"

The words burn bright into Liz's cracked skull. "These are the threads of life fully filled?"

"The word *threads* could also mean strands. Or maybe strings."

"You said threads."

"That's right."

"And?"

"Fully filled could have other meanings too. Life without limits. Eternal life. Hard to say at this point. Will need some help figuring it out."

"Eternal life?"

"Maybe."

"Is there more?"

"On the inside. Yes."

Liz waits.

"Best I can tell, it says *Good works do. Kind and loving be. Joy in pleasure seek.*"

The words reverberate in the kitchen like a shockwave, bouncing off the shiny ceramic tiles and cabinets until they dampen down to nothing but a memory.

"Good works do. Kind and loving be. Joy in pleasure seek? These are the threads of life fully filled?" says Liz.

"Sounds about right to me," says Gloria.

# 48

Hook's online discussion lasts for hours, gradually pulling in dozens of people with comments about her sneaky orgasm and the possibility of a big reward. But she's been smoking dope all day and a gray wave of exhaustion is building. Just as it starts to crash, Sinker and Eddie Junior show up.

"Get offa my laptop, bitch," says Sinker. He's not yet through the door, but from the two-hundred watt gleam in his eyes, Hook can tell he's been tweaking meth again.

"I'm sick of you fucking with my stuff all the time." Sinker wades in too close and his sour smell gags her. Eddie Junior sees things starting to unravel, but he can't pull Sinker away. The brother grabs the sister's hair and slams her to the floor.

Big mistake.

Before he knows what's hit him, she's ripped her Water Devil shark hook though the back of his leg, crippling him in a scream.

"Damn it," says Eddie Junior. "Now look what you did."

Hook slices her eyes at Eddie Junior, shutting him up. "Lay still while I get my damn cutters."

She unchains the hook from her belt and heads for the door, kicking it all the way open. She comes back with bolt cutters big enough to handle the hook running clean through Sinker's leg. His whimpering pisses her off. She presses on the hook and he screams.

She ignores him, talking instead to Eddie Junior. "You're gonna have to take him to emergency. I don't want him back tonight. You hear me?"

Eddie Junior watches while she clips off the barb and backs the hook out in a quick second. Sinker starts wailing again.

"Good thing I got me a spare," she says, fingering the shorn shaft of her hook . "You better get a move on."

"What're you gonna do?" asks Eddie Junior.

Hook looks at the blood on her hands. It seems like hers. She gives Eddie Junior a faraway look. "I'm gonna write me a goddamn poem."

Eddie Junior dumps Sinker in the emergency room parking lot thirty minutes later. He figures no good can come from actually going in, and he's probably right. The ER staff has seen enough of Sinker to wish he'd just go ahead and die, as long as it's somewhere else. But now he's lying on hospital property, blocking one of their ambulances, and they have little choice but to drag him in. Eddie Junior waits in the distance to make sure Sinker's picked up, then he heads back to the RV park. When he gets there, he circles around by Hook's trailer, sees the light on, and goes to the door.

"Hadn't you seen enough trouble tonight?" says Hook.

Eddie Junior takes her question as an invitation and bumbles in. His droopy pants pocket catches on the doorknob. Hook laughs despite herself. She's back at the computer, working on her poem, drinking a Mountain Dew.

"Come on, Hook. I didn't do nothing."

"Where'd he get that crank?"

Eddie Junior scans the room for an answer. "Over in Jacksonville?"

Hook stares him down, then lets it go, much to Eddie Junior's relief. He falls on the sofa, lying on his side so he can keep an eye on her. "What're you doing?" he says.

Hook's surprised she doesn't get mad. "Talking to my friends."

"What friends?"

"*My* friends, dip shit."

He scratches his head. "Sinker says you don't even know who they are."

She sashays to the cupboard and gets a Slim Jim. She peels the plastic off with her teeth and hangs the smelly stick of beef from her mouth like a cigar.

"What're ya'll talking about?" he asks.

Hook's brow darkens over a sneaky smile. "My stupid brother."

Eddie Junior winces. "You tore his leg up good."

"I meant to."

Eddie Junior gets up and pokes around the cabinets. "Got any more Slim Jims?" Hook watches him reach for the top shelf. His boxer shorts show baby blue above the waist band of his jeans.

"Got some jerky," she says. "Your favorite." Hook sings the words as she opens a drawer and lifts out a bag of Pemmican mesquite-flavored beef. She swings it back and forth like a tease. "You got any coke?"

It's not often Eddie Junior's holding coke, but Hook figures the odds are good tonight, and she's right. He just bought a bunch of meth and managed to finagle a clean gram of powder in the deal.

"Good coke for old beef jerky?"

Hook pooches out her bottom lip. "It ain't old, Eddie Junior. I just bought it last week."

Eddie Junior's eyes follow her to the bathroom where she picks up a hand mirror and a razor blade. She's talking a mile-a-minute the whole way. "Who else you gonna do it with?" She eyes him sweet. "Come on, Eddie Junior. Let's see what you got."

Five minutes later, Hook's climbed a few white lines to a place just short of happy. Eddie Junior's behaving himself. Sinker's gone. Her front teeth are numb. And her mind's buzzing with silliness. She doesn't even get pissed when Eddie Junior asks to read what she's writing. She just laughs.

"Play out another vine and I'll weed it to you."

"Huh?"

"I'm just goofing with you, Eddie Junior."

"Sounds stupid."

"Being as you're the prince of stupid around here, you probly got yourself a point."

"Damn it, Hook."

"Lay out another line and I'll read it to you." She says it extra clear.

Eddie Junior thinks hard for five seconds then does what she asks. She sucks up the coke and holds her breath for the rush. Then she starts to read.

*i stabbed my stupid brother after he pulled me on the floor by my hair. stuck a shark hook through the backside of his leg. he yelled like it hurt, which i bet it did. heh. i hope i didn't cripple him for life, but i wouldn't mind if he had to limp for a few months. asshat better keep his hands off me. next time i cut off his balls.*

Eddie Junior whistles. "Damn. Who you writing to?"

"I told you. My friends. They love hearing what a dumb shit my twin brother is."

"Don't sound like no poem."

Hook giggles. "That's cause it ain't. I hadn't got to that part yet."

"What's a asshat?"

"You're a asshat, Eddie Junior."

The young man's having trouble keeping Hook's smiling face and her rough words together in his mind, a strain that dulls his brightness to a pout. "I ain't so sure I wanna hear it."

She pats him on the cheek. "It won't hurt."

"I didn't do nothing, you know."

Hook gets up from the recliner and presses her forehead against his. She puts on her mean look, tightening her lips. "You got that crank."

Eddie Junior fidgets like a first-grader, but Hook can't stay upset. "Never mind. Just listen."

She wouldn't want to admit it, but she's excited about reading her poem to someone. It's one thing to write this stuff online, but Eddie Junior's almost a real person.

"Joy tried," she reads. "By Hook."

*plastic play stick shaky ride*
*sharp hook push in pain*
*snappy say place words to play space*
*eddie's home again*

Eddie Junior scans the room, surprised he's the only one in the audience. Hook takes a drink of Mountain Dew.

"You got my name in there," he says, not quite in accusation.

"So?" Hook takes another slug of Dew and wipes her mouth with the back of her hand.

"This is weird," says Eddie Junior. "I mean it." His worried look makes Hook smile.

"Fish is speared," she says. "I clean it."

The words crack her up and Eddie Junior laughs too, though he's not sure why.

# 49

After Hook reads her poem to Eddie Junior, they do some more lines and laugh until gray seeps into the morning sky. Hook is happy playing with words on Emisphor, thinking for the first time she might have a talent besides fishing.

By sun up, the coke has disappeared and Hook's feeling cuddly. She settles on the sofa with the laptop to show off her postings, leaning in so close that Eddie Junior gets worked up. She's too wired to notice.

"Think you'd ever go for a boy like me, Hookster?"

His seriousness catches her off guard. "What're you talking about?"

"You know."

She wrinkles her nose at him. "If I knew, I wouldn't be asking."

"If I flew, I wouldn't be crashing," says Eddie Junior.

Hook claps her hands in delight. "That's pretty good, Eddie Junior. Too bad it took you all damn night."

He chews on his thumb.

"What'sa matter?" Hook's cooing by now.

Eddie Junior tugs his ear. "I guess I kinda like you, Hook."

Maybe it's just the coke. Or maybe all the silliness. Whatever the reason, Hook doesn't get pissed. Eddie Junior might not be so bad. And besides, he still hasn't tried to touch her.

With that loose footing, she slips into her flirtiest voice. "Now just what do you got on your mind, Eddie Junior?" Her coked-up lips spread to a grin and Eddie Junior flushes red. She slides her hand over to his crotch and grabs a handful of blue jeans and balls.

"Oh sweetie. You ain't even got a hard on."

# 50

"Rise and whine, Frank Furter. Time for church." Liz digs through the blankets to uncover her husband's sleepy face.

She woke him briefly when she got into bed last night, just long enough to report what Gloria told her about the bracelet. He took it all in stride, figuring there was no other option. Having unloaded her burden, Liz fell asleep right away. Frank got out of bed and went downstairs.

"I'm sick," he says, trying to dampen her Sunday morning enthusiasm.

"You sound fine. What'd you do? Stay up all night?"

"Only till four."

"Poor baby."

"I was playing jump rope with the threads." He scrunches a pillow under his head. "Well, maybe not jump rope. More like Cat's Cradle." He hands her a three-by-five index card from the nightstand. "Here you go."

Liz furrows her brow, suspicious. "You spent all night doing this?"

"Just read it."

He cranes his neck to see if his words are still there. She scootches back and pulls the card from his prying eyes. She studies the rough blocky letters and thinks for the first time that his handwriting is the frail scratching of an old man.

"The threads of life fully filled. Okay."

"Turn it over."

"Do good. Be nice. Have fun."

She rolls her eyes in an exaggerated sweep. "You stayed up all night writing this?"

"Easy there O Possessed One. Focus on the clarity, not the quantity."

She reconsiders Frank's version of Gloria's original translation. *Good works do. Kind and loving be. Joy in pleasure seek.* "Hmmm," she says. "Do good. Be nice. Have fun." She drops the card in her bag. "I like it. Now get dressed. We're late."

It was six years ago on a cold October morning that Liz and Frank first tested the holy waters at the New Hope Unitarian Universalist Fellowship. Their home heat pump wasn't working, and Liz convinced him it would be warmer at church. The service turned out to be a toasty Halloween ritual, laid out for worship by a barefoot pagan priestess.

Frank's assessment was harsh. "We just sat through a church service with a witch for the preacher. And wood nymphs in tights with a fake bonfire."

"Don't be mean. The wood nymphs were cute."

"What about that witch?"

"That witch has an MFA from Berkley. She's brilliant. Come on. You liked some parts of it."

"I liked the part when they let us leave."

When he eventually joined New Hope, Frank wouldn't have predicted that his favorite part would be the Pagan Studies Circle, a quirky refuge for spirits seeking something more than mainstream mysticism. At New Hope, the UU Pagans happily coexist with the UU Christians, the UU Jews, the UU Agnostics, the UU Buddhists, and the UU Atheists. All of whom anchor New Hope just slightly to the left of tofu, according to Frank.

"Pagan studies? After all the grief you gave me about that Halloween service? And now you're joining them?" It was a Sunday morning, before church. Liz was making pancakes.

"I'm not joining anything."

"Oh right. You're not a joiner."

"I'm just dropping in every now and then."

"But you're not joining."

"Besides, there is something interesting about being around a bunch of witches."

"Now I get it. You have the hots for a pagan sorceress."

"I wouldn't call it the hots," said Frank. "More like the tepids."

"Tepids schmepids." Liz loosened her robe, dribbled maple syrup on one of her heavy breasts, then lifted her nipple to Frank's lips. "Let's put out that fire."

The official abbreviation for the New Hope Fellowship is NHUUF, which Frank read as *Enough* the first time he saw it in a church bulletin. This morning's visit drives the nickname home. The parking lot's overflowing, spilling a stream of open hearts into the modern sanctuary. Liz sails amidst the tide of shorter churchgoers with her husband like a dinghy in tow. His rumpled khakis and dull gray sweater make her bright blue dress all the more noticeable on this dreary October morning.

"Looks like a big crowd," Liz says to a woman walking beside her. The woman's shirt is covered with tropical cartoon fish. One green fish flops over her shoulder, eyeing a yellow fish swimming into her armpit.

"It's Halloween!" The woman's enthusiasm unnerves Frank.

"Our favorite," laughs Liz, elbowing her husband in the ribs. Having sat through five Halloween ceremonies in as many years, Frank looks forward to the annual show with a volatile mixture of dread and lust.

"I don't want to be here," he says.

"Such a grump." Liz stops in the middle of the walk and looks him in the eye. She wraps one long arm around his shoulder and whispers in his ear.

"Remember the threads? Do good, be nice, have fun? Let's have fun. Really. It's okay."

Frank wonders if he knows what fun is anymore. Or if he ever did. He wonders why he's not home in bed. His back hurts.

# 51

Hook spent Saturday recovering from her night with Eddie Junior. They talked and drank beer until sunrise, when she sent him home, mostly untouched. He left her too frazzled to sleep, so she watched TV and chatted online. Sinker called to say Hook should pick him up at the hospital the next morning. She told him to call again when he was ready. She knew she wouldn't be home. Eddie Junior asked her to go fishing with him. He'd wanted to change the subject after he couldn't get an erection, but Hook wouldn't let it go.

"I could get one if I had a mind to," he'd said.

Hook patted through his pants. "Course you could."

Eddie Junior willed himself hard, but no dice. All he could say was, "Don't go making jokes." That was the first time Hook had seen him embarrassed, and it almost broke her heart. She smiled like she was in love.

Streaks of gray fog laze in the dark canyons between the trailers in the RV park. It's five-thirty on Sunday morning and Eddie Junior's sitting in his new Ford pickup, honking for Hook to come out.

"Hold your damn horses." Hook's dressed and moving, but barely awake. She loads her gear into the truck bed and climbs in the passenger seat. Eddie Junior's all scrubbed and sweet.

"You clean up pretty good for a old man." Her voice carries the crackly thick of sleep.

Eddie Junior catches her eye for a second before he turns to look out the back window. "You better watch it."

"Or what." Hook puts her bare feet up on the dashboard. Glittery purple nails.

"Or no more coke." He throws the truck in reverse, and backs away. The Ford's high beams spotlight the worn-out Roadliner. The black circle of burned grass. The busted pelican planter on the porch. Hook's beat-up old truck. She can't believe this is all her life amounts to.

# 52

Sinker hobbles to the phone in the hospital lobby and calls Hook. No answer. He calls Eddie Junior. Nothing. Same with Doug Dipper. He slams the phone against the wall, catching the attention of a security guard, who's flirting with the receptionist on the other side of the lobby. The guard hikes up his holster and saunters toward Sinker, talking extra loud.

"I don't need you making no trouble, Sinker. You understand?"

"My stupid sister said she'd pick me up and she ain't even goddamn home."

"Not my problem."

"Guess I'll just have to hang around here then," says Sinker. He plops down, grabs a magazine, and sprawls his wounded leg across a side table.

The prospect of getting stuck with Sinker moves the guard to action. He calls the police station. A town cop shows up ten minutes later to give Sinker a lift.

Sinker's more than primed for a fight. After the cop drops him off, he busts through the flimsy trailer door, hunting for Hook. All he finds is a note on the refrigerator saying she's gone fishing with Eddie Junior.

"Suck ass bitch." Sinker spits the words so hard his throat hurts. He kicks the refrigerator with his good leg, loses his balance and falls, hitting his head on the counter, opening a gash above his eye. He presses a dishtowel against the cut and drags himself to his bedroom. He rifles through the dirty clothes on his mattress, hoping to find some pot. He's in luck.

Sinker smokes and stews for an hour before he finally decides that the only fair thing to do is to blow up Hook's truck. He finds a gas can in the storage shed, douses the driver's seat, and tosses in a match.

As the fire swarms across the vinyl upholstery, Sinker notices one of Hook's tackle boxes on the passenger-side floorboard. He runs around the truck and throws open the door, only to be greeted by a hot ball of flames. His hair catches fire and he rolls the ground, rubbing his head and face in the sandy soil. The burning truck feeds his fury, but there's no big bang. Good thing. He'd be dead if the truck exploded.

By the time firefighters arrive, Hook's truck is toast. They spray foamy stuff, mostly for show, and call the police. The cop who brought Sinker home shows up a few minutes later.

With his brain on overload, Sinker freaks out and tries to run. He doesn't get far on his shark-hooked leg.

"What the hell happened here?" says the cop. "You do this?" he asks, pointing to the smoldering truck.

"I didn't do nothin'."

"What's that gas can doing there?"

"None of your fucking business."

Grudgingly, the officer pushes Sinker to the ground and pats him down. He finds half a joint in Sinker's pocket. "Well, lookie here."

"Why're you hasslin' me?" says Sinker. "I told you I didn't do nothing."

"I'm not hassling you, " says the cop, clamping handcuffs around Sinker's skinny wrists. "I'm arresting your dumb ass. You're whole damn self oughta be against the law."

# 53

After the new Jesus put the finishing touches on his midnight marker madness, the boys crashed and stayed that way, waking groggy to the sound of sirens Sunday morning.

"They're coming to take us away," says Gary, sleep hanging heavy around his words.

Luke sneaks a peak through the Airstream window.

"They aren't after us," says the new Jesus. He pushes Luke aside for a better view.

Luke scoffs. "Just like it wasn't going to rain."

The new Jesus presses his head with his hands, trying to squeeze his headache away. "Fuck you, Luke."

"I'm glad your head hurts. S-serves you right."

"I'm serious," says Gary. "The cops are coming."

"Did you hear that from the dog lady, too?" snarks the new Jesus. His pushy chin demands an answer, but Gary declines.

"I asked you a question."

"I don't know who told me."

"And he doesn't have to know, either," says Luke. "You're Jesus. Why don't you know yourself?"

The sky's still angry, but the rain has let up. A thick column of black smoke lifts through the drizzle behind the trees on the other side of the RV park. And here comes Sinker running toward the beach with a cop on his tail.

"That's Michael," whispers the new Jesus. "The guy who made the sign."

"We could use a Michael." Gary's hobbling around the Airstream like he's walking on glass. Those nails did more damage than he knew.

"There's no Michael in the *Bible*," says the new Jesus.

"Bullshit," says Luke. "He's in Revelations. There's this war in heaven where he fights the devil. Michael's the big angel."

"What's the devil doing in heaven?"

"He s-snuck in as a dragon."

"Who won?" says Gary, opening the trailer door. Whiffs of burned oil and rubber carry on the breeze. The police officer has Michael spread-eagle on the ground.

"The cop did," says the new Jesus.

# 54

The NHUUF sanctuary is a bright, cheery room with creamy walls, a vaulted ceiling, cushioned pews, and wall-to-wall windows overlooking a healthy stand of beech trees. Sitting in the rear of the room, Liz scans the backs of a hundred heads and wonders what each hopes to hear today. The shiny bald head with brown hairs sproinging from its ears. The butch in front of him. The sensible pageboy in front of her. The gray pompadour. The gelled spikes. The chemo wig. The flat top. The hippy braids. All these heads with all their ears, sifting through the flow of words for something to give meaning to their Sunday morning existence.

The New Hope minister usually sits down front while the congregation assembles to the tinkly tones of a not-so-grand piano. But today his chair is empty, and the music comes courtesy of the Odd & Occasional Pagan Singers. Their eerie voices drift with musky incense across the makeshift altar. A JetBlo fog machine pumps manufactured mist from a door behind the singers. The crash of a heavy bronze gong announces a priestess who glides into the room, flashes of bare toes bright beneath her hooded robe. As she begins her signature prayer, a woeful chant of nonsensical pagan patter, Liz tilts her head in obeisance, fingering the bracelet on her wrist, sinking into something that feels like sleep. Threads tense inside her brain, a bundle of swerves impatient for unraveling at the drop of a hint. She startles to attention when the spooky priestess speaks.

"We come now to that time in our service for the sharing of joys and sorrows." She gazes around the room. "For some, the past week has brought laughter and wonder. For others, it has been woven with sadness. Such is the fabric of life."

Liz gasps. The bald head in front of her turns around worried, deep-set eyes flitting to Frank, accusing him of something he wishes he had done. Liz leans forward, head in hands, breathing herself calm.

"You okay?" says Frank. He rests his hand on her back. She shrugs it away. He scans the people moving forward to declare their miseries. He feels Liz touching his shoulder, stepping past him out of the pew. She takes her place at the end of the joys and sorrows line, holding the bracelet, shifting her weight from side to side. He guesses she's going to offer a sad report on Molly's death.

The first speaker is a short man in hiking boots and a Sierra Club tee shirt. "I ask that you pray for my mother who fell and broke her hip," he says. "She's ninety, and tomorrow she's going to have replacement surgery. Please keep her in your thoughts."

*Keep her in your thoughts?* Frank is certain the old lady would be better off in the hospital than in his skeptical skull.

Next is a worn-out woman filled with sighs. "My husband was laid off from IBM last week." Sigh. "He's a wonderful writer." Sigh. "And if anyone knows anyone who might be hiring writers?" Sigh. "Please call us." Sigh. "I'm pregnant." Sigh. "And he really needs a job." Sigh.

Then dear Deirdre, her eyes tearing before she starts to speak. Recently widowed, Deirdre has been a fixture at NHUUF for three decades.

"My sweet little dog is gone," she cries. "My sweet little Corky. She lived with me for eighteen years, and she died yesterday. I don't know what I'm going to do."

*Oh great.* Frank sinks in the pew, staring at a crack in the concrete floor. It reminds him of a snaky river. *She's stealing the show with her dead dog story.* As he studies the bends in the river below, the congregation quiets. He looks up to find Liz in the front of the sanctuary with every head and eye and ear in the church waiting for her words.

"Good morning. My name is Liz Forsythe." Her chest lifts with deep breathing. "I was walking on the beach last month, when I found this in the sand." She holds the bracelet high, like Unitarian show-and-tell. The heads in the pews bobble and wobble, the brains inside them wondering whether they're about to hear a joy, a concern, or a sales pitch.

"It has inscriptions in Aramaic. A professor tells me they may have been written almost a thousand years ago. It says *Do good. Be nice. Have fun. These are the threads of life fully filled.*" She surveys the sanctuary. "Do good. Be nice. Have fun," she says, her smile brightening the space around her. "These are the threads of life fully filled."

And while an old truck smolders on the soggy shores of Sunrise Beach, silence explodes in a Chapel Hill church. It's just what the shadow puppet wanted.

# 55

At the western-most tip of Sunrise Beach lies Miles Inlet, a treacherous gap that provides ocean access to thousands of boats docked along the intracoastal waterway, and a hot fishing spot for people lucky enough to have four-wheel drive. But Hook and Eddie Junior don't catch much this blustery morning. He breaks out the coke as soon as the big Ford rolls to a stop by the channel.

After his soft Friday night performance, Eddie Junior figures to take it easy on the drugs. But that doesn't mean Hook cuts him any slack. She lets him unbutton her blouse, but when he goes after her jeans, she slaps his hand. He yells out louder than a grown man should.

"What're you trying to do anyway?" she says.

"What'd you think I'm trying to do?" He rubs his forehead on the steering wheel. The leather cover still smells new.

Hook pokes him in the ribs. "You might be trying to get my pants off so you can get your hands on my sweet little pink parts."

Eddie Junior sits up and looks at her sideways. He can't stop a grin from spreading. "Well, there's that."

"Or you might just be trying to get yourself a woody."

He blushes.

"Or you might be trying to . . ."

"Okay, okay. I get what you mean. Jeez."

"Well?" Hook clicks her thumbnail against her front teeth.

"Well what?"

"Well, what're you trying to do?"

Eddie Junior looks cornered. "Okay." He takes a deep breath. "I'm trying to get your pants off so we can fuck." He smiles, proud of his answer.

Hook fingers her invisible beard.

"That there's a interesting idea."

She lifts her shirt to give him better access, but the very split second he digs in under her panties, Hook goes into meltdown. She shakes her startled head in a frantic "no" and cries out with a yelp.

To his credit, Eddie Junior shifts from horny to helpful smooth as can be. "What's the matter?"

"Something happened," she says. "We gotta go." She won't look at him.

With only minor grumping, Eddie Junior starts the truck and heads for the RV park. Neither of the missed-out lovers has much to say on the fifteen-minute drive, but Hook's fried brain is scrambling for some traction. She hasn't been hit like this since a year ago when she helped the cops find that drowned boy in the sound.

When they pull up to the trailer, Hook wants to scream at the sight of her burned-out truck, but she ends up crying instead. The only sliver of independence she's ever had is gone. She shouldn't have been out with Eddie Junior. She should have known nothing good would come of it.

Eddie Junior stretches across the big console and tries to give her a hug. He's interrupted by a knock on the window. It's one of the firefighters.

"Can I help you two?"

*You two.* That's the first time Hook's heard herself mentioned as part of a couple. She pulls away from her possible boyfriend.

"That's my truck." She closes her eyes.

"Do you know Michael Martin? The man they found here at the scene?"

*Michael Martin.* It's been years since Hook's heard Sinker's real name. "I guess I do. He's my damn idiot brother. And he ain't no man."

"Well, your damn idiot brother's in custody for possessing illegal drugs and resisting arrest. And if you decide you want to press charges, they might be adding arson to the list."

# 56

Sunday morning sirens laced with an acid hangover knock the new Jesus into the pits and he can't climb out. Plus he's having trouble stomaching Luke's cheeriness. They've moved from the trailer to the dunes, laying low in the cool, gritty wind, hoping the cop has gone for good.

"Let's head over to the pool and check out traffic from when the churches let out." Luke rubs his hands together exactly the way Mark hates. "Do a trial run for the baptizing."

"Cool," says Gary. He's almost back to his old self and doesn't want to referee another spat. "I'll bet Mr. Dipper has the pool all warmed up and ready to go. We can put up our new banner."

Luke and the new Jesus trade a nervous glance.

"I feel like shit," says the new Jesus, curling into a ball on the sand.

"We have to rehearse," says Luke.

The new Jesus drags himself to his knees and asks god to stop driving railroad spikes through his skull. But god seems to be busy with other stuff.

"I can't. I'm sick."

"That's just great, Mark."

The new Jesus growls at the sound of his old name.

"Just give us the sign," says Gary. "We'll take care of things."

Gary's feet hurt like hell on the ten-block walk to Doug Dipper's. He wanted to drive, but the Jeep wouldn't start. Dead alternator. When he and Luke get to the pool, they find Doug slumped in an Adirondack chair beside a bright blue circle of chlorinated water.

"I thought you dirt bags was gonna have a baptizing today," he says. "Where's the guy with the money?"

"We decided to wait till next week." Gary looks up to heaven. "It's been raining."

Every one of Doug Dipper's brain cells screams *I told you so* as he stomps down the deck stairs. He knew these dickheads would screw things up.

"Listen morons. You said today. I heated the pool. That's fifty bucks. You want to use it again next week? That's another fifty."

Luke looks panicky at the prospect of more cash outlays, but Gary fields the offer in stride. "Deal," he says, reaching in his pocket for a clump of bills. "Can we go ahead and put up our sign?"

Doug takes the money and smiles. "You can put up a damn cross for all I care. Just don't fuck up my pool." He climbs behind the wheel of his van and peels away.

Before the dust settles, Luke starts in on the third degree. He climbs the stairs to the deck and looks down at Gary over the railing, a raging preacher in pressure-treated pulpit.

"What the heck are you doing with that money, Gary Gray? Mark's s-supposed to be holding the cash."

Gary watches the steady flow of Sunday traffic passing the Pool Palace, the same big families that rolled by seven days ago, heading home from their weekly fixes. He imagines the miracle of them pulling up to the pool for their baptism next Sunday. There might be a good turn-out after all.

He forces his attention back to Luke. "I kept some just in case," he says.

"Just in case?" Luke calms his breathing, fighting back tears. "I gave you every nickel to my name. Just in case of what?"

"Come on, Luke. You had like fourteen dollars. It's for emergencies."

Gary nears the pool and looks up at Luke. He hears the quiet buzz of yellow jackets stirring under the deck. He backs away a few steps.

"That's a bunch of crap," says Luke.

"You don't trust me?" Unexpected anger sharpens Gary's voice. "Then keep it your own damn self." He throws the thin wad of money in Luke's direction, watching the worn bills swirl in the wind. Luke hesitates only a second before he scrambles to collect the cash.

"Dang it, Gary. You're getting weirder than Mark."

Gary ignores the complaint and carries the banner up on the deck, where Luke's fishing for dollars with a pool skimmer. He starts to unroll the sign.

"Wait," yells Luke. "Don't do that."

Too late.

# 57

When the UU Halloween service wraps up, one of the Pagan Singers steps from the back row of the choir out the side door. It's Nancy Kneedle, founder and general manager of WTCH, a public radio station specializing in strange. Having both a nose for news and, as it happens, a fondness for Frank, she senses a story in the making and figures to flirt her way to the source. She skirts around the side of the church and waits by the Sunday School building.

It was Nancy Kneedle's raw sexuality that first attracted Frank to the church's pagan circle, and her dependably lusty ways have kept him coming back for more. Nancy subscribes without apology to anything goes, as long as no one gets hurt along the way. Grinding her hips into Frank when they hug at circle meetings is well within bounds as far as she's concerned.

"You do this with lots of people?" Frank asked after their second dry hump.

"Frank Forsythe. You're jealous."

"More like curious. I'm new to this pagan stuff."

"Honey, this isn't pagan stuff. This is Nancy stuff. Just me being me."

Not knowing exactly what to do with Nancy just being Nancy, Frank kept quiet.

"Don't you like having that little wild feeling when it swells up all inside you?" she said. "I sure do."

"To tell you the truth, I like it a lot. But . . ."

"It's not going to turn into anything."

"Really?"

"You're not my type, Frank. Besides, you're married."

Frank couldn't decide if he was relieved or disappointed. "You didn't answer my question."

"Which question?"

"Whether you do this with lots of people."

She smiled and patted his cheek. "Only one at a time."

When *We're Talking Chapel Hill* first signed on in the early nineties, Nancy's start-up station had its work cut out. Its main competitor, funded by the University of North Carolina, appealed to the Tarheel faithful with a bland blend of classical music and sanitized news. Counterpunching like a bantam-weight boxer, Nancy went after local intellectuals with non-stop talk, sharpened to a cynical edge. When she joined the Pagan Singers a few years ago, she dreamed up *Midnight Pagan*, the first of several fringy call-in shows that made the station a high-powered magnet for mystics and weirdoes. Not the least of whom was Preacher Joseph J. Peters of nearby Rougemont.

"You realize, Mizz Kneedle, that your radio station is an abomination," the preacher said in an editorial on his own little Christian network. "It cannot be allowed."

The warning spawned what would become Joe's *Ditch the WiTCH* fundraising campaign, igniting the indignation of his right-wing mailing list and setting the stage for a full-fledged radio showdown. Fortunately for Nancy, Preacher Peters was better at raising money than raising hell, and his attack soon fizzled. WTCH doubled its audience after the assault, securing itself as a safe haven for the coven of crazies Nancy employed.

"That was some tale you told," says Nancy, herding Liz and Frank into an empty classroom. "Wouldn't you like to share it with a bigger audience?" She looks at Frank, but he's pacing away. "We could do a whole show about your bracelet. Maybe on our Halloween midnight special?"

# 58

With Sinker stuck in jail, Hook has some welcome time to herself and her online friends. They're full of suggestions about how to rid the world of her miserable brother.

Hook: sinker sploded my durn truck. ima keel him.

James: let him eat snake

Hook: he was doin crank

James: meth mouth?

Hook: this aint all that helpful

Justagrl: poor hooker

Hook: i need wheels

James: did you get a reward for saving that lady's butt?

Hook: nope

Justagrl: did you ask her?

Hook: nope

James: you got her email, right?

Hook: im not doing it

James: it's your shot at big bucks

Trixiebedlam: dig ducks

James: oh jeez

Trixiebedlam: pig fucks

Hook: hey trix

Trixiebedlam: fig trucks

Justagrl: ask her

Trixiebedlam: rig lucks

# 59

*Turn or Burn Sunday.*

The flaming red words on the banner hit Gary right in the gut. He slumps like a punch drunk fighter, then rolls to his back beside the pool. He'd been over this hell business with Luke and Mark a thousand times, and he'd always been extra clear. No weeping and wailing. No gnashing of teeth. No fire and brimstone. No fountains of blood. No lakes of fire. No hell. No way.

And now this stupid sign.

"Hey," says Dog. The old woman sits at Gary's feet, spilling goodness and light all over the rain-slicked deck. She slides her hat back on her head, setting loose a glowing wash of clean yellow light that brightens the dreary day. "You sure spend a lot of time laying around."

Gary wonders if she saw the sign.

"Not your worry." Dog breathes deep, stirring up a whistle of wind in the afternoon air. "You gave up being Jesus. You're Gary Gray, the finder. Gary Gray, the motherless son."

He's unsettled by Dog's words, but her smooth voice somehow calms him all the same. He wonders how she knows so much about him.

"Oh, I know a few things." She clucks like a happy chicken and hugs his feet to her heart. "You sure got your sole messed up. Let's see what we can do."

Gary closes his eyes and wishes his wounds away.

"Anything else?" Dog says.

"I was wondering if you wanted to take over."

Though Gary casts the words in Dog's direction, it's Luke who reels them in.

"Me take over?" Luke cries for joy and kneels beside Gary, cradling his head. "These things have I told you, that when the time shall come, ye may remember that I told you of them."

Luke has the whole New Testament memorized and half the Book of Mormon, but this isn't him talking. Quicker than a second coming, he's stepped into Jesus' shoes.

"O all ye that are spared because ye were more righteous than they, will ye not now return unto me, and repent of your sins, and be converted, that I may heal you?

Gary runs his jittery hands along the edge of the banner, trying to gather his wits. "Which one is that?"

"Third Nephi."

Gary lifts up on his elbows and stares at his feet. They're good as new.

# 60

"What the hell are you thinking?" Frank can't believe Liz has agreed to do *Midnight Pagan*. Nancy's gone, and he's still pacing. "You're going on a radio show to tell the whole damn world about your pelicans and threads?"

"It was one pelican, Frank. One. And besides, other things have been happening, too."

"Oh really. What now? Talking kingfishers?"

"Talking puppets."

Frank stops in his tracks. "Puppets?"

"One puppet, actually. The one pinned to our bedroom wall. Sita. Friday during the storm."

Frank screws himself tight into a ball of fury. "And what did this puppet supposedly say?"

"It said, 'I know you hold the threads, and now you must release them.'"

Frank swallows the sour spreading in his throat.

"What?" Liz is the one who's angry now.

"I'll tell you what. Call Nancy. Call her right now and tell her you've changed your mind." He holds out his cell phone.

She crosses her arms tight. "I'm not doing that. We're recording the show tomorrow." Liz takes a deep breath and searches for an olive branch. "At least it's not live."

Frank reaches for the twig. "That's a relief."

"What are you so worried about?"

"I'm worried about what's going to happen when half the world hears you've found some kind of secret sign from god."

"Damn it, Frank." She blushes mad. "This doesn't have to have anything to do with god. Nothing. That's all your crap."

He tries to breathe. "It might be, but as your PR guy, I can tell you this. Going on *Midnight Pagan* does not seem like a very smart idea."

She gathers herself. "Those words you wrote? Do good, be nice, have fun? People should hear them. They really should. That's what it means to release the threads."

He presses his thumbs into his eyes, forcing his voice to quiet. "Listen to what you're saying."

"What am I saying?"

"What you're saying is crazy." His voice is too loud, too clear.

Liz lifts the bracelet to her cheek, feeling the silvery song. "I don't care if it is," she whispers.

# 61

Hook doesn't approve much of charity, especially when she's the intended recipient, so the idea of getting a reward from Elizabeth Fancy Pants didn't sound all that positive when her online friends first brought it up. But they've raised the subject again, and she's entertaining the possibility. Her truck's totaled. Her brother's losing what little sense he ever had. And to top it all off, now Eddie Junior wants to get his hands in her pants. He'd even kissed her goodbye when he left the other night.

"I don't like you thinking you can just go around kissing me like that," she'd said. They were standing on the porch, looking at her crispy Ford Ranger. A hint of burned rubber oiled the evening air.

"Kiss you like what?"

"You know. All that tonguey stuff. I didn't give you no permission to do that stuff."

"Then why'd you kiss me back?"

"What're you talking about? It was just your magination."

He thought she was teasing, but wasn't as sure as he wanted to be. "Yeah, well. It ain't my magination that I better go on home. You're getting smart-assy and that's always a danger." Eddie Junior kissed her again before he said good-bye. Hook did the tonguey stuff that time.

Later that evening, she downed a couple of beers and wrote an email.

*you don't know it but my brother and me are the ones who saved you from getting drowned. i found your name cos i cleaned your condo for irene. sorry for snooping in your drawers, but its the only fun part of being a maid. i figured you might want your hat*

*back, so i left it there. i wouldn't mind a reward for my braveness.*
*don't bother with sinker though since he tried to feel you up. hook*

She knows her scheme isn't going to work the instant she clicks send. She sees the message whipping across the North Carolina sandhills at light speed, eager and enthusiastic. She sees it scrambling through a jumble of wires and cables, searching for Liz's address. She sees it tumbling into the great black morass of misguided messages that never get found and read.

# 62

With his feet feeling better and the day warming up, Gary wants to hang the banner and go for a swim. But as the next new Jesus, Luke isn't ready to take the plunge.

"We can't use this stupid sign," he says. "It goes against everything you believe."

"Hey!" says Gary. "You're not stuttering!'

"Really?" says the next new Jesus.

"Say something."

"She sells sea shells down by the she shore?"

"Told ya."

"Oh my god," says Luke, dancing on the deck. "It's a miracle."

Gary smiles and offers up a hug. "It is indeed."

Luke grins. "What about the sign?"

"You're the next new Jesus, do what you want. Use it, or don't use it. Either way is fine. But don't worry so much, okay? Remember the pansies?"

"They were lilies."

"I knew that," says Gary, not sure if he did. "I'm just trying to say that things will work out. All is well."

The next new Jesus picks up one end of the banner and lifts it over the deck railing. The letters dance like candles in the wind.

Mark's friendly sign maker might not have much judgment when it comes to slogans, but he sure knows how to make a sturdy banner. This heavy-duty vinyl strip has six brass grommets and enough nylon line to make the job quick and easy. The banner fits perfectly on the railing, with the flaming red arrow pointing straight to the stairs going up to the pool.

"Walk out a ways and see how it looks," says Gary. "We gotta catch people coming and going."

The next new Jesus backs across Doug's splotchy grass, edging toward the street twenty yards away. A truckload of just-released Christians rolls by, red-rubber-necking the new black messiah like he's a five-car pile-up.

"Go all the way to the street," yells Gary, pointing for him to keep walking. "Make sure you can read it."

The next new Jesus takes a few more tentative steps, his eyes on a red Silverado with big chrome wheels. The truck passes slow enough to make the latest son of god hold his scared breath. Gary sees the fear, and it breaks his heart. Luke the first disciple. Luke the black lily in a white man's field. Luke the next new Jesus.

"Hang on." Gary runs to join him. "'I want to see it too."

That Sunday's service at the New Gate of Heaven Church turned out to be a ball-buster. The preacher hadn't met his October quota, and the pressure was on for two saved souls. It took him awhile – they had to sing all the verses of *Just A Closer Walk With Thee* twice – but things finally clicked, with a new Christian to spare. A family of three came forward at the very last minute.

For Sergeant Stone and the other Gatekeepers, it was a miraculous accomplishment, coming back from two-down on the last Sunday of the month. They celebrated by polishing off a bottle of Wild Turkey on the preacher's back porch.

Stone heads for home when the party breaks up, pumped and primed, looking to kick some ass. That's just how it is with John Paul Stone. He'll fight for god. He'll fight for country. He'll fight for anything, especially when he's drunk, which he most certainly is when he sees the next new Jesus and Gary Gray prancing on the grass in front of Doug Dipper's Pool Palace.

*Oh my god. It's them faggots.*

Gary reaches the next new Jesus in no time and they twirl together on the lawn, oblivious to Sergeant Stone and his drunk-clenched fists. If they'd seen those fists tearing at the air inside Stone's red truck, they'd have left the Pool Palace right then and there.

But they didn't. All they saw was a perfectly straight

banner, a warm swimming pool, and a chance to practice a little baptizing.

"You really like it?" says the next new Jesus, framing the banner with his hands, like a movie director.

Gary looks through the viewfinder. "It's okay."

"Gives me the creeps," says the next new Jesus. "I told Mark it was a bad idea."

"Some people have to be scared into being nice."

"If ye know these things, happy are ye if ye do them," says the next new Jesus, following Gary up the stairs to the deck. He watches Gary skip to the edge of the pool and somersault into the water, clothes and all. He takes off his glasses, slips off his shoes, and eases in after him.

After weeks of ocean bathing, the next new Jesus floats underwater like he's in heaven, a dark angel swooping through the spread of Gary's legs, tickling his tiny toes. He dunks Gary in a few practice baptizings, wondering how John the Baptist would have done it. He savors the water and the chance to swim with the love of his life.

"You really think I can do this?" says the next new Jesus, squinting without his glasses.

Gary squats low under the surface then jumps up like a cheerleader. "The next new Jesus, he's our man, if he can't do it, nobody can. Goooooooooo, Jesus!'

Luke picks Gary up on his shoulders and lunges around the pool like a bull. "Walk on water," he says. "Go on, I gotcha."

"You're the one who should be walking on water." Gary laughs and dives into the soft blue wet. When he comes up near the edge of the pool, he's staring straight into the barrel of John Paul Stone's twelve-gauge Winchester Black Shadow shotgun.

After Sergeant Stone saw the boys jitterbugging on the lawn, he took no time to plan his attack. Like a Marine on patrol, he slipped into automatic, idling his truck around the block, rolling to a quiet stop under the live oaks behind the Pool Palace showroom.

He willed himself invisible, became a holy ghost. He reached into the backseat for a pint of Jim Beam and his shotgun. He slugged down half the bottle and shook his eyes into focus. He watched the black guy cover the hippy's nose, bend him over backwards, lift him out of the water, then kiss him on the mouth. Stone flipped open the glove compartment and grabbed a couple of shells.

Gary looks beyond the flat black gun barrel, settling on Stone's flushed face, where the heat of anger and alcohol has taken a splotchy toll. Gary smiles and slides back under the water, scooting away to the middle of the pool where the next new Jesus is doing handstands. Gary pulls him to the surface and draws him close.

"Sergeant Stone." Gary whispers the words and turns the next new Jesus to face a blurry black suit holding something that looks like a cannon.

"Does he have a gun?"

"Yep."

The next new Jesus gulps.

"I asked him to follow me," says Gary. "And here he is. Pretty cool, huh?"

The next new Jesus smiles through his white clenched teeth and pees in the chlorinated water.

"Don't worry," says Gary. He frog-kicks to the edge and swoops from the pool in a puddle at Stone's feet. The Marine steps away like he's dodging a skunk.

"You came," says Gary.

"Don't talk to me, faggot." Stone stares him down, wobbling a little, backing up till he's leaning against the railing.

"Be not afraid," says Gary, beaming with open arms.

"What are you doing with that nigger?"

Stone watches Gary with one eye, his other on the next new Jesus, who's inching toward the other side of the pool. He feints a lunge and the next new Jesus echoes with a yelp, shielding his face with a hand.

Gary slaps Stone on the back. "You're one scary dude, Sergeant Stone."

*I'm gonna kill me a goddamn hippy*, thinks Stone. He trains his gun on Gary's chest.

"Mark says we could use a John," says Gary. "Are you interested?"

"What you could use is a fucking coffin."

Gary sighs. "Blessed are they who don't say fucking all the time."

Stone ducks away from a yellow jacket buzzing too near his

face. "You're that crazy one." He forces a slurred laugh. "Where's the spic?"

"He couldn't make it today," says Gary. "You could stand in for him though."

A pint of booze doesn't normally throw Stone this far off his game, but something's out of whack today, like there's voodoo in the air. Stone pulls a Ka-Bar knife from his belt and holds it high to break the spell.

"Sure. I'll stand in." Stone glares at the banner hanging behind him, then rips his seven-inch blade through the vinyl, splitting *Turn* from *Burn* with a single swipe, shredding *Sun* from *day* with another.

"I didn't like it either," says Gary. He stoops to pick up the pieces. "Hey. Maybe we should try *Sun Burn Day.*" He makes goo-goo eyes and arranges the words on the deck.

Stone knows the hippy's messing with him, but he's not sure what to do. When in doubt, kick ass. "Get over here, nigger," he yells.

When Luke starts to climb from the pool, Stone stabs his knife into the railing and swings the shotgun like a pointer. "Stay in the water. Where I can watch you."

Gary settles at Stone's feet, Buddha-style. Yellow jackets skim along the railing, agitated by the knife play. When Stone reaches back for the Ka-Bar, five angry wasps spring on his hand like a trap.

John Paul Stone is one of a very few good men who could die from the venom of yellow jackets, which is why he carries a supply of injectable epinephrine everywhere he goes. Except today. He'd been late for church and rushed from home without it. Even in his drunken state, he knows his ass is grass. He drops his knife and gun and dives in the pool, leaving the stingers behind. His arm begins to swell and his breath goes shallow in anaphylactic shock.

Unlike suicidal honey bees, yellow jackets don't die after stinging their prey. They can drive their serrated stingers repeatedly into human flesh, pumping exotic poison deep into the wounds. Stone hits the water with a dozen deadly holes drilled into his hand.

It takes a miracle for Gary and the next new Jesus to drag Stone's body from the pool. By the time they flop him on the deck, he's knocking on heaven's door, but Gary's not ready to let him go.

"He was going to kill us," says the next new Jesus. The boys are kneeling beside Stone the Gatekeeper, Gary holding his swollen hand like a priest. The next new Jesus wanders away to find his glasses. Gary closes his eyes and cries to high heaven.

"Shouldn'a messed with wasps," says Dog.

"He's going to die."

"Sooner or later."

Gary hugs the swollen hand to his chest.

Dog squats beside them. "You ask him to join up?"

"He's not interested."

"Ask him again. See what happens."

"I'll try."

Dog bonks Gary on the head with a gentle fist. "Didn't you see *The Empire Strikes Back*, where old Yoda tells Luke there is no try?"

"There is no try?"

"There is no try. Do. Or do not."

Gary takes in Dog's words and focuses on Stone's cold heart.

"Hey there, John Paul. This is Gary. I was talking with Dog. We were hoping you'd stick around for awhile. You don't have to be our John or anything. Just don't die."

The barest of breathing shows Stone's still alive.

"You're good at this," says Dog.

"It's not me."

"I wouldn't be so sure."

Gary winks. "I couldn't be so pure."

"Maybe you oughta call nine-one-one," says Dog.

Mark's just waking when Luke and Gary get back to the Airstream. The thrill of Stone's resurrection has Luke buzzing.

"You should have seen it, Mark. That dang Stone was good as dead."

"Praise the lard," says Mark. He's having trouble drumming up enthusiasm for the miracle he missed.

"Gary saved him." Luke beams with pride, ignoring Mark's

smart-assiness. "The man departed and told the Jews that it was *Jesus* who had made him well."

"It was Dog," says Gary.

"And I've stopped stuttering."

"Stop calling me Mark and stop talking so loud."

"You *are* Mark," says Luke. "We voted. Gary's Jesus again." Luke had found it easy to surrender his throne when John Paul Stone sat straight up from all the hand-holding, surprised he wasn't dead. The sergeant was nearly back to normal when the ambulance arrived, though he didn't say a word. The paramedics told Gary there was nothing for them to do.

"That's bullshit," says Mark. "I get to be Jesus for at least another week."

"We voted." Luke spoke with more confidence than he thought possible.

"What about your turn?" says Mark.

"I had my turn. And I gave it up. Gary should be Jesus. He's the one."

"Don't I get to vote?" Mark's not as mad as Luke thought he'd be about the recall campaign. He liked the Jesus perks well enough, but the truth is, the robe never quite fit. Mark had been lucky to last a week.

"It's two against one," says Luke.

Mark sticks his tongue out at Gary with a smile wrapped around it. Gary grins and takes Mark's hand, kissing it with a generous bow. "Think you can get us another sign?"

Following the resurrection of John Paul Stone, the strain of musical-chairs-Jesus pushes the sweepers into an uneasy truce. Though Mark accepted Gary as Jesus again, he has some misgivings. He'd reigned over their best week ever in fundraising, and his early retirement has seen the last few days fall off. Plus he isn't convinced Jesus really worked a miracle with the wasps. The boys are sweeping the Piggly Wiggly parking lot when he brings the subject up again.

"You weren't there, Mark." Luke pokes at a squashed black snake on the asphalt. "You didn't see those stings." He waits till a minivan passes and kicks the snake into the weeds.

"Then why'd you call that ambulance," snarks Mark. "The real Jesus didn't need nine-one-one when he brought what's his name back from the dead."

"I told you, we called them just in case. Just. In. Case."

"Just in case of what? In case sergeant grunt decided to blow your fucking heads off?"

Luke relives the fear of John Paul Stone ordering him around with his shotgun, remembering how he peed in the pool, how he'd wanted Stone to die. He prods at the snake with his broom.

"Blessed are they who don't say fucking all the time," grumbles Jesus. "I'm freezing."

"You shoulda got some good shoes when we told you," says Mark.

Luke tried to buy Jesus a pair of Nikes from the thrift shop the day before, but Jesus wanted flip-flops. And now he has cold feet.

"He can wear what he wants," says Luke.

Sick of the sniping, Jesus plops on the grass at the edge of the parking lot, hugs his knees and closes his eyes.

"Those friends of yours sure do like to argue," says Dog.

Jesus nods.

"Stone could have been faking," says Mark. "Right, Jesus?"

Right Jesus. Left Jesus. Go Jesus. No Jesus. The recycled savior is buckling under the weight of his divine burden. And all he really wants is warm.

"You need some hot coffee," says Dog. "Maybe a game of darts."

"Should we stop by Tall Paul's on the way home?" says Jesus.

"That sounds right," says Dog. "Just make sure you're there at midnight."

"It's Halloween," says Luke. "There might be a party."

"Now you're talking," says Mark. "I'll start believing in miracles again if you keep this up."

# 63

Though annual Halloween celebrations in downtown Chapel Hill are known for their drunken debauchery and unruly crowds, the real action this Thursday night is elsewhere.

After a hot time in his tidy church office that evening, Preacher Joe drives Rachel Rose home on a winding country road. Rachel chugs down her sixth glass of Sonoma chardonnay with one hand and switches on the radio with the other. The smooth sound of Nancy Kneedle announcing the Halloween edition of *Midnight Pagan* fills the car. She slaps Joe when he reaches to change the station.

"You have to keep up with the competition, Big Joe." Rachel always gets her way when she calls him Big Joe.

Sprawled in the back of Doug Dipper's black Dodge van on Ocean Drive, Sinker rests uneasy, while Nancy's mysterious theme song blasts through eight new Blaupunkt speakers, rumbling inside the van like an earthquake. When *Midnight Pagan* went into syndication two years ago, a nearby community college station picked up the freaky program and Doug became a regular listener. The station had been promoting tonight's special all week. *The Mysterious New Secrets of Eternal Life.*

"Whyn't you play something besides this crap?" yells Sinker.

In a lapse of judgment, Doug had agreed to pick Sinker up when he got out of jail. "Whyn't you shut the fuck up?" he mimics. Doug's madder than he should be, mostly with himself.

"Least let me come up front," says Sinker.

"I said shut the fuck up," says Doug, turning up the volume.

And in the quiet back room at Tall Paul's Bar and Grill on Ocean Drive, Mark sits on a worn wooden barstool while Jesus and Luke play a game of darts. When the Coors clock clicks to midnight, the languid voice of Nancy Kneedle spills from the radio behind the bar.

*Tonight we have an exclusive treat – or could it be a trick? – for* Midnight Pagan *listeners all across America. Is the story you're about to hear the goddess' truth? Or is our guest just a merry prankster? Listen and find out as we talk now with Elizabeth Forsythe about the mysterious new secrets of eternal life – written on a silver bracelet she found at North Carolina's Sunrise Beach.*

Before Nancy's words can penetrate Joe Peters' preoccupied brain, Rachel chokes on a gulp of wine, spluttering a splatter on her gray linen suit. "Jesus, Joe. Did you hear that?"

Before those same words can settle across the red Stainmaster carpet in the back of Doug's van, the swimming pool king slams on the brakes, throwing Sinker forward, smashing his face into the floor. "Jesus, Sinker," says Doug. "Ain't that the lady you tried to rape?"

And just as the off-and-on savior nails a triple-twenty with his second dart, Mark jumps from his stool and wrestles him to the floor.

"Oh my god, Jesus. It's our bracelet."

NK:  Last Sunday at the New Hope Unitarian Universalist Church, you told the congregation a remarkable story. Would you repeat it tonight for our listeners?

LF:  I was walking on the beach last month, when I saw something in the sand. It was a silver bracelet covered with engravings. One expert says it may be a thousand years old. We're going to have it analyzed.

NK:  Very strange.

LF:  That's what I said.

NK:  Do you have it with you?

LF:  Sure. Have a look.

NK:  Whoa. Folks, this thing's amazing. It's like Raiders of the Lost Ark, only real. Solid heavy silver. Mysterious engravings everywhere. Spooky. Check it out on our website. WTCH.org. There's a picture. You'll love it.

NK:  Does this expert know what he's talking about?

LF:  She. I think so. She's a professor who seems pretty familiar with things like this.

NK:  What's her name?

LF:  I'd rather not say.

NK:  Because . . .

LF:  I don't really want to get her involved.

(beat)

NK:  In what?

LF:  Whatever. You know.

NK:  She interpreted the inscription on the bracelet?

LF:  It's written in Aramaic.

NK:  What does it say?

LF:  It says: *Good works do. Kind and loving be. Joy in pleasure seek. These are the threads of life fully filled.*

NK:  *Good works do. Kind and loving be. Joy in pleasure seek?*

LF:  That's right.

NK:  When you told the story in church last Sunday, you said something different.

LF:  I did. My husband used to be in advertising. He shortened it to do good, be nice, have fun.

NK:  Do good. Be nice. Have fun.

LF:  Right.

NK:  So. You found this bracelet on the beach and it turns out to be a thousand years old and it's covered with ancient writing.

LF:  That's pretty much it.

NK:  Wow. I don't know what to think about all this.

LF:  Me either. Here I am, a perfectly normal person with a perfectly normal life. And all of a sudden I'm in a recording studio for a show called *Midnight Pagan* talking about the threads of life fully filled.

NK:  What do you think it means?

LF:  I'm sure it means different things to different people, like anything else.

NK:  For example?

LF:  (laughs) I have one friend who thinks these could be new commandments.

NK:  Do *you* think these are new commandments?

LF:  Not really, though I do like the idea of some new ones.

NK:  Say more.

LF: From what I can see, the commandments we have don't say much about happiness.

NK: How so?

LF: I was raised in a family of Southern Baptists, born again and baptized at the age of ten. Sometimes it seems like I spent half my life worrying about going to hell. No one ever talked about fun.

NK: So, Elizabeth Forsythe. Are these new commandments?

LF: I don't much like the word.

NK: What do you call them?

LF: Threads. The threads of life fully filled. Just like it says on the bracelet.

NK: It really says that?

LF: There could be other interpretations, but . . .

NK: Like what?

LF: For example, "life fully filled" could be interpreted to mean eternal life or maybe life without limits. And "threads" could mean strands or strings.

NK: You're talking about eternal life here?

LF: (laughs) You're good.

NK: Just doing my job.

LF: And I'm just telling you what the professor said.

NK: Why? Why *are* you telling us?

LF: You mean right now?

NK: I mean why are you telling anybody at all? Aren't you going to stir people up with these new commandments, these threads? What are you hoping to accomplish?

LF: I really like the idea of doing good, being nice, and having fun. It seems like a decent way to live a fulfilling life. Plus you can actually remember it. It's just six words.

NK: An evangelist!

LF: Not likely.

NK: A reluctant prophet?

LF: Don't be silly.

NK: We talked about doing this show as a live call-in, and you said you'd rather not. Why is that?

LF: I've just said all I have to say about this, plus some things I probably shouldn't have said. If I took calls from listeners, I'd just be repeating myself. This isn't about me or what I think. The threads speak for themselves.

(beat)

NK: Have you thought about what the bracelet might be worth? Could be millions, don't you think?

LF: (laughs)

NK: Liz, thank you for being on our show. It's been fun talking with you. And good. And nice.

LF: Thanks for having me.

NK: Well, there you have it. Do good. Be nice. Have fun. These are the threads of life fully filled. And as our reluctant prophet and gracious guest this evening says, they pretty much speak for themselves. So, what do *you* think? The *Midnight Pagan* phone lines are hereby open. You know the number: 1.800.666.WTCH. We'll be right back after a quick break, so call Nancy now.

# 64

As Jesus, Joe, and a million other *Midnight Pagan* listeners get their first taste of the threads, the reluctant prophet herself listens to the show in her Chapel Hill home, warming by the fireplace with Frank, Oscar, and her sister Faye, who's come to town for the weekend. A stop-smoking hypnotherapist of minor notoriety in Richmond, Faye is always dropping in for visits, though this time Frank invited her to help him carry the heavy load of Liz. The sisters have a habit of easy banter that often smoothes things out, plus when Faye's around, Liz has someone to pick on besides her husband.

"Look at your poor toes, Faye," Liz said that afternoon over margaritas. She licked a clump of salt from her glass, sliding into their mother's Richmond drawl. "You keep wearing those pointy high heels and I swear, you're gonna end up with bunions just like Mama."

"My shoes look a hell of a lot nicer than those Birkenshock boats of yours. You don't wear those things to work, do you?"

"Birkenstocks. And you have no idea what you're talking about. You've never even tried them."

"And I never will. They're ugly as sin."

"That's just like you, Faye. It's always about looks. Always about what men think."

"You have no room to talk."

"Excuse me?"

"You and your tits and your low-cut blouses?"

"That's ridiculous."

Sooner or later, discussions between Liz and Faye always get around to boobs and boys. Liz has all she needs of both, while her little sister keeps coming up short. Born a year later than her busty sibling, Faye Forsythe was near the back of the line when they handed out cup sizes and reliable men.

"Come here and give me a back rub," said Faye when their dueling died down. "You're bound to owe me for something."

When the interview wraps up, Frank wants to escape. "I don't want to hear anymore of this," he says. He's worried that his hots for Nancy Kneedle somehow fueled this fiasco, and he's eager to end it.

Liz rocks quietly by the fireplace, bracelet in hand, while Faye shushes Frank from the sofa. "Hand me the phone."

"You're not calling in," he says.

"Lighten up, Frank. Everything's fine."

"Everything is NOT fine," says Frank. "Everything is not one goddamn bit fine."

"Come on, Frankster. You like pagans," says Oscar. "Remember?"

"And I just happen to know they're all flat-out nuts."

"I'd like to hear the show," says Liz. She hasn't spoken since the broadcast began and her words pull them all up short.

Frank slumps in a chair, stuffing the phone under a pillow. The sweet smell of hickory burning in the fireplace barely masks the tension in the room.

NK: Hello, Rhonda in Roanoke. Welcome to *Midnight Pagan*. What's on your mind?

Rhonda: Hi, Nancy. Love the show. And your guest tonight? Fantastic. I just wish I could talk to her. Those threads? They're amazing. I mean, what could be simpler? Do good. Be nice. Have fun. Kind of says it all, doesn't it?

NK: Think so?

Rhonda: Well, not absolutely everything. I mean, how could they? But they're close enough for me. A philosophy of life you can put on your bumper.

NK: Thanks, Rhonda. (beat) Gary. From Jacksonville. Right here in North Carolina.

Gary: Actually, my name's not Gary. I just didn't think you'd let me on . . .

NK: Okay, Gary. What should we call you?

Gary: Jesus?

NK: As in Christ?

Gary: Like I said, I didn't think . . .

NK: Jesus in Jacksonville. Sorry, friend. It looks like you called the wrong show. Sharon in Chicago. You're on *Midnight Pagan.*

Sharon: I don't understand where this woman is coming from.

NK: What do you mean, Sharon?

Sharon: If these threads are supposed to be so great, how come they don't work? I'm good and nice, but I'm not having fun. I don't get it. She says have fun. Sure. Anyone can say that.

NK: I'm not sure the threads work that way.

Sharon: And what do you mean by good? Some people would say killing murderers is good. Or not paying taxes. Or snorting cocaine. Or anything. It's just not that simple. Nothing's that simple.

NK: You see a problem with knowing what good means?

Sharon: What does anything mean? Nice? Is it nice to tell a mother her baby is cute when he's really ugly?

NK: I'm just guessing you have the same thoughts about fun.

Sharon: Fun's the worst.

Frank huffs. "I've had enough." He turns to Liz, but she's closed her eyes. He gets halfway up the open staircase and looks out over the living room for a sign of support. Nothing doing. "I'll be in bed if you need me," he says to no one in particular.

NK: Well, look who's on the line. It's my old pal, Preacher Joseph J. Peters, from down the road in Rougemont. Joe? Is that you? It sounds like you're on a cell phone. Out kind of late, aren't you?

Joe: Mizz Kneedle. You know I consider your pagan practices shameful, but tonight you have crossed the line. Th'idea that this woman is claiming to have found three new commandments is an assault on the very foundation of our Christian culture. You have gone too far.

NK: Come on, Joe. What do you really think?

Joe: This may be amusing to your pagan friends, but I fail to see any humor in what you're doing.

NK: And just what is it you think we're doing, Preacher Peters?

Joe: You are providing Satan with the perfect soapbox, Mizz Kneedle, plain and simple. You're spreading evil throughout the land.

NK: Are you saying my guest tonight is Satan?

Joe: She may not be Satan herself, but she . . .

(beat)

NK: Joe? Are you there?

(beat)

NK: Looks like the good preacher is experiencing some technical difficulty, so let's take a quick break. Be right back.

Nancy Kneedle would have laughed out loud into her Heil Classic studio microphone had she known exactly which technical difficulties Joe Peters was experiencing when Rachel Rose lunged across the cushy console to wrestle the phone from his hand, blocking the road from his view. The speeding car sailed over the shoulder, through a barbed-wire fence into a soggy cow pasture, where it banged over a boulder and sunk to its axles.

Rachel lifts herself from Joe's crumpled lap and steps out onto the muddy meadow.

"I will not, I repeat, I will not let you get away with calling one of my employees Satan," she yells. "I won't stand for it, Joe Peters. Not for one goddamn second."

Joe struggles to get out of the car, but the driver's door is jammed. He beckons Rachel back.

"Come on, dolly. I didn't call her Satan."

"Don't you lie to me." Rachel spits the words. "I heard what you said and I know what you were going to say next. And I'll tell you what, buster. It's a damn good thing I stopped you. Because if you had said it, if you had actually said what you were getting ready to say, you can bet your skinny old ass that would be the last you'd see of me."

Knowing his car is totaled, and calculating the same potential damage to his affair with Rachel, Joe backpedals. "Now, sweetie, you know I didn't mean anything. It's just that damn Nancy Kneedle. That woman has a way under my skin, and I just can't seem to control myself. I'm sorry as I can be."

Rachel swings like a drunken pendulum back toward the car, back toward Joe. "You're really sorry?"

"I truly am. And I wouldn't do nothing, nothing at all, to hurt your friend."

"You promise?" She crawls in the door.

"I do dearly promise, sweet pie. Now let me see if you're okay."

"Are you alright?"

"My door's stuck."

"You stay put." Rachel hikes up her linen skirt. "And crank that seat back. I need me a little licking."

# 65

Tall Paul's Bar and Grill has stood like a house of flimsy cards on a sandy corner of Ocean Drive for at least fifty years. The windowless shack holds a few grimy booths, a carved-up bar, a worn-out pool table, and no more than a dozen regular customers. Though it's Halloween night, the place is all but empty. A drunk gunnery sergeant playing solitaire at the bar. Two old guys sipping beers in a booth. And the faintest trace of an old lady with angel wings drifting round the room. When the boys come in, the customer base nearly doubles.

"Hey, Tall Paul," says Jesus. "Big crowd tonight."

"Boys." From a dozen previous visits, Tall Paul knows all about the sweepers and their mission. So the kid thinks he's Jesus. Big deal. After decades in the bar business, Tall Paul's seen enough strange to last a lifetime. Plus the boys drink nothing but Cokes and coffee. Way better margins than beer.

"Cricket," calls Mark, heading for the dart board, where Tall Paul always keeps a good set of house darts. "Which of you wants to be massacrated first?"

Luke opts for the honor, just to get it out of the way. He and Jesus indulge in the game only to keep Mark in good spirits. They never win.

The boys throw darts for couple of hours, trying Cricket, 301, and Follow the Leader. Luke wants to quit, but Jesus says no. Dog told him to stay until midnight, which is when Tall Paul stops feeding the jukebox and switches on the radio.

Gary's lining up to nail a must-have bulls-eye when the Dog lady floats toward him. He doesn't recognize her in the angel outfit.

"How're those feet?" says Dog.

"What're you doing here?"

"Checking things out."

"You look like an angel."

Dog winks and whispers, "Halloween."

That's when *Midnight Pagan* starts and Mark goes nuts.

None of the boys had any idea what the inscriptions on the bracelet meant until that very moment. But if you thought they'd be in awe of the news, you'd be wrong. Jesus takes the threads in stride, happy the gospel is spreading. That's why he calls into the radio show, just to say thanks.

Mark steps right into calculating the revenue potential. If they can only get the bracelet back.

And poor Luke is surprised to find himself torn. Sure Jesus found the threads in the first place, but the soft-spoken woman on the radio was the one who discovered what they meant. Who to follow?

Tall Paul closes the bar at one and the boys wander back to the Airstream. A cold front has moved in, which does nothing to dampen their arguing about what to do next. Mark wants to go to Chapel Hill and find the bracelet, but the Jeep's not running. It needs a new alternator and maybe a water pump. They can't afford either, and they can't even get to Jacksonville for more fundraising.

"You heard what that lady said," says Mark. "The bracelet could be worth millions."

"She didn't say that, Mark."

"It's not hers to keep."

"Sure it is," says Jesus. "I lost it. She found it. Pretty simple."

"But what if it *is* worth millions?" says Mark. "Think what we could do with that kind of money. We could really start that church of ours." He bats his eyes at Luke, pandering like a whore.

# 66

Upstairs in bed, Frank is too upset with himself to sleep and too upset with Liz to join the late-night Halloween fun. He hears the doorbell ring. He hears Liz welcome her friend and doctor, Sarah Stern.

"Sorry I'm late," says Sarah.

"I'm so glad to see you."

Frank imagines them hugging as he mimics his wife's enthusiasm with a scrunched up nose and a waggly head, marveling at the childish brain running his old man's body. The brain insists that he pout upstairs, and the old man gladly complies.

Sarah slumps into a kitchen chair and slides easily into the conversation.

"Did you hear the show?" says Oscar.

"How about that nutcase preacher?" says Faye.

"Easy," says Liz. "That's my boss's boyfriend."

"Rachel goes out with that guy?"

"More like in and out," says Oscar, making the universal hand sign for intercourse.

"Now *that* is not nice," says Sarah.

"It's fun, though," says Oscar, his mind sailing to the threads.

"Definitely not nice," says Liz.

"Ah ha," says Oscar. "Venn diagram." He grabs a pen and draws three interlocking circles on a paper towel. "That little space where the circles overlap? That's the sweet spot. Good. Nice. And fun. All at once."

"I'll drink to that," says Faye.

"Red's open." Liz points with her chin to the cupboard. "Pour me one too. Eggs are almost ready."

Oscar studies the label on the bottle. *Paz Dos.* "The perfect wine for the second coming."

Liz's brain tightens in a tangle of knotty threads. "The what?"

"The second coming. We *are* in the presence of a prophet, albeit a reluctant one." Oscar wraps an arm around Liz's shoulders. "And this particular prophet just happens to possess the mysterious secrets of eternal life."

"Watch it, buster."

Faye circles the table with a steaming skillet of huevos rancheros, the yummy edge of chili powder sharpening the kitchen air.

"Who wants more wine?" says Oscar.

"All around," says Sarah. She rings her glass with a fork. "It's been quite a Halloween. But before things get too spooky, I'd like to offer this toast. To my dear sweet Liz. To all of you. And to the threads of life fully filled. Do good. Be nice. Have fun." Sarah smiles and lifts her glass in the warm kitchen light.

"Do good," says Faye.

"Be nice," adds Liz.

"Have fun." Oscar grabs a chunk of cornbread and stuffs it into his mouth, triggering the feeding frenzy the friends have been waiting for.

"This is the second coming, Oscar. Not the last supper," says Faye.

Liz cringes. "I wish you all would stop saying that."

"We're just having fun," says Faye.

"Not me. I'm totally serious," says Oscar. He drains his glass and sits up straight. "I've dealt with more ecclesiastical mumbo jumbo than you can imagine over the past five years. And to make a very long story short, I love these threads. They really could be the three new commandments. God knows we need them."

"Wow. He *is* serious." Faye pats the back of Oscar's beautiful hand.

He crams a forkful of eggs into his face and muffles. "He is indeed."

Later Liz catches Oscar alone in the living room and asks what he knows about halos.

"My dear, you were born with one," he says.

She pokes him in the belly.

"It's true," he says. "Some people – the saints among us – have them. And some don't. You do. Anyone can see that."

"I'm serious." She threatens to tickle him and he pushes her hands away.

"You're serious. Hmmm." He pretends to think. "*The Halo Effect* was required reading for a seminar I took in New York last year."

"There's a book called *The Halo Effect*?"

"Probably. Though I really did go to a seminar once about the golden rings – not to be confused with the golden arches."

"What'd you learn?"

"Off the top of my head, heh, I can tell you this. Halos go back to pagan practice. Some people think of them as auras. Cranial lights."

"So regular human beings can have halos?"

"Indeed."

"Do they come and go?"

"Of course."

"And are they visible to everyone?"

"You're really interested in this."

"I am."

"Well, dear. I'm afraid I've already told you more than I know."

# 67

Things settled down for Hook once Sinker got arrested, mostly because of Eddie Junior. After five years living a hundred yards apart, romance stirred the salty air between them. Last Monday morning, there he was again, pounding on her door.

"I brung you a bicycle," he yelled, loud enough to bother neighbors if there had been any. "Ain't you supposed to be at work?"

Hook bumbled to the door with squinty eyes. "What're you doing here, Eddie Junior?" She tugged at her nightshirt to make sure everything was covered.

"If it ain't Sleeping Beauty." He smiled bigger than usual.

"You say something about a bicycle?" asked Hook.

"I said you might need one now that your truck's got torched."

"You said you brung me one."

"Yeah, well."

Hook put on some hot water for instant coffee. She checked herself in a wall mirror and tousled her hair out of bed head. Eddie Junior sat at the kitchen table, fingering a cigarette burn in the Formica.

"You making coffee?"

"You bring me a bicycle?"

"I did, but it's busted. I thought you should look at it first. Make sure you want it before I fix it up."

Hook needed a few seconds to think this through. She wanted to get mad just for the hell of it, but he was being too sweet. She bought some time slamming cupboard doors.

"Come look at it." He flipped through a tattoo magazine.

"Right now?"

"You gotta get to work, don't you?"

"You ain't my damn daddy." She knew the words were too heavy.

"You ain't no yam patty," he said, straight as can be.

She looked at him and melted.


Hook came when they fucked for the first time that night in Eddie Junior's bedroom. It upset her. Eddie Junior figured he'd done a pretty good job from all her yelling and squealing, but then she pulled away.

"What's wrong?" he said.

"I don't know what the hell we're doing. You're old enough to be my . . ." She stopped short of another comparison to her dead daddy.

"I'd have to been having sex when I was eleven," said Eddie Junior. Then he laughed. "Didn't start till thirteen."

Hook sat up and scanned the room. "Sure is neat and tidy around here. You clean up just for me?"

"Yes ma'am, I did. I been hoping you'd let me get my hands on them pretty pink parts, so I changed the sheets and everything."

"You're mighty damn sure of yourself."

Eddie Junior breathed deep and got serious. "I know what I want."

"You want to get laid. It don't take no rocket scientist to figure that out."

"You're just about perfect for an old man like me."

"You ain't no old man, Eddie Junior." Hook grinned and lifted up the sheets to see if he was getting hard. "More like middle-aged."

By Tuesday morning, Eddie Junior's middle-aged member was rubbed good and raw. Hook was sore too. It was the last day of her period and she wasn't worried about getting pregnant. Plus Eddie Junior said he hadn't slept with anybody else for a couple of years. It felt like the truth, so she let him go bareback. They smelled like old goats.

"Get up and fix us some breakfast while I take me a bath," said Hook. Her tone left no room for discussion.

That night they drove to all the way to Morehead City and ate at the Sanitary Fish House on the waterfront. Eddie Junior enjoyed the chance to show off his social skills, and Hook was happy to let him call the shots. He was being so nice he didn't even order a beer, in honor of her still being underage.

"You can drink if you want," said Hook. She liked the idea of seeing a legal beer in his hand. "You can't be worried about setting no bad example." She kicked him under the table.

"That's alright," he said. "Sweet tea'll be fine.

Hook looked at him lazy-eyed and started to fall in love.

Wednesday brought a continuing fuck fest, made all the more frenetic because Eddie Junior was leaving the next day for a fishing trip. He'd turned Hook into an orgasm machine, though he didn't always get there himself. Hook couldn't understand why he was being so nice.

"You hadn't yelled or bitched these whole three days," said Hook. They were lying in his bed with the lights out, having just screwed for the second time since supper.

"So?"

"I ain't used to nice. All my old boyfriends just wanted to screw me up the ass."

"I figured that'd be a bad move with all them angels watching." He rubbed her tattooed shoulder to acknowledge their presence.

"You mean you'd want to?"

"Can't say I didn't think about it. Never done it though, so no big deal. Thing's are okay when you don't know what you don't know."

Hook nuzzled up to his armpit. "Eddie."

He yawned and patted her on the butt. "Steady."

She closed her eyes and said a private prayer.

She heard him starting to snore and whispered, "Ready."

# 68

Frank's Halloween sleep was punctuated by Liz coming to bed late and getting up early. So when the phone on his nightstand rings at nine the next morning, he's not the pleasant conversationalist Erica Eisner is hoping to find. The pushy woman says she's a senior producer for *Larry King Live* in Los Angeles. She wants to speak with Liz.

"She can't come to the phone."

"When would be a good time to call back?"

"Anytime after sunrise."

"You'll make sure she gets my message?"

"Will do. Erica Eisner."

"Mister . . . ?"

' Forsythe. Frank Forsythe. Her sleeping husband."

"Mr. Forsythe. I'm sorry I woke you, but I really do appreciate your help with this. Larry heard about your wife's interview last night and . . ."

"I'll give her the message."

He switches the phone off and stares at the hit-and-run handset. Ninety seconds ago he was asleep. And now, Larry King.

When the phone rings again, his "good morning" is beyond sarcastic.

"This is Gene Jordan. From the *New York Times*. May I speak with Elizabeth Forsythe, please?"

"She's busy." Frank sounds like he gets calls from the *Times* every day. "You'll have to call back."

He presses the phone off. He pulls the covers over his head and blanks his mind. He hears Liz padding up the steps, breathing heavy from her morning walk. He hears her clothes fall to the floor beside the bed. She settles in between the sheets, spooning her sweaty body up around him. Her strong hand moves over his stomach. The phone rings again. She flinches. He wilts.

A bold Italian accent booms from the answering machine. "Good morning, Mrs. Forsythe. I am calling for Cardinal Craven in Washington, D.C., regarding your bracelet. I will try again to reach you."

When the machine clicks off, Liz flops onto her back and stares at the ceiling. "What was that about?"

"There were two other calls. Let's see. There was Erica from *Larry King Live*. And Gene from the New York *Times*."

"Stop joking."

"I'm serious."

"What'd they say?"

"They wanted to talk to you."

"What did you say?"

"I told them you were possessed and that they should steer clear."

"You did not."

"I told them you weren't here and that they should call back."

"When?"

"Sometime when you're at work. Speaking of which, aren't you going to be late?"

"I'm taking the day off. I figured I'd be in no mood for ambulance-chasing after *Midnight Pagan*."

"No kidding."

"What should we do?"

Frank doesn't bother to think. "Let's fuck."

# 69

The first morning in November finds Hook anxious and squirmy. With Eddie Junior gone on his fishing trip, the reality of her lonely life settles in dark. Irene's shut down until Thanksgiving week, so she doesn't even have a job. She worries she might be pregnant and wonders if the past three days were some kind of whacked-out dream. She wants to go fishing and remembers she doesn't have a truck. She tries to go online. No web access. She calls the cable company. They cut off service because of past-due bills. She storms through the trailer looking for drugs and finds a tab of acid. What the hell. She starts to trip, hard and mad. Fancy Pants never emailed back. She throws the laptop against the wall. *Slaptop*. She presses the Water Devil into her forearm. She watches an angel bleed.

Things get worse that afternoon when Sinker hobbles in on crutches and sees his laptop busted on the floor. He swears at Hook and tries to hit her with a crutch. She kicks his hurt leg on the way to her bedroom.

"I thought you was in jail."

"You thought wrong. I got out last night. Doug picked me up."

She eyes the scrapes on his neck. "Doug-the-ding-dong Dipper? Some friend you got there."

"You don't know shit."

Hook does her best smirk. "I know he's a cocksucker."

"That cocksucker's gonna make us rich."

Hook wants to smack his smug-ugly face. "Bullshit."

"You wait."

Sinker hobbles to the window and parts a pair of mildewed curtains enough to see the swimming pool king sitting in his van. He remembers Doug told him to be nice to Hook.

"And if you want in on the deal," says Sinker, "you better stop being such a goddamn bitch."

Hook's intrigued despite her better judgment. With so many things falling apart in her life, she might as well hear what the cocksucker has to say.

"You know your truck got burned up?" Doug steps over the cracked computer and shakes his head. "I thought you was moved outta here, Hooker."

"I'll be gone soon enough." Her words carry more certainty than she feels.

"I heard about your run-in with old Bobby. He's telling everyone you tried to stick Henry in the balls."

"If I'da tried to, I'da done it."

"No need to get pissed at me. I just thought you might not mind getting a bunch of money right about now."

Sinker chimes in. "Tell her your plan."

"You don't know jack shit about my plan, dickhead." Doug rifles through the refrigerator, grabs a beer. "Let's smoke some dope before we head on out to Commieville."

Sinker hops to his bedroom and comes back with the goods.

"What's Commieville?" Hook puts on a mask of casual.

"Chapel Hill, dumb ass. Where them pinkos live."

"What're you going there for?"

"Cause that's where you and me and Sinker is gonna find us a sweet little silver mine."

# 70

After a half-hour of thrashing, Liz is a sweaty mess. She scoots into the shower, while Frank slides into post-orgasmic sleep. When she emerges washed and robed fifteen minutes later, the phone rings again. She picks it up before Frank wakes enough to say, "Let it go."

"Good morning," Liz whispers on her way downstairs to the kitchen.

"This is Elizabeth Forsythe?" The lilting voice has French undertones.

"That's me." She's distracted, looking for orange juice she can use to stir up a flax seed cocktail.

"I am happy to have reached you, Ms. Forsythe. Please hold for one moment. His Holiness the Dalai Lama would like to speak with you."

Liz flies back to the bedroom. "Frank! You won't believe who called." She jumps on the bed with wet hair and orange juice breath, forcing her sleepy husband back to life.

"Bugs Bunny?"

"Be serious."

"Okay. Howard Hughes."

"Just for that, I'm not telling."

"Come on. The suspense is now officially killing me. Who was it?"

"It was the Dalai Lama."

Frank sits up. "*The* Dalai Lama? Holy shit."

"Holy something, that's for sure."

"What did he want?"

"He wanted to say hi." Liz beams. "He heard about the threads and thinks they're great. 'Exciting,' he said. Especially the have-fun part. He thinks people are way too serious. 'All the time, too serious,' he said. And then he laughed. He was so sweet."

"That's it? That's all he wanted?"

"He talked about getting together, but I told him I wasn't sure."

Frank slumps back down into bed. "The Dalai Lama wants to meet you and you told him you're not sure?"

"Well, I'm *not* sure, Frank."

"What does that have to do with anything?"

Liz bristles. "So now you're all certain about what I should do. You and Oscar. If he talks about the three commandments one more time, I'm going to smack him."

"He's *joking*."

"Oh no he's not. It's like he's the one who's possessed, not me."

"I think you're both crazy."

Her bristles sharpen. He holds his tongue.

"I know the interview pissed you off," says Liz. "But guess what? I *did* release the threads. Just like I was supposed to."

"Like you were *supposed* to?" Frank actually sputters. "Liz, this whole business is getting way out of hand."

"Damn it, Frank. Stop being so petulant."

"Petulant?" His voice oozes sarcasm. "What happened to being nice? Huh?"

"Being nice evaporated when you started behaving like a jerk. And yes, I said petulant. Ever since I shared the threads at church, you've been whining about every damn thing I do."

Frank releases his most impatient sigh.

"Are you going to help me with this? Or are you stand on the sidelines and be a pain in the butt?" Liz grabs the bracelet from the nightstand and circles it around her wrist. Frank stares at her, wondering why this woman is so angry, why things are spiraling out of control. He's not quite sure what they're arguing about. He's not quite sure he wants to know.

"I don't have to stand anywhere to be a pain in the butt," he says, pulling the covers up over his head. "I can do that perfectly well while I sleep. You just go off and talk to your cardinals and your lamas and leave me out of your holy bullshit. I've had enough."

# 71

With no banner to post and no Jeep to drive, the boys settle into an uneasy routine on Sunrise Beach. The fall chill has caught them off guard, and Mark's pushing for a run to Chapel Hill. It's morning in the Airstream, with stale Froot Loops on the menu.

"We *have* to go," Mark says, opening the fridge for milk. "And we're gonna go. It is written. That bracelet is ours."

"Written where?" says Luke.

"Right here," says Mark. He grabs a piece of paper and scribbles *Go to Chapel Hill*. He wads the paper in a ball and swallows it. "I can feel it inside me," he says, rubbing his stomach.

Mark's silly enthusiasm finally wears Jesus down. "Okay," he says, "You get the car fixed and we'll go. I wouldn't mind seeing our old bracelet again."

"We're not going to *see* the bracelet, Jesus. We're going to *get* it," says Mark. "It belongs to us."

"Not us," says Luke. "It belongs to Jesus." He rests a hand on Jesus' arm, feeling for affirmation.

Jesus shrugs.

"Speaking of getting, where's that new banner you promised?" says Jesus. "We're still doing the baptism, right?"

"We are?" says Luke.

"Sure," says Jesus. "That was a good plan. Maybe we can get enough offerings to fix the Jeep."

Mark softens at the compliment. Though he'd bragged about how the baptizing plan was god's idea, they all knew he'd made it up. God never said squat to Mark.

"I might see Michael on Sunday."

"Cool," says Jesus. "And in the meantime, maybe we can catch up with Sergeant Stone. We could still use a John."

"He tried to kill us," says Luke.

"I bet he's changed," says Jesus. "It can't hurt to ask."

"Can't hurt? You saw that knife."

Jesus laughs at the image of John Paul Stone shredding *Turn or Burn*. "He sure didn't like that old sign."

"What're we gonna put on the new one?" says Mark. "Do good. Be nice. Have fun?"

"Do. Be. Have." Luke claps like he's solved a riddle. "Perfect."

"Do behave," says Jesus.

"Or doobie have," says Mark, doing a Groucho Marx imitation with his eyebrows and an invisible cigar.

Later that day, the boys walk to Eddie's pier to use the pay phone. It's busted, but Big Eddie lets Jesus borrow his cell. The savior listens as crackly static fills the air between Sunrise Beach and Chapel Hill. Liz's voice comes on the answering machine saying she's sorry she missed the call. Jesus believes her. He leaves a message in Jesus' name.

"Damn it. Don't tell her who you are," snaps Mark. "She'll think you're nuts."

Jesus blows a raspberry. "She might be right."

# 72

After her harsh words with Frank, Liz wanted escape. She hopped in her new little car and drove twenty miserable minutes to downtown Chapel Hill, swinging back and forth between second-guessing her anger and fuck-you-ing her husband. Their growing spats over the past few weeks have left her worried – and being nice has fallen by the wayside.

She parks on Franklin Street and follows the uneven brick sidewalks toward the UNC campus, passing through a stream of garbage from last night's Halloween brawl. She steps over a cardboard angel wing and a tin-foil halo taped to a wooden stick. A crumpled poster in the gutter declares the end is near.

She makes her way toward the quad, passing Howell Hall where Frank once worked. She thinks about him still asleep, wondering if he'd even care that she's gone.

Minutes later she stops in the shadow of Silent Sam, the bronze statue of a Confederate soldier celebrating North Carolina's rich tradition of racism. Legend has it, old Sam's rifle fires only when a virgin passes by.

Today what's firing is Liz's brain, a hot twist of thwirling threads tightening in her skull like a messianic migraine. If she really released the threads like the puppet said, why do they have such a hold on her heart? She slumps at the base of the statue, trying to find her breath.

"Liz? Is that you?"
"Gloria? What are you doing here?"
The old professor smells like tangerines. She's wearing black jeans, a rust-colored turtleneck, and sensible walking shoes.

"Church elders meeting this morning. God's always calling about something."

"Don't I know it." Liz squeezes her head in her hands, trying to contain her headache.

"Are you alright?"

"Not really. I'm afraid this thread stuff is getting out of control."

Gloria reaches down to pull Liz up. "Let's hear all about it," she says, nudging Liz forward across the quad. It takes Liz less than five minutes to finish her full report.

"Quite a story," says Gloria. "That pelican business was interesting, but goodness, the Dalai Lama? No wonder things are strained with Frank."

"Are they ever. He's somewhere between depressed and mad most of the time. Or else asleep."

"Have you considered what it might be like living with a modern-day Moses?" Gloria laughs to ease the tension.

"Don't you start, now. I'm no modern-day anything. I'm a sold-out fundraising hack caught up in a tangle of threads. My husband thinks I'm possessed, and I'm not so sure he's wrong."

Passing near the Old Well, an unassuming water fountain that is UNC's main historical attraction, Gloria leads Liz to a granite bench. The cool stone slab keeps them on the edge of their seats as students trickle by.

"What are you going to do now?" says Gloria.

"I can honestly say I have no idea."

"So who should I ask?" Gloria smiles and hugs her.

Liz thinks it through. "Maybe I'll just do good, be nice, and have fun," she finally says.

Gloria cocks her head and smiles. "It's a philosophy of life you can put on a bumper sticker."

Liz cringes. "You heard the show?"

"Nancy Kneedle's a good friend."

"I'm not sure I should have . . ."

"Nonsense. You made a perfectly good decision. And it certainly seems you released those pesky threads."

"Maybe."

Gloria watches Liz go from thoughtful to sad in the space of a breath. "What is it, sweetie?"

Liz studies the brick pavement before she brings herself to

open up again. For the first and last time, she tells the whole sad tale of her roller-coaster life. Raised in the church. Finding god. Finding boys. Getting pregnant. Having an abortion. Moving to Chapel Hill. Falling in love. Getting pregnant again. Marrying in a hurry. Watching her body change. Hearing Frannie's heartbeat. Painting the nursery. Buying teddy bears. Seeing Frannie dead. Leaving god behind. Feeling the world collapse.

She finishes the story and discovers the telling hasn't helped. She wipes her eyes. Bells and buzzers echo across the campus, turning the trickle of students into a wave that washes through the bright November morning.

"My butt's gotten cold and flat," says Liz over the din. "Let's walk some more."

"My butt's been cold and flat for years."

"You have a cute butt." Liz pats her soft and low.

"Thank you, dear." Gloria laughs and takes Liz by the arm. "I guess I should get back home and apologize to Frank."

"Might not be fun, but good and nice? For sure."

# 73

"Damn it, Hook." Doug Dipper just finished his third joint and he's starting to whine. "You gotta come with us. There ain't no way that lady'll see us without you."

"She sure don't want nothin' to do with me," says Sinker. He's about to pass out, and Hook wishes he'd just go ahead and do it.

"No shit, Sherlock," says Doug.

"This don't make no sense." Hook still hasn't heard anything resembling a plan.

"You said you oughta get a reward for saving her ass," says Doug. "Right?"

Now it's Sinker whining. "What about me?"

"And don't forget about that bracelet," says Doug. "It's worth a fortune, and that lady said she found it right here on the beach."

The hint of something shiny flashes bright in the back of Hook's brain.

"It was silver?"

"That's the one."

"Dibs on half," says Sinker.

"You ain't getting shit," says Hook.

"That's right." Doug needs an angle, and siding against Sinker might do the trick. Hook's been smoking hash and throwing down shots, and she might just fall for his divide-and-conquer plan. He goes for the close, like he's selling sand filters.

"I wouldn't want that reward to get away from you, not after all you done." He tugs at his dick. "How about this. Anything we get, you and me'll split. Fifty-fifty."

Hook flashes back on negotiating with Bobby Beak. "Sixty-forty."

"Damn you're hard." He pretends like he's thinking. "Okay.

That there's a deal. But we gotta get going. I don't want you backing out on me."

"What about me?" says Sinker.

"What about you?" says Hook.

"How about we don't turn your dumb ass in for attempted rape? That good enough?" says Doug.

# 74

When the phone rings at home later that morning, Liz answers it without thinking.

"Liz Forsythe? This is Jim Johnson from the Chapel Hill *News*. I'd like to talk with you about that bracelet you found."

"Yes?"

"That was an interesting interview you did last night."

"You heard it?"

"Online this morning."

"Well then, Mr. Johnson. I'd say you know all there is to know."

"Would you answer a couple of questions for me?"

"I'd rather not. But thanks for calling."

She clicks off the phone and goes to the kitchen. The answering machine is blinking like a time bomb. Four new messages. She switches it off and mutes the ringer. She decides to take a nap.

Liz awakens on the sofa three hours later to an afternoon sky that's turned gray, darkening her house and her mood. She hears the toilet flushing upstairs, and remembers she owes Frank an apology. Though she's not in the mood for making amends, she climbs the stairs to the bedroom. There's Frank, standing naked by the bed, pale as a peeled potato, dark gray circles under his dull brown eyes. It smells like he just threw up.

"You look terrible."

His voice wavers as he scoots under the sheets. "I'm sick. It's probably stomach cancer. Chills. Vomiting. Diarrhea. "

Liz can't help laughing. "Sounds like food poisoning."

"I haven't eaten since that lasagna yesterday. Remember?"

"*You* had lasagna. I fell asleep."

"You did?"

"It could have been spoiled."

"Oh great. Lethal leftovers."

Liz ignores the dig. "I'd better call Sarah."

A few minutes after six, the best-friend doctor bursts through the front door. Liz leads her to Frank, then leaves them alone. After a thorough examination and more questions than Frank wants to answer about bodily discharges, Sarah confirms Liz's diagnosis.

"And we need a stool sample," she says.

"Oh man," whines Frank. "Can't I just wait and see if it goes away?"

"Plus antibiotics. Here are some freebies to hold you over. If you're like this tomorrow, you'll come to the office."

"Do you have anything for a headache?"

Sarah gives him a sample pack. "Take a couple of these."

"Tylenol?"

"It's what doctors recommend." She snorts out a laugh and starts collecting her things. Frank tries to peel away the foil backing, but his wobbly hands won't stay steady long enough to get past the child-proof packaging.

"Need some help?"

"I can't get this stupid thing open." He's looking away from her, gazing out the window. These days, Frank spends more time staring out this window than even he thinks is healthy, too easily seduced by the silver-white bark of a beech tree standing near the house. Sarah sits on the bed and waits for him to face her.

"What's going on?" The question is too casual and too forced, all at the same time.

"What do you mean?"

"You know what I mean."

"I've been throwing up all morning. And I can't open a goddamn package of pills."

"Your hands were shaking out of control. That has nothing to do with headaches or diarrhea or anything."

As he searches for what to say, a sad wave rolls through the room. He and Sarah both look at the fingertips that betrayed him.

"Remember my first physical? It started about a year before that. Mostly my right hand. And only in certain positions. Like when I'm writing or holding a fork. It didn't seem like a big deal."

"And now?"

"And now it's both hands. Plus walking. Sometimes I'm not sure when my feet are hitting the ground."

"Have you noticed any patterns?"

"It's worse when I'm tired."

"The walking problems?"

"Just in the last few weeks. When we were at the beach I felt like I was tripping in the sand."

"What else?"

"It comes and goes."

Sarah watches Frank while she gathers her thoughts. He looks like a little boy caught lying. She brushes the image away.

"Tremors like these are common in men your age." She speaks with every bit of reassurance she can muster. "And most of the time it's nothing to worry about."

"But what about when it *is* something to worry about."

'Usually there are other symptoms."

"Like green triangles with yellow edges floating in your peripheral vision?"

Sarah rests her hand on his thigh. "Not like that at all."

"Like memory loss?"

"That's pretty normal, unless . . ."

'Unless what?"

'Unless it's accelerating."

"I'm not sure. And I'm not sure it's just memory. I seem more depressed than usual too."

"That's pretty bad." She tries to smile.

"That's what worries me."

"Anything else?"

"You mean besides the fact that my wife thinks she's the prophet of the holy threads?"

"That's not fair, Frank."

"I can't stop getting mad at her. My mind is wobbling like my hands."

Sarah sits silent.

"Do you know what's wrong with me?"

"That, dear friend, is going to require some tests."

After several hours of more chills and pills, Frank falls asleep. In exchange for Sarah keeping quiet about her worries, he promised he'd call to make an appointment in the morning.

While he snoozes, Liz checks the answering machine downstairs.

*Friday. 12:41 PM.*
Liz? This is Rachel. I heard you on the radio. Plus I got a call from an old friend, Cardinal Craven in Washington. We should talk. Sunday morning maybe?

*Friday. 12:47 PM.*
Hey doll. You too, Frank. This is your wonderful sister. You guys around this weekend? I'm thinking of driving down tomorrow and staying over till Monday. Sorry I was so tough on you, Frankly. Forgive me? See you tomorrow.

*Friday. 1:43 PM.*
Hello? This is Jesus. I called the radio show? Anyway. I'm on a borrowed cell phone, so I'll have to call you back. Peace.

*Friday. 1:45 PM.*
This is Nancy. You won't believe what's happening. Call me.

Liz switches off the kitchen light, seeking the quiet of the dark. She often tiptoes to the living room at night, searching out the sounds of silence, thinking through the lives she hasn't lived and wondering what she's missed. With the easy promise of procreation pushed off the table, she had looked elsewhere for fulfillment. But tonight, those elsewheres offer scant comfort. Her hypochondriac husband is drifting into depression. Work weighs heavy. And her very own mind is beginning to teeter. Time for sleep.

She places a foot on the first carpeted stair tread and hears the crunch of tires on the gravel driveway outside. No car lights. She would have seen them. No one should be here. Not tonight. She hurries to the front door and locks the deadbolt. She grimaces at the clunk of brass falling into place. The gravelly noise stops. She works her way toward the back door, which is not locked either. She freezes at the sound of a man's voice on the screened porch. She can't make out his words. She flinches when the low grumble of the refrigerator wheezes into the starkest kind of silence. In the still darkness, she hears what sounds like pee splashing on the slate patio. She hears the voice again.

"What the fuck you doing?" A long fart then a muffled giggle. A zipper whisking shut.

She reaches into the pantry and wraps her hand around a twenty-eight ounce can of crushed tomatoes.

# 75

Doug Dipper's Dodge van rolled into downtown Chapel Hill at eight o'clock Friday night with Hook and Sinker sleeping in the back. They stopped for a bucket of extra-crispy Kentucky Fried Chicken, three pints of baked beans, and a gallon of sweet tea. They inhaled the stuff, walked across the street to Sonny's for a six-pack of beer, and drove north out of town toward Morgan Mountain. When they came to a road-side cemetery, Doug eased onto the graveyard lane for a last-minute planning session.

After a few hours of convincing bullshit from Doug, Hook had decided to join the boys in earnest. She figured becoming an instant millionaire might have some advantages, and with Eddie Junior gone fishing, she didn't have anything better to do. Now they're making a quick visit to the home of Elizabeth Fancy Pants Forsythe, just to get acquainted. At least that's what Doug said. Hook's too hung over, too stoned, and too car-sick to care either way.

"Do what I say," whispers Doug as they approach the back porch. The full moon's hidden behind a thick layer of clouds. No lights anywhere.

Sinker, who's so drunk he can barely walk, pulls out his dick and pisses on the flagstone patio.

"What the fuck you doing?" says Doug. The splattering is followed by a sonorous fart that echoes across the yard.

Hook giggles and covers her mouth.

Sinker slides up his zipper.

Doug slashes his hand wildly, signaling quiet. But despite his altered state, he knows it's no use. His plan is not going to work. He should not be here with these fuckheads.

Not being one to surrender easily, though, Doug sends Hook into the breach. He motions her forward as he eases open the kitchen door.

"Go on," is what Doug Dipper whispers.

"Go on," is what Liz hears.

"Go on," is what Hook does, across the gray tile floor.

And when the faintest shadow of her bony body slides across the pantry door, Liz slams a can of crushed tomatoes into her unsuspecting face, dropping her criminal skull to the floor like a wounded grackle.

Liz hears the voice outside again. "Hook? You okay?"

Nothing.

"Hook?" A louder voice.

Nothing.

"I'm getting the hell outta here." A panicked voice.

"What about Hook?" Another panicked voice.

"I'm leaving and I'm driving and if you don't want your dumb ass stuck in jail again, you better come along."

Retreating footsteps give Liz room to breathe. She hears car doors slamming shut and wheels rolling away on the gravel. She edges back against the pantry shelves. The can of crushed tomatoes slips from her sweaty hand and clickety-clacks across the tiles. She reaches for the light switch.

Lying on the floor like a Barbie akimbo is a barely breathing woman in a shambles. Bubbles of blood spume from her nose, and a sea of pee spreads around the crotch of her faded black jeans. A menacing five-inch-long hook hangs from a key chain on her black leather belt. The sleeves of her brown hooded sweatshirt are pushed up to her elbows, revealing a swirl of blue-green angels on her skinny arms. Her short oily hair is raven black.

*The woman from the beach?*

Liz's steady hands have wrung the necks of English sparrows, and she is not intimidated by the bag of bones lying on the floor. But she is alarmed. This is the second time this tattooed person has crossed her path.

She takes a roll of duct tape from the pantry and stoops beside the body. She wraps its smallish ankles with five tight loops, then its knees, taking care to avoid the pissed-on pants. She flips the body over and tapes its arms together from wrist to elbow. She takes the fishhook from the belt and sets it on the table. She steps back to survey her work. She wants this bloody mess out of her house.

Liz grabs the shoulders of the body's sweatshirt, a fistful of fabric in each hand, and drags it through the open back door to the screened porch, down two steps to the patio outside. The body puts up no resistance. She drops it on a bed of fallen leaves and walks back to the kitchen. A smear of blood on the floor creeps her out. She gets a sponge mop from the pantry and scrubs the floor with straight Lysol.

When she's finished her cleaning frenzy, the house is quiet. Except for the pounding of her heart. And the whispers in her brain.

*Dogoodbenicehavefun.*

Almost in a daze, Liz finds herself in the hall closet digging out a sleeping bag. She takes it outside and spreads it over the body. When she passes back through the kitchen, the clock on her microwave oven reads 12:34. She tries to remember the last time she saw that number, tries to remember what day that was, what day this is. Can't remember anything. She starts upstairs for the second time tonight and feels a plea from out behind the house. She continues up to the bedroom.

"Frank?" She whispers. "Are you awake?"

His labored breathing pisses her off.

The plea gets stronger.

*Dogoodbenicehavefun.*

She grabs the Louisville Slugger by Frank's dresser and goes back downstairs, stopping at the front hall closet for a jacket and a flashlight. A minute later, she peels back the sleeping bag. The light makes the face of the body squint. The squint makes the body cry.

"You're blinding me."

Liz savors her torturer status for a second before she moves the light away from the woman's eyes.

"Who are you?"

"My head hurts."

"I said, who are you? What are you doing here?"

"Where's my brother and Doug?"

"Listen you. I'm the one with the baseball bat. You better start talking."

*What am I doing? I should call the police.*

"I wasn't gonna hurt nobody."

"What's your name?"

"Hook."

"Hook?"

"Yes, ma'am." Hook slips into submissive. After years of working around the reckless will of Sinker, she knows full well when to fold.

"What are you doing here? Why were you in my house?"

"We were looking for that bracelet. Me and Sinker's the ones that drug you outta the surf."

"Who's Sinker?"

"My brother."

"You attacked me."

"That was Sinker."

Liz glares as her temper flares. She towers all of her six-foot height over Hook's scared self.

"You were right to hit him." Hook's searching for the best words to offer. "You were right to hit me, too. I shouldn't a been in your house in the first place. I knew it was a stupid plan."

"Who else was with you?" says Liz.

"Doug Dipper."

"The swimming pool guy?"

"That's him."

"What does he have to do with this?"

Hook wonders if she should keep answering these questions, but can't think the problem through. She's stoned, drunk and smashed in the face, and even if she weren't, she still wouldn't know what to do. Sinker and Doug would tell her to keep quiet. But they're the ones who got her into this mess in the first place.

"Doug heard you on the radio talking about the bracelet from the beach. Sinker said we found it first. Doug said it's ours."

Liz sags under the weight of Hook's truth. "That's an interesting story. But it doesn't change the fact that you broke into my house."

"What're you gonna do?"

*Dogoodbenicehavefun.*

"I'm going to let you decide. You can either sleep out here tied up. Or I can call the police right now. Take your pick."

"That's my only choices?"

"Best I can do, Ms. Hook."

It takes Hook two seconds to think it through. "Could you least bring me a pillow?"

# 76

Liz sleeps fitfully, pushing Frank out of bed before six. He's feeling better, and goes to get the paper, only slightly surprised to find the front door locked. The cool morning brightens his spirits until his stomach starts to growl. Until his eyes start to squint. Until his feet start to falter. Until his mind starts to float. He wonders if he'll be able to hold food down today. He wonders why Liz has been so mad at him lately. He wonders what kind of testing Sarah has in store. He wonders why he's wondering so much.

Cars speed by on Morgan Mountain Road, thirty feet from where he's standing. He makes a note to pester the county sheriff for more patrols. He finds a sample box of fruit-flavored Cheerios sealed in the plastic newspaper wrapper. He rips open the box and shakes the pinkish O's into his mouth. He spits them on the ground.

Returning to the house, Frank loops around the back to go in through the kitchen. His old sleeping bag is spread on the ground. He grabs the damp nylon and turns away in one smooth motion. His eyes catch something on the ground, jolting a spike of fear through his body with a yelp.

The sound of his alarm rushes Liz to their bedroom window.

"It's okay," she yells. "Don't do anything. I'll be right there."

An hour later, Liz sits in the kitchen with the intruder, the giant hook lying on the table between them. Hook's bruised face makes Liz wonder if there are two cracked skulls in her kitchen. Frank duct-tapes Hook's arms to the chair.

"I *know* we should call the police." Liz takes the phone from

Frank for the third time. "But not yet. We need to think this through."

"What's to think through?" Frank slips into pathetic. "She tried to break into our house. The others could come back. They could have guns."

"They ain't got guns." Hook's bloodied nose muffles her voice like she has a cold. "And they ain't coming back neither. They're drinking beer on the beach by now." Liz can see Hook wishes she was with them.

"I'm calling the police," says Frank.

"You'd be in your rights." Hook turns meek, which is easy considering her circumstances. "But I sure hope you don't."

"I don't care what you hope," snaps Frank.

Liz scolds him with a stare.

"I know what I done was stupid," says Hook. "But I wasn't trying to hurt nobody."

"I still don't understand what you were planning to do. Sneak around the house until you found what you were looking for?" says Liz, pointing at the hook. "And what's this about?"

A high-pitched hello rings in from the living room.

*Oh shit,* thinks Frank. *Faye's here.*

*Oh shit,* thinks Hook. *Another one to worry about.*

Liz catches Hook's fidgety eyes. "It's just my sister," she whispers.

By ten, Liz, Faye, and Hook are talking like old friends, while Frank stands guard by the door with his baseball bat. Over his strong objections, Liz and Faye untied Hook and let her take a shower. She changed into some of Faye's stockpiled clothes and ate a bowl of Grape Nuts, cringing with every crunchy chew.

"You have to promise you're not going to try anything," Liz said during their quick negotiations. "And I mean anything. You have to behave."

"I won't do nothing." She looked at Frank. "I swear."

Hook, it turns out, falls freely for the threads. Liz gives her the Cliff Notes version, and Hook takes the three commandments to heart.

"I don't guess I been all that good," she says, "but I do mostly try to be nice." She looks around for agreement, which is hard to come by.

"Like when you break into someone's house?" says Faye.

"Maybe not that."

"And that brother of yours," says Frank.

"He ain't me," says Hook emphatically. She will not get dragged down by Sinker again.

"Well." Liz and Faye breathe the word in unison, almost like a sigh.

"You still got it?" says Hook.

"Got what?" says Liz.

"That bracelet."

"I do," says Liz. "It's upstairs."

"Can I see it?"

Liz and Faye exchange a might-as-well glance. When she comes back two minutes later, Liz finds everyone looking at a newspaper spread on the table in front of the couch.

"This is just great," says Frank, full of I-told-you-so.

"It's not that bad," says Faye. "Here. Let me read it to you."

### Bracelet Said to Hold New Commandments
#### By Jim Johnson

Chapel Hill – When stories about three new commandments surfaced last week, the Chapel Hill rumor mill shifted into overdrive. At the center of the stories is a silver bracelet covered with mysterious inscriptions. The finder? Elizabeth L. Forsythe, associate director of development for Duke University.

"It's quite fantastic," said Nancy Kneedle, general manager of WTCH-FM, where Forsythe told her story during a Halloween broadcast of Midnight Pagan. According to Kneedle, there are three threads: Do good, be nice, have fun.

During the broadcast, Forsythe rejected the suggestion that she had discovered new commandments, saying instead that the bracelet holds "the threads of life fully filled." Forsythe maintains the bracelet could be a thousand years old, a finding she said was confirmed by an unidentified scholar.

Some clergy, however, are skeptical about the claims.

"This is the Devil's work," said Joseph J. Peters, the minister at Calvary Mission Church in Rougemont. Peters said he saw the bracelet a week before its church debut.

"No good will come of this," said Peters. "And these are

certainly not commandments. God would not be worrying about people having fun. It makes a mockery of the Word."

When asked about the threads, Forsythe declined to comment.


Hook's angels dance when she points at the bracelet. "Yessir. That sure is it." Her declaration hs heavy in the room, but she's oblivious. "What you think it's worth? Doug says millions."

"I'm not sure how much I'd trust Doug Dipper," says Liz.

Hook seems to take the advice to heart. "Still. If you get a bunch of money, could you maybe give me some?"

Liz throws a look in Frank's direction. His pained expression annoys her. She turns to Faye and finds a sympathetic nod. "We'll see," she says.

# 77

The boys dive into their daily chores with new resolve. Though the weather's turned cool, it's a sunny day, and things are looking up. After Froot Loops, Mark heads over to Signs by Tomorrow, where Michael promised to meet him and make another banner.

Meanwhile, Jesus and Luke are on the trail of John Paul Stone to see if he's okay. They stop first at Doug Dipper's Pool Palace, but find no sign of anything. Their pool is drained, shut-down for the winter.

"There goes our fifty bucks," says Luke. He sits with his feet dangling and pouts, swinging his broom like a pendulum, stirring the air. The sharp odor of chlorine edges out the thick scent of vinyl for worst place. He wonders if he smells pee.

"Let's leave Mr. Dipper a note." Jesus settles in beside Luke. "I bet we can get him to fill it up again."

"He won't do that, Jesus."

"Dog said it doesn't hurt to ask."

Luke looks around nervous. Last week's gun play shook him up more than he knew. "I don't like all this Dog business."

Jesus scans the sky. "She was a good weatherman."

"She was a dang ghost."

Jesus sinks into a low spooky voice, wiggling his fingers like spidery webs. "I think I am possessed." Then he rolls his eyes back in his head and keels over.

Luke knows he's faking, but can't find the humor. Things are starting to unravel on him. The bracelet. Elizabeth. The threads. Dog. He can't make sense of it all. He looks over at Jesus, lying like a mummy. He shakes his head and wonders for the millionth time what he's doing here.

"You really think we should be going go to Chapel Hill?" Luke says. "That lady won't give us the bracelet back."

"We don't need it," says Jesus.

"Then why're we going?"

Jesus shrugs. "To be nice and have fun?"

"You and those threads."

"It'll be good to go." Jesus sits up and holds Luke's hand. "For us. Won't it?"

*Us.* Luke knows that means Mark, too. Not just the two of them. And it hurts. "There you go, letting Mark get his way again. It happens every time. You just can't say no."

A fast cloud moves in to block the sun, dropping the temperature a few degrees. Jesus cuddles up against Luke. "You can have your way, too, you know."

Sergeant Stone's red Silverado seems big as a fire truck when the boys find it parked in Tall Paul's skuzzy gravel lot that afternoon. Jesus has to jump to reach the running board so he can peek in the window. There's not much to see through the mirrored glass, just a decal with a cross dripping blood and the words *Semper Fi.* Always faithful.

"Get down from there," says Luke. "What if he comes out?"

"What if who comes out?" says Sergeant Stone. Dang if he hasn't snuck up on them again.

Dodging death last Sunday had left its mark on John Paul Stone, but he wasn't quite sure what it meant. And his blurry memory didn't help things either. He could picture getting the drop on the faggots. He remembered the yellow jackets, but everything else was a blur of bright. Somebody holding his hand. An old lady whispering nonsense. The worst part was the coming back from the warm white light.

"Sergeant Stone!' says Gary, hopping down from the truck. "You're good as new."

If you've never almost died, it's hard to imagine the trip. Not the pain part, that's easy enough to grasp. It's the head game that throws you. That impossible rush from here to there with time stopped cold and fast. No gates to open. No lectures to endure. No scales to balance. No anything. Even for an asshole like John Paul Stone, it's a wild free ride that splashes into nothing but light, no questions asked.

But the quick bounce back to life knocked Stone off balance. Why hadn't he passed? The EMTs told him he was lucky he wasn't dead. They said the faggots saved him. Fuckin' faggots.

With nowhere to turn but god, John Paul Stone prayed like a saint all week, the first honest praying he'd ever done. On his way to work. At the rifle range. Standing guard duty. Commissary shopping. He even visited his preacher for some extra horsepower. They met after weekly prayer meeting to sip some whiskey and talk things though. The preacher told John Paul not to fret. He said Stone's ticket to heaven was already punched. God's only son had come to earth to save him from his sins. Yep, he said, John Paul Stone had long since grabbed the golden ring. There was nothing else to do.

"But what about the queers," said Stone. "I'da killed that nigger one if I hadn't got stung."

"That's alright," said the preacher. "Queers oughta be killed. You did good."

Despite the encouragement, Stone didn't feel like he'd done good. Not one bit. His brush with nothing spooked him.


"What're you doing here?" says Stone. His Gatekeeper suit looks none the worse from its emergency dip in the pool last week, either that or he has a duplicate.

"We came to see if you might want to help. We're still looking for a John."

"You're fucking crazy."

Stone hasn't said nigger or faggot yet, which is a relief to Luke. Maybe Jesus is right, maybe he's changed.

"That was a close call you had," says Jesus. "Good thing Dog showed up."

Stone wants to slap the little shit just for being, but his strength fails. He looks toward the bar where his buddies are still inside. He can't let the other Gatekeepers see him with the homos again. He fishes keys from a pocket and presses a button. Four chrome posts jump to attention, unlocking the truck in a second.

"Get in," he says to Jesus. Then he turns on Luke. "Back seat, black boy."

# 78

Frank got grumpier after dinner and put his shaky foot down. He said Hook had to sleep in the basement. He said it's the only room they can lock from the outside.

"She'll be fine," said Faye. "Just relax. And pass that bowl of mush." She took the dish and snooted at her sister. "Do you cook cauliflower for every meal, or is this special punishment just for me?"

"I know she'll be fine." Frank slit his eyes. "She'll be locked in the basement."

"It's okay," said Hook.

"There's no bed down there," said Faye.

"Yes, there's a bed down there," mimicked Frank. "I'm not a total asshole."

Faye stuck her tongue out at Frank when he turned his back. Hook laughed and winced from the hurt.

Hook found the basement arranged beyond reason, courtesy of Frank's occasional need to impress foreign exchange students. When she reached the bottom of the wooden stairs, she decided she could live here just fine. A tidy twin bed, a nightstand with a reading lamp, a small chest of drawers, a card table with a folding chair, a round braided rug, and a washer and dryer. Even a bathroom with a shower.

"Sure is nice," said Hook.

"Don't bother anything," said Frank. "And don't get too comfortable. It's just one night." He looked at Liz for agreement and got a frosty stare.

Locked away, Hook started poking around. A bookshelf stacked with light bulbs and wrapping paper. A dark corner's worth of karate trophies. Boxes bristling with photographs, all lined up by year.

She flipped through the first box of baby pictures. Liz and Faye playing naked in a backyard wading pool. Old cars on a farm. Tractors.

She pulled out the dark heavy box from the year she was born. She sifted through pictures of Liz, pregnant and glowing. Frank putting a crib together. Liz in front of a hospital. Liz flashing a peace sign on the way into delivery. The frozen smile in the picture squeezed the breath from Hook's lungs.

Later after Liz has gone to bed, Frank is messing around in his office when Faye comes in with a bottle of chardonnay in one hand and a wooden pipe in the other.

"Let's finish this off and smoke some pot," she says, standing in the kitchen door.

"When'd you start that again?" Frank points at the pipe with his chin.

Faye used to be a pot head, but stopped five years ago after a rough New Year's Eve party in Richmond. He thought she was still on the wagon.

"I haven't started anything again. I brought it just in case."

"In case of what?"

"In case I wanted to get high, Frankly."

She lights the pipe and passes it to her brother-in-law.

Frank indulges on rare occasions, and tonight seems rare enough indeed. He draws on the little pipe, closes his eyes, and holds his breath. The effect is immediate. His guard is down and his mind is loose. He heads to the pantry in search of a snack. Before he can decide what to eat, he starts to rearrange the shelves. He finds a bag of dog treats. He wonders where Molly is.

Meanwhile, Faye takes over the living room, dimming the lamp and kicking off her shoes. Frank arrives just in time to see her slip her black bra out through the sleeve of her wrinkled linen blouse.

"God that feels good." She rubs the sides of her ribcage. "You have no idea how lucky men are. You don't have to be trussed."

"You don't either."

"Are you kidding?" She sits up.

"I see women without bras all the time."

"You see them because you're always looking at their tits, Frank. Which totally makes my point."

She throws the bra at him and slumps back on the sofa, closing her eyes and resting her brain in the quiet space of her home away from home.

Frank studies her familiar features. She's six inches shorter and forty pounds lighter than Liz, but clearly borne of the same strong stock. Her hands and feet. The angle of her cheekbones, the shape of her knees. Her hips. He pictures her private parts, too, wondering exactly where the similarities end.

"What's going on, Frank?"

"Huh?" He imagines she's added mind-reading to her professional repertoire.

"With you and Hook. What's got you so worried?"

Frank flashes to Liz and Hook giggling in the kitchen. He can't recall Liz being so genuinely happy in the past twenty years.

"I'm not so worried," he says. "I'm scared shitless."

# 79

Mark was excited about the chance to hang with Michael, get a new banner, and maybe dig up some more dope. So he's flat-out bummed when he gets to the shop and there's no sign of his friend. He presses his face against the locked glass door, looking for hope. There's none to be found. Fuck. He stomps off in the direction of the trailer park, riding his broom like a hobby horse. He's sick of it all. Scummy garbage. Pizzas. Money worries. Broken-down car. No way to get to Chapel Hill. Double fuck.

So imagine his surprise when a red Silverado pulls up close behind him with Jesus and Luke sitting inside.

"Markie," yells Jesus. He's hanging out the passenger window waving. "We found our John."

As one of the original Gatekeepers at the New Gate of Heaven Baptist Church, Sergeant John Paul Stone has been born again more times than he cares to remember. But not a single one of the previous soul-savings compares to what just happened in the cushy leather seats of his tricked-out truck. No sooner had he pulled away from Tall Paul's when all heaven broke loose, a buzzing rush of cosmic yellow jackets dancing on his heart, pushing him once again toward the light.

"Are you okay, Sergeant Stone?" said Jesus.

Stone choked the steering wheel with sweaty palms like a man driving through fog. "What do you want with me?" His face went red and tight. "How come I didn't die?"

Luke ahemed from the back seat. "And Jesus said to him, 'Today salvation has come to this house, because he also is a son of Abraham.'"

Stone threw Luke a drop-dead look. "No one's talking to you, boy." Then he shifted his glare back to Jesus. "You said Dog showed up. What the hell's that supposed to mean?"

Jesus smiled. "This old lady who used to come around sometimes."

"She's not real," said Luke.

Jesus pffffted.

"She was real enough to save good ol' Sergeant Stone."

"That was you, Jesus," said Luke. "Not Dog."

Stone swerved to a side street and stopped in a skid. He reached back and grabbed Luke by the shirt. "Did you just call this little faggot Jesus?"

Luke couldn't talk, but he managed to stammer out a nervous nod. Stone pushed him away. Jesus scooted to the far side of his seat, scrunching his eyes shut tight. He felt for the door handle, but the automatic locks clunked home. He turned and found Stone draped over the steering wheel, humming an old Baptist hymn.

*He lives.*

Jesus stretched across the cab and touched the sergeant's beefy back. "All is swell," he said.

Stone felt that hand like the kiss of an angel. He could barely bring himself to breathe.

# 80

The household wakes happy to a blustery Sunday morning. Except for Frank. He's achy and feeling put out. Even with Hook locked up overnight, he wouldn't relinquish his Louisville Slugger.

Hook's helping Liz hang laundry out back, the first of many chores Liz has planned. A gusty breeze offers the promise of perfectly dried sheets.

"What'll happen when you get back home?" Liz drags a yellow duvet cover out of the basket and hands one end to Hook.

"What's this thing?" Hook sticks her hand inside the open end of the big cotton cover. "Looks like a giant pillow case."

"It goes over a comforter," says Liz. "A duvet. I guess it is kind of like a pillowcase."

"Duvet." Hook throws Liz a crooked smile. "Man, you sure got it rough around here."

By two-thirty, towering gray clouds have filled the sky, and Hook has earned Frank's grudging trust. First by phoning her brother, then by killing a copperhead.

On the brother front, Hook called Sinker to say she was okay. She said he should stay put and do nothing. She said everything would be fine unless the woman's crazy husband called the police. Frank was proud of how she handled it.

But it was in the snake department that she really won him over. They were sweeping leaves off the courtyard in front of the house.

"You can put that bat away," said Hook. "I told you I won't cause no trouble."

"Okay, Ms. Hook." Frank wanted to finish the clean-up

before it rained. "We'll just give you a little test." He leaned the bat against the door and took up his newest cornstraw broom. Hook used an older broom, doing her best to follow his lead.

"What do you think about them threads?" asked Hook. "You think they're commandments?" She pushed a pile of leaves around with dramatic flourishes.

'Use short strokes," said Frank.

"They seem like it to me." Hook stabbed at the ground with her broom, trying to dislodge a squashed worm.

"Seem like what?"

"Beam like nut." The joke sneaked out before she could stop it.

"What?"

"Sorry. I'm just goofing around."

"What're you talking about?"

"I'm talking about those threads."

'Use short strokes," he said again. "Like this." He was demonstrating his technique with a flurry of quick scalloped movements when two steely words landed in his ears.

"Don't move."

He looked at the bat on the porch.

"There's a copperhead by your foot."

Frank resisted the urge to run while Hook eased over to the porch, picked up the baseball bat, and baby-stepped back to where he stood.

"Hold still." She cocked the bat above her head and looked him square in the eye. Electric images of wild tattoos flashed through his brain as she slammed the Slugger on the ground inches from his foot, smashing the head of the four-foot-long snake into a mangled mess. Before Frank could jump away, she dealt three more blows to the writhing reptile, splurting snake blood over the clean swept bricks. She collected the snake with a bare hand, carried it out past the driveway, and threw it in the woods. She came back and picked up her broom like nothing happened.

"Sorry about that mess." She wiped her hands on Faye's old jeans. "I don't know if killing snakes is doing good or being nice."

Frank's heart raced, but Hook went back to sweeping.

"I tell you what though, I'd sure like one," she said a minute later.

"One what?"

"One of those lifes fully filled. I sure would."

"It might not even mean that."

"Huh?"

"The words on the bracelet. They might not really mean life fully filled. They might mean eternal life. Big difference if you ask me."

"I'd take either."

"Either what?" Faye came out the door carrying a wooden tray with brimming glasses of tea.

"Either glass." Frank was ready to change the subject. He stepped toward Faye and stumbled over a brick, knocking the tray from her hands. Quick as a snake smasher, Hook caught one of the glasses with barely a spill. Faye saved the other from crashing, but dumped the tea on her brother-in-law.

The wet sweater was problem enough for Frank, but it was Faye's easy laughter that did him in.

"Goddamn it." He stomped across the porch and slammed the door shut with an eighty decibel "Shit."

"Oh, oh," said Faye. She and Hook watched as unexpected cars came down the driveway toward the house. "Frank's going bullshit, and it looks like there's going to be a party."

# 81

Mark, Luke and John Paul Stone sit like they're strapped in electric chairs, not yet shocked, but ready for oblivion. It takes the words of Jesus to break the awkward silence.

"Good news, Mark. John Paul's thinking about helping us with the baptism."

"He's joining us?"

The question hangs in the air while Stone shifts into drive and pulls back on the road. After a few quiet minutes, they're parked at the Doug Dipper's Pool Palace, still quiet as ghost crabs.

"I ain't joining nothing," says Stone. "I said might help. Period."

"That's cool," says Jesus. "Helping's good."

"Except the pool's drained," says Luke. "And we're running out of money."

"And we don't have a sign to put up," says Mark. "Michael wasn't there."

"We'll be okay," says Jesus.

"Yeah, right," says Luke. "That's what you said when we lost the dang bracelet."

"Which is exactly why we're going to Chapel Hill," says Mark. "Maybe Sergeant Stone can drive us."

The jumpy conversation gives John Paul Stone more than a few second thoughts. With each passing word, his fragile faith fades like a fevered dream. He can't figure out why he's sitting here with a truck full of faggots. He tries to focus on Mark.

"What the hell are you talking about?" he mumbles.

"We lost the bracelet at the beach," says Mark. "We're trying to get it back."

Stone blinks slow, forcing his brain to a lower gear. He's not driving the faggots anywhere. Especially not to hippy heaven.

"Don't worry," says Jesus.

He pats Stone again, but the kiss of his hand has turned to a cattle prod. The big sergeant stares at Jesus like they'd never met, shivering hard as he falls from grace.

"Get the fuck outta my truck."

# 82

When Liz peeks through the bedroom curtains at the cars coming up the driveway, the threads of life fully filled spin her heart into a jewel of joy. She pulls on a white cotton caftan and slips the bracelet strong around her wrist. Standing in front of the wall of mirrors, she runs a quick brush through her short blonde hair. Glimmers of light dance in the air around her. She stretches her natural smile extra wide with every stroke, pumping swirls of endorphins into play. She searches her own blue eyes for some kind of direction, glancing at the puppet still pinned to the bedroom wall. There are no words of wisdom. Sita is speechless.

Liz comes down the stairs to her husband, sister and four unexpected guests. Sarah the healer. Rachel the dealer. Nancy the wheeler. Oscar the kneeler.

"This is a surprise," says Liz, smiling and wondering at the same time.

"My idea," says Rachel.

"You wouldn't let us come if we asked," says Nancy.

"I'm here to check up on Frank," says Sarah.

"I'm here for breakfast," jokes Oscar. His wisecrack starts a ripple of uneasy laughter, which grinds to quiet when Hook comes up from the basement. She's been folding the last of the laundry.

"Everyone, this is Hook," says Liz. "She's staying with us for awhile."

"Didn't mean to interrupt." Hook knows they're staring at her bruised face, wondering what the hell she's doing here.

"You didn't interrupt anything," says Faye.

"Ya'll talking about them threads?" Hook whispers to Liz, but everyone hears.

"Sure seems that way." Liz hugs her close.

"One heck of a story," says Rachel.

"Yes," says Nancy. "But we haven't heard *all* the gory details."

"Off the record?" says Liz. "I'm not ready for any more reporters."

"Deal," says Rachel, nodding toward Nancy.

It takes Liz less than ten minutes to tell her whole surprising story, and she's glad to have it out. The beach. Hook and Sinker. The pelican. The bracelet. The car wreck. The threads. Sita the puppet. *Midnight Pagan.* Larry King. The Cardinal. The Dalai Lama. The newspapers. The phone calls. The crushed tomatoes.

"You forgot that baseball bat," says Hook. She catches Frank's eye, and he almost smiles.

"Our website is getting visitors from all over the world," says Nancy. "Seven hundred thousand hits in twenty-four hours. I've never seen anything like it."

"That's ridiculous," says Frank.

"It is not ridiculous. People loved hearing about the threads," says Nancy. "They loved your interview, Liz. They're calling you the reluctant prophet."

Liz chews a thumbnail.

"The prophet needs a scribe," says Oscar. "I can handle six words. Do. Good. Be. Nice. Have. Fun."

"And I'll be your PR guy," says Nancy, giving Oscar a high-five.

"I don't need a PR guy," says Liz. "Besides, Frank already volunteered." She glances over Nancy's shoulder at her husband. He's never looked so glum.

"I withdraw my application," he says under his breath. No one else seems to notice, but the words turn Liz cold.

"Guess that leaves me with fundraising," laughs Rachel. She rubs her hands together like a sneak.

Later in the kitchen, Sarah grills Hook about her head injury. There had been a trickle of blood from her ear, and Sarah suspects a fracture. All Hook can think of is no insurance.

"In the meantime, stay away from cans of tomatoes," says Sarah. "A bump on the head could kill you."

An hour later, Frank reached the limits of his tolerance when Liz agreed to go on *Midnight Pagan* one more time. Nancy seduced her, plain and simple, and the prickle of jealousy only added to his upset. It happened while Hook was telling a story about the hammerhead shark she caught off Eddie's pier in August. Halfway through the fish tale, she smacked her thigh and changed her tune.

"I guess killing sharks doesn't do much good," she said. "Ain't nice, either. It's fun for sure, but that don't seem to be enough no more." She paused for a beat to push up her sleeves. Tattooed angels swarmed the room.

"Hook, you could come on the show, too." Nancy's one-track mind was on a promotional roll. "You both found the bracelet, you know."

Hook and Liz looked at each other and Hook shrugged off the beginnings of a grin. Liz said right then and there that she'd go on the show if Hook would.

It was his wife's casual "okay" that stomped Frank through the kitchen and out the door to his truck, driving him away from home in search of reason. He ended up at the Chapel Hill Public Library, an hour before closing.

At one of a dozen Internet terminals, his trembling hands type *threads life fully filled* into Google. In three seconds he has access to more than two thousand web sites reporting on Liz's *Midnight Pagan* debut. He can't bring himself to follow the ominous links.

He enters a new search for *hand tremors* plus *memory loss*. It produces hundreds of hits on sites covering a host of ailments including Parkinson's disease, Grave's disease, Wilson's disease, Alzheimer's, DLB, brain tumors, chemical poisoning and alcoholism. It takes him thirty minutes to conclude that he's DLB all the way. Dementia with Lewy Bodies. Gait disturbances. Shuffling feet. Poor balance. Awkward falls. Hallucinations. Depression. Confusion. Memory loss. Slowness. Muscle stiffness. Trembling. Mood swings. Symptoms overlap with Parkinsons and Alzheimers. Lewy Bodies. Tiny protein deposits that disrupt brain functioning by interrupting neurotransmitters. Dementia. With Lewy Bodies. A progressive, degenerative disease with no cure.

Frank gets home around midnight, relieved to find no lights on. He won't have to deal with anyone, especially his rock-star wife. He stops at his desk to check email. There's a new file on his laptop screen called *Threads*.

- Liz call Dalai Lama? Guest on *Midnight Pagan*?
- Rachel contact Cardinal Craven.
- Bracelet for sale?
- Appraisal? Check with Gloria
- Nancy call *Larry King* and set up *Times* interview

Frank guesses it was Nancy's lust for fame that pushed the plan ahead. She'd done a good job, though he can't resist a few improvements.

- *Times* interview first
- Embargo until after *Larry King*
- Buy url: www.lifefullyfilled.org
- Insure the bracelet!

Frank spends another hour online, digging deeper into his self-diagnosed disease. He prints out a page of DLB symptoms, highlighting thirteen of the eighteen he can reasonably claim. He reads the sad story of a Brit whose DLB diagnosis triggered three unsuccessful suicide attempts before he finally drove his car into a telephone pole. He drops the paper in his recycling box and turns his attention to sleep. Steering clear of Liz seems like a good idea, so he opts for the couch. His mind shuts down quickly, despite the press of Lewy Bodies.

He wakes with a start at seven-thirty to sounds upstairs. With stiff limbs and bad breath he grabs his shoes and hurries for the door. Liz calls from the bedroom. He bumps his toe and swears. He jogs to his truck in stocking feet. He drives halfway to the road before he checks the rearview mirror and sees Liz standing in her nightgown on the porch. He almost stops. He wishes he had dry socks. *Spin doctor.* The thought spikes through his mind in an angry burst and he presses on the accelerator. His wheels spew wet gravel until he peels onto Morgan Mountain Road. A horn-honking garbage truck barrels around the curve behind him. He speeds to get away. A minute later his cell phone rings. He doesn't answer. He turns on Sunrise Road and stops at the Dot 'n' Dash for gas and a Snickers. He calls Sarah's office to say he won't be there for tests this morning. He turns his phone off.

# 83

The woman Frank left behind is drowning in the drama of his early morning escape, in the squeal of his tires and the blasts of the horns. She spends too long imagining that nothing out of the ordinary is happening, that her husband is just going out for coffee. She stands too long on the porch getting cold. She goes in the house and dials his cell phone.

No answer.

She fixes a cup of tea and tries again.

No answer.

Goes upstairs and pulls on a pair of jeans and a flannel shirt.

Calls again.

No answer.

She goes to his study, finds his amendments to Nancy's plan, sees a sticky note on his desk about Monday morning tests.

She phones Sarah's office. The receptionist is in a snit. Frank had just called to cancel his appointment. Liz waffles between sorry and mad before she settles on depressed. She grumps around the house for a while, trying to savor the solitude, but not quite getting there.

She starts cooking breakfast, putting a whole pound of bacon in her favorite pan. It takes only a couple of minutes for the sweet aroma to seep into the basement, coaxing Hook up to the kitchen, wearing Faye's pajamas.

"Where's that husband of yours?" Hook's sleepy-eyed, the bruises around her eyes and nose softened to muddy brown. "He come home last night?"

"Sure he did." Liz puts on more cheeriness than she feels. "He had a doctor's appointment this morning." Not quite a lie.

"I was hoping to use his computer."

"He won't mind." Liz pours two glasses of orange juice and sets them on the table.

"Wonder where that thing really came from?" Hook points at the bracelet on Liz's wrist. "Seems kinda weird laying on the beach like that."

Liz hands it to her.

Hook flashes back a month to the finding and the fainting and the falling in the surf. Unfamiliar images of pelicans and puppets slide into her thoughts. She closes her eyes and presses the silver to her cheek.

*Dogoodbenicehavefun.*

Hook laughs like she's tripping. She grabs the table to steady herself and knocks a glass of juice to the floor. It shatters in a golden burst. She watches the pulpy mess stream around her feet, slivers of glass sprinkled through like stars in a bright orange sky. She kneels without thinking to pick up the pieces. Liz squats beside her with a wad of paper towels.

"Careful now," says Hook, slipping into taking care, her guardian angels mopping up the juice. "Don't need no more blood on this nice kitchen floor."

Hook cleans up the dishes while Liz damp mops. When they're finished, Liz tries to call Frank again. Frank, who's not where he's supposed to be. She guesses he might be heading for the beach and dials the condo number, leaving the sweetest message she can conjure up.

Hook says she really needs to go online for a few minutes. "Hang on," says Liz. "Just let me print a copy of our plan." Frank's printer is out of paper. She grabs some sheets from his recycling box and puts them in the tray. The phone rings.

"Good morning." Sarah's voice is chirpy. "I tried you at work, but they said you were out. Everything okay? Frank didn't show up for his tests."

Liz covers the phone and tells Hook to come back in a few minutes.

"He's gone. I don't know where."

"Oh sweetie. Is there anything I can do?"

"I don't think so."

"What's going on?"

Liz takes a deep breath and searches her heart. "I don't know.

I guess I'm just tired of being possessed."

The reluctant prophet hangs up the phone and takes the plan from the printer. The hint of yellow highlighter bleeds through the page. She turns it over and sees a list of symptoms for something called DLB. Her heart collapses like a sand castle in a sea of sorrow.

# 84

Hook logs on Emisphor and finds a new name adding comments to her journal. Uncleneddie. He's left her a love poem.

*hook shook take a look uncle neddies hott*
*wink pink no time to think*
*you is all i got*
*came home early*
*miss my girlie*
*where'd you get to got?*

Hook squeals delight around the house, runs upstairs to Liz's room and barrels through the door. "You won't believe what happened." She's smiling big and happy.

Liz has been staring out the window at the beech tree. She pushes Frank to the back of her mind and turns on her best listening.

"He wrote in my journal," says Hook. "He misses me."

"That's really sweet," says Liz. "What's his name?"

"Eddie Junior." She says it again to herself.

"You want to call him? You can use the phone, you know." Liz watches herself tumble into mothering and doesn't even consider trying to slow the fall.

"I think I'll just stay online."

"Whatever you want."

Hook's almost out the door when she stops. "What'd you mean by that?"

"By what?"

"By whatever I want." Her question isn't pushy, she just wants to know, but it pulls Liz into a spell of serious thinking. She pats the bed for Hook to sit down.

"I know we got off to a rough start. But it's really nice having you around now." She reaches to touch Hook's hair, stops, pulls back. "What I mean is, you can do whatever you want. You can go home. You can call Eddie Junior. Go online. Stay here. Whatever you want."

*Stay here?* That stops Hook cold.

"Do I have to decide right now?"

All Hook wants is to get back online to look for Eddie Junior.

Hook: got me a boy fiend

Solitude: awwwwww, where you been hook?

Trixiebedlam: tell us tell us

Hook: plus i found miss fancy pants. she's reeli nice

Solitude: yikes . . . did you get a bunch of money?

Solitude: crunch some honey

Trixiebedlam: what about the boy?

Hook: not yet, but i might

Uncleneddie: hey hookster

Hook: {{{eddie junior}}}}

Uncleneddie: where the heck are you?

Hook: chapel hill. long story

Uncleneddie: can i call you?

Hook: brb

Trixiebedlam: so your hooks boyfriend?

Solitude: you hurt hook and i'll kill you.

Uncleneddie: dont worry

Hook: liz says not to give her number out.

Uncleneddie: liz?

Hook: the lady on the radio

Uncleneddie: what radio?

Hook: its nice here

Uncleneddie: kiss nice rear

Hook: miss twice dear

# 85

Walking back to the trailer that afternoon, Luke is mostly relieved that Sergeant Stone had thrown them out of his truck.

"I don't care if he's the next, next, next new Jesus or not," Luke says. "That guy gave me the creeps. Nigger this and faggot that. Disgusting."

"He was changing," says Jesus. "You saw what happened."

"All I know is he had a truck," says Mark. "He could have taken us to Chapel Hill."

"Chapel Hill." Luke spits the town's name like a bitter seed.

"You wanna stay here? It's getting cold, Luke. Even if we don't get the bracelet, we might as well get moving. Go south or something."

"Goeth upon thine hill for that which I have told you stands strong against the night," says Jesus.

Luke scours his memory for book and verse, but can't place it. "Goeth upon thine hill?" he says. "That's not in the *Bible*."

Jesus yucks.

"Dang it, you got me. That was a good one," says Luke, bopping Jesus on the head like a brother. "Now make us up a nice hot dinner."

Jesus folds his hands in prayer. "As the living Father hath sent me, and I live by the Father so he that eateth me, even he shall live by me."

"John six fifty-seven," says Luke.

"There you go with the 'eat me' again," says Mark.

Sinker – known as Michael to the boys – is drunk from an all-day binge with Doug Dipper when he stumbles toward the Airstream that evening. He'd been heading for the beach, but missed a turn and ended up on the backside of the trailer park. Though Luke and Jesus hadn't yet met the sign maker, Mark knows him well enough to smile big when he knocks on the door.

With little in common beyond first initials, it's hard to explain the crazy sparks between the two young men, but it's easy to feel the heat. Luke and Jesus go wide-eyed as the two M's hugged like it had been forever.

When he first connected with Michael a couple of weeks ago, Mark's motives were purely mercenary. He'd stopped by Signs by Tomorrow to see about a banner, and Michael agreed to make the sign for the price of a blow job. But the transaction evolved quickly into a full-fledged crush, the likes of which neither young man had ever felt. They somehow managed to drag the best out of each another, finding simple acceptance with no questions asked. They'd met only three times – always at the store – but that had been enough. When they were together, Michael escaped being Sinker, the dumb-ass brother of Hook. And Mark got to be Markos, a Latin lover and the disciple of no one. They shared a little sex, a lot of dope, and just enough lies to stand each other.

By nightfall, Mark has moved into the Roadliner with Michael, leaving Luke and Gary to themselves in the Airstream. Michael lets Mark take over Hook's room and doesn't even ask for money, he just wants love.

# 86

When Frank doesn't come home that night, Hook asks questions Liz can't honestly answer. "It's them threads," says Hook. She and Liz are in the kitchen eating grilled cheese sandwiches.

"I'm afraid you might be right," says Liz. "Plus he's worried about his health."

The phone rings so hard it feels like ESP. They both know it's Frank.

"I'm at the beach," he says, sounding like he's in the next room. Liz motions Hook to go ahead and eat.

"There's something I need to tell you," he says. "I know you'll think I'm being a hypochondriac, but I'm pretty sure I have this weird disease called Dementia with Lewy Bodies."

"I saw the paper in your office."

The phone line hums, filling a space that's lost for words.

"What do you think?" He sounds farther away.

"I think you should have gone for the tests Sarah scheduled this morning. And I think you're getting carried away like you always do. How many different kinds of cancer have you had over the past fifteen years?"

"This is different."

"How?"

"I wouldn't mind having cancer, but I do not want to have Dementia with Lewy Bodies. I don't want to have dementia with anything. And I don't think I'm making it up. I fit the profile. A little young, so it could take years before I lose it."

"There have to be other explanations."

He's standing on the balcony of their condo, looking out along the curving coast, remembering the Sunday five weeks ago when Liz found the bracelet. "That's a pretty good plan you put together yesterday."

"Rachel did most of it. She knows that Cardinal who called, thinks I should meet him. She said the Catholic Church might want to buy it. He's coming Thursday morning. Are you going to be back?"

"How's Hook?"

"Sarah thinks she has a skull fracture, but there's not much we can do."

They fall silent again.

"Did she tell you she was in our condo?" Frank throws the question like a smoke bomb, and Liz can't see what to say.

"She was the cleaning person," says Frank. "Wrote in the guest book and signed her name with a little hook. She left your hat on the hall tree."

Nothing again.

"Are you okay?"

Liz makes light. "I'm feeling, you know, pretty normal. No animals are talking to me. Or puppets. Like a fog lifting."

"Maybe I should come home."

"I'm worried about you."

"It's okay." His voice has moved away to the other side of the world.

"You've always said you wouldn't want to live if you had some terrible disease. It scared me when you first said it, and it's really scaring me now. Especially since you don't actually know if you actually have some terrible disease."

"It's okay. Don't worry."

"You promise?"

Liz sits at his desk, looking over the collection of ephemera that her husband has become. A slew of diplomas in cheap black frames. Books stacked on the corner of the desk. A photo of her wrapped in a towel on the beach. Another of Frank and his brother, two sad kids in front of a spindly Christmas tree. A sheet of paper with DLB symptoms highlighted in yellow.

Frank has turned quieter than nothing.

"Please come home," she says.

# 87

On most Tuesday mornings, Liz has multiple meetings on her mind. An eight-thirty staff meeting, a ten o'clock planning session, and a noon working lunch for prospect profiling. But today she's dodging Duke again. With Frank safe and at least temporarily sound, she turns her attention to Hook.

"Don't you never go to work?" says Hook, who's been awake for hours. She's reading the comics on the sofa in the living room, a bright blue afghan spread across her lap.

"Good morning, young lady." Liz settles in beside her.

"You do got a job, right?"

"Yes, I have a job. I help Duke University raise money. I told them I wouldn't be in for a few days."

"What's it for?"

"What's what for?"

"The money."

"Mostly to pay salaries to famous professors."

"Do they make a lot?"

"It depends who you ask."

"How much?"

"Some get two hundred thousand. Or more."

"For a professor?" Hook drops the paper. "Damn," she says, catching Liz's eye. "I mean durn."

"I can't complain about my job. I work with some wonderful people. But I'm not having a lot of fun. And I've been starting to wonder if I'm really doing that much good."

Hook gets up and heads to the kitchen. She stops in the doorway and looks back.

"You take time off anytime you want?"

"More or less."

"If I did that, they'd fire me so quick."

"Where do you work?"

Hook got sad. "I used to work at Bobby's Superstore in Beaufort. In the stockroom. I got fired cause I let Bobby Beak see my tits."

Liz isn't sure which path to follow, but dodging the tits seems like a good idea. "Bobby Beak? Is he related to Bill Beak?"

"Bobby's the creepy older brother."

"Do you know Bill Beak?"

"He comes in the store some. They're both worthless in my book."

"I ran into Bill after you fished me out of the ocean."

"Yeah, he works at your condos."

"I told him what happened. With you and Sinker. And I saw him talking to Doug Dipper."

A smile dawns on Hook's face. "So that's how Dipper found out about all this. Ho-ly shit." She covers her mouth to hide the swear.

Liz stretches her arms behind her back, feeling the need for exercise. "Want to go for a walk?"

"Where to?"

"Wherever. Looks like a nice day."

"How long's it gonna take?" Hook eyes the kitchen door. "I'm kinda hungry."

"Let's eat first. After that, we're free. I don't have anything to do today, and Frank said he won't be back till Thursday. Let's have some fun."


The two women walk out the back door later that morning, curving to the west, up the hill behind the house. At the edge of the meadow near Molly's grave, they stop and sit.

"That's where we buried our dog," says Liz. "Over by that rock. She was a dachshund."

"What's a dachshund?"

"A hot dog. You know, a weenie dog. Long body. Short legs."

Hook lights up in a flash of recognition. "I seen 'em on the beach all the time. Happy little dogs."

Memories of Molly splashing in the surf trigger a trickle of tears that Hook can't help but notice. She squirms and looks at the ground. She laces her fingers together and fidgets.

"Sorry," says Liz. "I don't usually get like this."

"No big deal." Hook picks at the bark on a stick as a gust of fall-filled wind climbs the hill, crackling through the beech trees. "I'm kinda used to doing stuff," she says. "Not just sitting around."

"We can go back if you like."

Hook scratches at the ground with her stick. "Maybe we should talk about those durn threads."

Liz waits.

"You really gonna do those things you said? Going on the radio and all?"

"I'm not sure. It was fun making plans, but we'll just have to see how things play out."

"What am I supposed to do?"

"I'm not sure you're supposed to do anything. Just be yourself."

"Who cares about that?"

"I care, Hook." She turns the bracelet on her arm.

Hook throws a dirt clod at a post thirty yards away. She hits it.

"You said yourself the threads are cool," says Liz.

"Nobody cares what I say."

"You'd be surprised. Frank does."

"Frank." Hook puffs. "He'd just as soon beat me with a bat."

"That's not true. He's your biggest fan."

"I shouldn'a killed that snake."

Liz imagines someone eavesdropping on their conversation. Hook's chaotic trains of thought jump tracks without a hint of hesitation.

"This whole business is getting complicated," says Hook. "Doing good, being nice and having fun. How's anyone gonna do all that?"

"I think it's more like a promise. If we can do good, be nice, and have fun, we get to have a life fully filled. Whatever that means."

Hook fidgets even more.

"What's the matter, sweetie?"

Hook looks at her straight. "How come you never answered my email?"

Liz is surprised to find herself surprised one more time. "You sent me an email?"

"When I cleaned your condo for Irene. I found a card with your name and sent you a message."

Liz thinks it through, trying to take the news in stride. "Where was the card?"

Hook blushes. "In your bedroom."

"Oh sweetie. That was an old email address. I never got your message."

"I brung your hat back, too."

"No wonder things are working out so well." Liz leans over and rubs Hook's back like any mother would. "That was my good luck hat."

# 88

With Markos moved into Michael's trailer, the boys settle into something that borders on normal. Michael works days, leaving Mark, Luke, and Jesus to do whatever fundraising they can manage without transportation. They're picking up twenty bucks a day, saving every penny they can to repair the Jeep. With no pool available for the big baptizing, they've focused their attention on a run to Chapel Hill. Another hundred dollars and they'll be ready to roll.

If Michael and Mark weren't such accomplished liars, the dots between Hook and Jesus and Liz and the bracelet might have been easily connected. But that didn't happen. Michael claimed his sister was away at college, and Mark sidestepped the Jesus question with an easy dodge.

"He's not really Jesus," Mark said the one time Michael asked about it. The two were looking at porn on another stolen laptop. Mark had control of the mouse and opened a new website featuring more dicks than you can count.

"Look at the size of these cocks," said Mark, unzipping his pants and freeing his own Doug-Dipper-sized dong. "I got one of those."

# 89

Liz stretches out on her side of the bed, leaving an open space for her missing man. She's talking on the phone to Faye in Richmond. "I guess I feel like I'm not in control anymore," she says.

"You want to know what I think?" asks Faye.

"You're going to tell me anyway."

"Well, for starters, of course you're not in control. Which makes you exactly like every other human being alive on this planet. We live. We die. And in between we have so little control it hardly matters. Shoot, we can't even control what we think."

"You don't have to be mean about it."

"I'm not trying to be mean, just clear."

"Oh, that's clear enough," says Liz. "We live and then we die. Boy oh boy. What fun."

"And along the way, we try like hell to sustain the illusion of control."

"That's ridiculous."

"You'd never say you're in complete control of everything, right?"

"Maybe."

"Well, if you're not in *complete* control, then you're not in control at all. It's like pregnant. You either are or you aren't."

Liz goes stiff. "Well, I'm neither."

"Oh shit. I'm sorry, hon."

"It's okay."

"You sure?"

"It's just that Hook's brought up some mother stuff I thought was long gone. Frannie would have been her age you know. It's been twenty years."

After a couple of long, sad beats, Faye reaches for another subject. "How's Frank doing with all this?"

"Besides running away to the beach?"

"He just needed a break."

"Maybe, but he says he has some new kind of disease. Looney Bodies."

"Dementia with Lewy Bodies."

"You've heard of it?"

"Of course I have. But Frank seems young for that one."

"He said it wouldn't be a real problem for a while. But he also said he wouldn't want to live if he had it."

"He really said that?" Liz can tell she's thinking like a therapist.

"Yep. Back when we were doing living wills. But tonight he said he wouldn't kill himself without telling me first."

"What a guy."

"I'm just glad he's talking at all."

"You want me to come down and help out? I'm free till next weekend."

"We'll be okay."

"I'm happy to come."

"Really?"

"You know how much I love being with you guys. Shoot, I'd move in down there in a heartbeat if you'd let me."

"Frank couldn't stand both of us all the time."

"Are you kidding? He'd love it."

"You think so?"

"He's always wanted to live with two women. Plus you wouldn't have to drag him around everywhere. You could drag me instead."

"Come on then. Let's talk about it."

Faye hears a distance in her voice. "You're not worried about him killing himself, are you?"

"No. Well, maybe. A little. After what happened with his brother. I can't help it sometimes."

"See what I mean about control?"

# 90

On Wednesday, Liz and Hook go shopping. Their trip to the mall materialized because Hook couldn't stand wearing Faye's old clothes any longer. Especially her underwear.

"I don't wanna be mean or nothing," Hook said over breakfast. "But your sister's underpants ain't exactly my style. You all got any thrift shops around here?"

Liz had no enthusiasm for used-underwear shopping. "Why don't we go to the mall and see what we can find. My treat."

The quiet little Civic rolls along the rural roads until it reaches a snarl of traffic on the outskirts of Chapel Hill. The car coasts to a stop beside one of the town's fire stations, where a light blue fire engine fills the driveway and a lump of scrap metal sits on the lawn, passing for sculpture. Her mind brimming with more important matters, Liz shakes off the urge to comment. Four days with Hook feel like a lifetime of comfortable years, and she wants to know more about the young woman beside her.

"I've been wondering," says Liz. "Hook's not your real name, is it?"

"Look at that durn fire engine," Hook ignores the question without embarrassment. The color reminds her of Eddie Junior's boxer shorts.

"They call it Carolina blue. It's UNC's color."

"Where we going?"

"I thought we'd start at Dillard's. They'll have lingerie. Then we can hit a few more stores before lunch."

Liz turns into the heart of downtown Chapel Hill, which borders the UNC campus. She wonders how Frank's doing. Too much is happening too fast. She almost wishes she could stop time, but then she remembers the time-life rule.

Hook squirms in her seat and clears her throat. "Mary Martin." The words creak out barely loud enough to hear.

"Excuse me?"

"Mary Virginia Martin. That's my name. After a woman who played Peter Pan in some old movie. Least that's what daddy said. His uncle was a dancing tree in the show, and he got a crush on her. I hadn't seen the movie, but that's where my name comes from."

"Your name is Mary Martin and you've never seen Peter Pan? Good gracious. We have to stop by the video store."

"Just don't start calling me nothing like that. Hook's what I go by."

The revelation of her official identity cuts something loose in Hook, triggering a tsunami of stories, punctuated by some wild fishing tales. Not wanting to interrupt the flow, Liz takes a roundabout route to stretch out their trip. As they circle past a blur of suburban sprawl, the stories get deeper and sadder. Hook's wrapping up her monologue with the saga of Bobby Beak's final harassment when they pull into Dillard's parking lot.

"I'm glad I'm done with all that," says Hook. She gets out of the car and slams the door before Liz can respond.

Liz sits for a few seconds, feeling Hook's aching heart inside her own tight chest, wishing she knew more about mothering. She follows Hook to the store, digging up all the cheeriness she can find.

"Let's go find some panties, girl."

It would be hard to guess what the two saleswomen at Dillard's cosmetic counter are thinking when Elizabeth Lena Forsythe and Mary Virginia Martin stride up to the snazzy Lancôme display and start sampling the wares. But it's a safe bet they're not imagining big commissions. Rarely will two more unlikely cosmetics customers spend so much time having so much fun buying almost nothing. Liz looks like an old hippy in a loose cotton cardigan over a faded rayon dress, without a speck of make-up. Hook's wearing her worn black jeans and brown sweatshirt, same as always, with the added liability of a bruised face.

"I don't think we're going to buy much," Liz admits after

they've run through the eye shadow and blusher collection. "We're just warming up for lingerie shopping."

"If it's bras you're after, I'm your gal," says the saleswomen named Dottie. The big-busted broad has been busy gossiping with another clerk, but the prospect of selling some expensive lacy things on this slow retail morning pushes her into gear. Well-trussed in industrial strength undergarments, Dottie takes Hook's elbow and ushers her through the store like Peter Pan leading Wendy through the Island of Lost Boys.

"Good thing your mama brought you out today, honey," she says. "If you don't get some support, you'll end up dragging the floor. What size are you, sweetheart?"

"Thirty-four C?"

Dottie stops and turns and takes Hook's left breast firmly in her hand. "Honey, you're a D if you're a day," she says. "And some underwiring wouldn't hurt you none either."

Three hours and two hundred dollars later, Hook proudly carries her purchases out through Dillard's heavy glass doors. A couple of bras, four thongs, a pair of jeans, a royal blue silk blouse, and a twenty-dollar Lancôme Juicy Tube lip gloss.

Hook had needed some convincing to splurge.

"I don't know why you're doing all this." She stood in a dressing room, staring at the full-length mirror, naked except for Faye's old panties and a new Bali bra. Liz sat outside on the chair normally reserved for weary salespeople.

Hook scanned her tattoos in the mirror without much interest, like they might belong to someone else. She noticed the fading outline of an angel drawn on her chest, wondering for the first time whether she really wanted another permanent piece of art on her twenty-year-old body. She dropped her eyes to the pile of new clothes on the floor by her feet. When she bent down to pick up a blouse, she looked under the door, relieved to see Liz's tapping toes a few yards away.

Liz caught a glimpse of Hook's bare feet on the gray carpet and smiled. "You need new underwear. I can afford to buy you some. Which means I get to do good and be nice. And we both get to have fun."

Hook responded by pulling on a rich blue blouse of raw silk and a tight pair of stone-washed jeans. She looked in the mirror, hardly recognizing the person staring back. "That lady thinks you're my mama," she said before she opened the door.

When Hook's green eyes and blue blouse and black jeans came squarely into view, Liz couldn't hold back her tears. She got up and stretched her hungry arms around Hook, pulling her close and hugging her breath away.

"I know," Liz whispered. "I like how it sounded."

After a late lunch, a swirl through the PTA Thrift Shop, and a quick stop at the video store, Liz and Hook head for home.

"What would you like for supper?" Liz glances at the dashboard clock. It's almost four. She feels the pressure of a deadline. Frank's coming back tomorrow.

"Don't matter to me. Whatever's fine."

"How about we order a pizza and watch Peter Pan?"

When she finally lays eyes on her namesake singing and swinging on wires in Wendy Darling's soundstage bedroom, Hook falls into a fit of giggles.

"He ain't nothing but a goofy little girl," she says.

"She's pretty though, like you. Especially with pizza all over your face."

Hook's been struggling with stringy mozzarella, trying to keep the mess off her new silk shirt. Liz helps her out, dabbing at the tomato sauce on her chin with a napkin.

"You don't look so bad yourself." Hook's grinning like a goofball. "Even if you are old enough to be my mama."

The dancing trees are the highlight of the show. "So now you know where your name comes from," Liz says through a yawn. "It's kind of cute."

"What's cute?" says Hook.

"That you'd be calling yourself Hook all these years – though you're actually named after Peter Pan."

"I don't know about that. But I tell you what. It sure does feel like I'm in that Neverland." She rocks to her feet and gathers their plates.

"What would you think about sticking around here for awhile?" says Liz.

"What for?"

"Oh, I don't know. The threads maybe? We can go on those

shows together." She hesitates. "And, well, I guess I just want you to. I'd like it."

"I'd kinda like it, too." Hook's on her way into the kitchen, Liz following. "But Frank won't."

# 91

At five o'clock the next morning, Frank Hunter Forsythe bumbles out of his beachfront bed four hours earlier than normal. He takes a quick shower, shaves, and climbs into his truck for the drive home. Unless he gets stuck in Research Triangle Park traffic, he'll be home by eight-thirty.

…

At five-forty-five Faye Forsythe slides into her Lexus convertible with a thermos of coffee in hand for the three-hour trip from Richmond to Chapel Hill.

…

At six-fifteen Joseph J. Peters awakens alone in his bed and jerks off to some Polaroids of Rachel Rose, who'd made the mistake of telling him about the Cardinal coming to visit Liz and see the bracelet. After dressing in his most preacherly attire, he heads to the Roxboro Road Waffle Shop for two eggs over easy, potatoes with onions, bacon, wheat toast, and four cups of hot black coffee. The good pastor has an early morning party to crash, and he wants to do the Lord's work with a full stomach and a caffeine buzz.

…

At seven-fifty-five, Liz Forsythe smells something fishy cooking in the kitchen and goes downstairs to find shad roe, bacon, toast, and hot tea sitting on the table. Hook stands by the stove in her new shirt and jeans, proud as can be.

…

At eight-twenty-two Frank calls on his cell phone. He's stuck in traffic near the airport and won't make it home until nine. Liz tells him to take his time, not to worry.

...

At eight-twenty-nine, Sarah Stern pulls up to Liz's house, as promised, to check on Hook. She settles in the kitchen for a cup of tea, using up the last of the milk in the refrigerator.

...

At eight-forty-four an ice blue Jaguar races up behind Frank's old truck on Erwin Road, riding his bumper, trying to pass on the narrow, two-lane highway. Annoyed by the tailgating, Frank slows below the speed limit, enraging the Jaguar's bald-headed driver, who eventually passes on a short, straight stretch, narrowly avoiding a head-on collision with a school bus. A minute later, the Jag squeals through a hard right turn and accelerates onto Morgan Mountain Road.

...

At eight-forty-seven, Frank notices he's almost out of gas. He pulls into the Dot 'n' Dash to fill up.

...

At eight-forty-nine, Liz calls Frank to get him to buy some milk. He doesn't answer his cell phone. She grabs her keys for a quick run to the convenience store. As she backs out of her parking spot, Faye pulls up. Liz rolls down her window to say good morning, to say she'll be right back.

...

At eight-fifty-one, Joseph J. Peters' two-ton Jaguar screams around a blind curve on Morgan Mountain Road at sixty-two miles an hour and slams into the flimsy driver's side door of a mist-green Honda hybrid, obliterating the little compact as it leaves a gravel driveway. The Honda's tall blonde driver does not see the speeding car until it's inches from her face. Despite the Jaguar's many advanced safety features, the Preacher's pudgy neck snaps like the neck of a murdered English sparrow.

...

One hundred yards away in the kitchen of a flat-roofed house, three worried women hear a jolting smash outside on the road. Each stops for a split-second to wonder what has happened. The one holding a dish of M&Ms drops to the floor like a wounded angel, banging her already cracked skull against the smooth gray tiles.

...

At eight-fifty-three, Sarah Stern kneels beside Hook to administer cardiopulmonary resuscitation. She unbuttons the collar of her shirt, tilts her head back, pinches her nose closed, breathes into her mouth, and prays.

...

At eight-fifty-seven, Liz's sister Faye dials 911 to report the fall of Hook. The dispatcher says there's already an ambulance going to that address.

...

At eight-fifty-eight, the Orange County deputy sheriff sets a flare four hundred yards east of the crushed cars. As Frank's truck approaches, the deputy waves him down.

"Bad accident," warns the deputy. "Have to ask you to turn around."

"But I live right there." Frank points to the small hill that passes for Morgan Mountain. "My driveway's just around the curve."

"Sorry. Can't let you through."

Frank eases his truck onto the narrow shoulder of the road. A limousine pulls up behind him. The deputy delivers the same bad news to Cardinal Craven and his driver who have stepped out of the limo. Frank introduces himself and says the house is close enough to walk. They begin a minor pilgrimage, with Frank stumbling only twice on the smooth black asphalt.

...

At eleven minutes after nine, the three-person entourage rounds the most dangerous curve on Morgan Mountain Road. Frank sees the back end of a vaguely familiar Jaguar smashed into the driver's side door of an unrecognizable little car. A spew of black smoke mercifully blocks his view. He blinks and the smoke erupts into flames.

# 92

An automobile fire can generate more than one thousand six hundred degrees Fahrenheit, the same temperature at which silver will melt. Neither Liz nor her precious bracelet survive the morning inferno. Nor does Frank. His trembling mind slipped into hiding at the sight of the accident, and not even the combined force of the women at home has been able to coax it out.

Until Jesus calls again.

It's a week after the wreck and Hook's still living with Frank and his Lewy Bodies. Faye asked her to stick around for a few days and Hook figured it would qualify as doing good and being nice. The funeral's over, but Faye had to go home for a couple of days, leaving the widower and the motherless child competing for saddest, wondering what Liz would do to cheer things up.

"Forsythe residence." Frank refuses to take any calls, so Hook answers the phone.

"Hello? I'm trying to reach Elizabeth Forsythe."

"I'm sorry." Hook's words catch in her throat for the hundredth time. "She was killed in a car accident." She says it just like Faye trained her.

Hook hears the caller whisper something to another person. Then he comes back on the phone. "I'm sorry to hear that. We were worried."

"Yeah, well. Whatever. You wanna leave a message for her husband?"

The caller whispers again, but Hook can't make it out. And she's not in the mood for guessing games. She's online with Eddie Junior and she wants to get back to flirting.

"Hey," she snaps. "You want to leave a message or not?"

"Please tell him that I called? Jesus from Jacksonville? It's about the bracelet."

"That bracelet ain't nothing but a durn blob of silver," says Hook. "Melted in the wreck." She hangs up. That makes about a dozen crank calls over the past week, and Hook's sick of it.

Frank comes in the kitchen as she's putting down the phone. "Who was that?"

"Another nutcase."

Frank eyes her like the father Liz wanted him to be.

"Said he was Jesus." She hands Frank a warmed-up bowl of SpaghettiOs. "Wanted to talk about that bracelet. Didn't sound like no Jesus to me."

"Any Jesus," says Frank.

He reaches into his pocket and fingers the lump of silver that was salvaged from the burned-out car.

# 93

Mark insisted they were going nowhere without the bracelet, so the minute they got the Jeep fixed, he was ready to roll. One more call to Chapel Hill and they'd be set. Michael had to work all weekend, so it was a good time for a road trip. Jesus said they should call ahead, which he did. The girl who answered the phone told him Elizabeth Forsythe was dead.

"She hung up on me," says Jesus.

"Of course she did," says Mark. "That always happens when you tell regular people who you are."

"She said our bracelet got melted in a car wreck. That lady got killed."

"Oh my god," says Luke.

"She's lying," says Mark.

"Why would she lie about that?"

"We're going to Chapel Hill," he says. "Tonight."

The two-lane road leaving Sunrise Beach has a curvy stretch through cotton fields where you can see the night sky in all dark directions, except for where the TV tower blights the horizon. Its pulsing white strobes will just about hypnotize you if you watch too long, which is exactly what happens to Mark. It's the Sunday before Thanksgiving and he's driving west toward Chapel Hill. He misses a curve and lands the Jeep on the swampy edges of Nowhere Creek.

The boys manage to escape the slow sinking wreck with their stuff and their brooms, but the car's gone for good. Luke stomps out of the marsh in a huff, brackish water squishing from his shoes.

"Dang it, Mark. What're we going to do now?" He slumps down on the grassy shoulder. His voice says he's ready to quit.

"Ask Jesus. He knows everything,"

"I told you we shouldn't be going after that stupid bracelet," says Luke. "It already killed one person."

"It's ours," says Mark. "Render unto Caesar."

Jesus trudges toward them using his broom like a staff. He sees the lights of an oncoming car and ducks behind a spindly cedar. He shines the flashlight up under his chin, pretending he's a zombie. "Here comes our savior."

# 94

After the call from Jesus, Hook's sense of responsibility for Frank wears thin. She promised Faye she'd help for awhile, but she really wants to see Eddie Junior.

Frank wants a change too. He can't even walk down the driveway to get the paper. The stain of burned oil pumps panic through his brain every time he ventures out. Now he's holed up in his study, where Hook finds him Sunday morning.

"You going to that church of yours today?" She walks in with a cup of coffee and a plate of toast, the beginnings of a morning ritual.

"That was Liz's church. I went along for the ride." Frank doesn't look at her. The memory of hundreds of friends at the memorial service hangs too fresh in his mind. They all wanted to help, but no one could. The day after the service, Frank buried Liz's ashes next to Molly, with Hook, Faye and Sarah as the only witnesses.

Hook blows on her coffee and walks to the window. The bright red maples and yellow sweet gums have faded fast. Another fall is over.

"Speaking of rides," she says.

"Hook, listen."

"Come on, Frankly." She picked that up from Faye. "You and me ought to go to the beach. Hanging around here ain't doing you no good. Besides. I gotta check on things."

*Dogoodbenicehavefun.*

The threads slip into Frank's ears on the laughing voice of Liz. He watches Hook stare outside like a kid on a snowy day. He thinks she's looking for a way to leave him behind. He thinks that might be a good thing.

The two-lane road approaching Sunrise Beach has a curvy stretch through cotton fields where you can see the Milky Way on a good dark night. That's what Hook's babbling about during most of their drive to the beach. She's hanging out the window having fun, yelling the names of constellations, when the truck's headlights shine on two men on the side of the road. Frank swerves in the middle of the Big Dipper, and bangs Hook's head against the door.

"What the heck are you doing?" she yells, louder than she knows she should.

He slows way down. "I almost hit somebody."

"There's people out here?" She twists around to the rear window. It's too dark to see much of anything.

"Two guys on the shoulder."

"Stop and help."

"Stop and help? Are you crazy?"

"It's the middle of the durn night in the middle of durn nowhere. They can't be out here on purpose."

Hook decides at that moment to be a person who always says durn.

Frank stops two hundred yards away and spies the boys in the mirror. "They have a flashlight."

"See if they want a ride."

"Oh come on."

"Durn it, Frank. What about doing good and being nice?"

"What about being stupid and getting killed?"

Hook's used to snotty comments from years with Sinker, so this one is easy to ignore.

"Least you can do is let them ride in the back. Just to Dolphin Golfin' by the bridge."

The men come closer. Three of them now. One's carrying a long stick.

"Lock your door," says Frank.

"Huh?"

"They can ride in the back. Just yell out the window."

Hook opens the door and the dome light comes on. Frank grabs her arm and she spins to face him, fit to kill. They burn stares in each other till he closes his eyes. It's the only time he's ever touched her.

He whispers a wish. "I just don't want you to get hurt. That's all. I'm sorry."

She sees right through his eyes to his cracked heart. She shuts the door and angles her head out the window, yelling for the men to get in the back. She pulls herself in and rolls up the window. The three new bodies rock the truck and, after a few seconds, Jesus smacks the roof. Frank eases onto the road and picks up speed. It's darker than Luke.

When they reach the miniature golf course by the bridge, Hook twists in her seat to get a look at the cargo. There's a face smashed against the glass with its cheeks puffed out and its tongue sliming on the window. She lets out a screech of panic. Frank sees the face, too, and slams to a stop. He rolls down his window half an inch.

"Get out," he yells. "Get. Out."

It's midnight and the boys can't think of anything better to do than climb the Dolphin Golfin' fence and set up camp inside the fake volcano. After Mark and Jesus fall asleep, Luke sneaks to the pay phone at the eighteenth hole to call home. He talks to his daddy, still without a hint of stuttering, and it all turns out like the prodigal son. The old man says he's driving up from Charleston and will be there by sun-up.

The minute he awakens, Mark announces he wants to be Jesus again. He says they need money. He says they have to keep trying to get the bracelet, even if it's nothing but a melted lump.

"I don't see why," says Jesus.

"Why what?"

"Why you're so obsessed with getting the bracelet. Why you want to be Jesus again."

"Because it's ours," says Mark. "And because you suck at being Jesus. You let us get in a wreck."

"You suck at being Jesus, too," says Luke.

Mark does a smart-ass curtsy with a bullfighter flourish. "It's my way or the highway."

Mark's threat gets tested ten minutes later when Luke's daddy drives up to the miniature golf course in a gold Mercedes with a bag of Egg McMuffins and some hot coffee. The old man's in no mood for chit-chat though, and he tells Luke to get his ass in the car right that minute. When Mark smells the cooked grease and eyes the cushy seats, it takes him all of two seconds to open the back door and scootch inside.

"Come on, Jesus," says Luke. "Hop in."

"So you're supposed to be Jesus," says Luke's dad. "You little shit." And before Jesus can answer, he slams the car into reverse, spinning his wheels and spitting gravel all over everywhere.

Jesus stands still for a full minute, watching his disciples scream away. Then he climbs to the eleventh hole by the waterfall. He kneels on the green plastic turf and wraps his arm around a goofy concrete pelican holding a beat-up trash can.

*What's wrong?* he almost thinks.

*There goes the second coming.*

*Are you sure?* he almost asks.

The pelican does not answer. It has said too much already.

# 95

The creepy face in the back of the truck reminded Hook of Sinker, reminded her that she wasn't quite ready to go home. Frank said she could stay at the condo with him. It was clear he wanted her company, and she was happy to go along. They got settled in around two in the morning and fell dead asleep.

Hook gets up early and makes coffee, trying her hand at Liz's unfinished jigsaw puzzle. Frank wakes up scared she might be gone, relieved to find her in the living room.

"Been up long?" He can't believe he's making small talk.

"Long enough to finish three seagulls and starfish." She doesn't look up from the puzzle. "There's sausage. And coffee."

The kitchen's separated from the living room by a counter with barstools. Frank puts three greasy links on a paper towel and settles in to watch Hook work.

She stops puzzling and talks to his face. "What you got planned today?"

"Take you home I guess. Get some groceries."

"You don't gotta take me nowhere. My trailer's not half a mile away."

He imagines Hook's a college girl home for fall break. He stills himself, hoping time will slow and extend her visit. Hook feels him looking for Liz.

"Are you okay?" she says.

"I miss her."

"Me too."

# 96

Jesus lives in the Dolphin Golfin' volcano for three days until the chill of Thanksgiving whistles through his fiberglass cave. He wakes up wondering how the real Jesus spent forty days and forty nights without vending machines. He makes the two-hour hike to the RV park, shredding his feet to pieces.

It's a cool day, overcast with soggy salt air. When he reaches the Airstream, the emptiness of the aluminum shell hurts his heart.

He wanders over to Michael's trailer where he finds Mark's friend crashed in a raggedy recliner, dead to the world. The whole place has lost its edge without Mark's laugh. And sweet Luke's charm.

He smells roast turkey.

"Who's that out there, Eddie Junior?" Hook's leaning over the sink in Eddie Junior's kitchen. There's a man out front sweeping the street, looks like a stoned-out beach bum.

"I got my hands full right now." Eddie Junior's dragging a twenty-pound turkey from the oven with Frank's half-hearted assistance. Layla's pretending to supervise. Zeke's watching football.

"Sure was nice of Big Eddie to get you this turkey," says Layla. "And then you doing all the cooking."

"Didn't have much choice." Eddie Junior isn't complaining, just being honest. "Mr. Forsythe here got roped in, too."

Frank drifts to the sofa and hides behind a tattoo magazine.

"Stop whining or I'll go get Sinker right now," says Hook. They all agreed the brother could come to dinner, but they wanted to delay his arrival as long as possible. "You know you're having fun."

"Whoopee." Eddie Junior spins a finger in the air.

"I guess you'd rather be at JJ's," says Hook.

"Wouldn't bother me one bit," says Zeke.

"Well go on then." Hook blows him a raspberry.

Eddie Junior aims the electric knife at Frank. "You gotta be better at this than me, Mr. Forsythe."

Frank can't make up his mind about Eddie Junior calling him mister. He likes how it makes him a father figure, but not how it makes him feel old. "The turkey needs to set for a while," says Frank, hearing Liz in his own voice.

"Didn't you know that, Eddie Junior?" Hook smooches him a kiss before she pulls on a sweatshirt and heads for the door. "I'm gonna see what this guy's up to."

"Wait a minute," says Eddie Junior.

He's been saying that a lot since Hook moved into his spare room two days ago. She'd knocked on his door on her way home to get clean clothes.

"Who is it?" he'd yelled, still in bed.

"Who you want it to be?"

Then the door flew open and the happiest man she'd ever seen grabbed her like a teddy bear. He kept feeling her hair and her face and her arms to make it real.

"I been missing you, girl." He nuzzled her neck.

"What's the matter, Uncle Neddie?" Hook purred. "You need a little rubbing?" She slid her hand down to his crotch, sending shivers up his spine.

"What're you doing here?"

"I need to pick up some stuff. I'm staying with Frank in his condo for a couple of days." Eddie Junior knew all about Frank from their online chatting. "I guess I ain't quite ready to move back with Sinker."

"Man, you look good. Even with that busted nose." He grinned and slipped a hand under her new silk shirt and squeezed a roll of flesh on her tummy. "Got you a little love handle."

She bonked him on top of the head. "That ain't gonna get you nowhere."

"I got a poem for you," he said.

"You do not."

"I sure as heck do. Come here." He covered her eyes with

his hands and walked her through to the back of the trailer. He bumped up against her butt. She wiggled her hips to show she liked it.

"Ready?"

She nodded and he set her eyes free on the prettiest room you can imagine in a singlewide. Fresh paint, new carpet. Lacy white K-Mart curtains. The latest *Tattoo* magazine on the dresser. A card and two Tootsie Rolls on the pillow. She eyed him over her shoulder, unwrapped a chocolate slug and popped it in her mouth. She pulled it out wet and teased his lips.

"No teeth," she said. "I might want it back after I read this here card."

He took the candy with his tongue. "You're not carrying that dang hook of yours. That's a relief."

She smiled and shrugged and picked up his poem.

*footsie tootsie chewy gooey*
*sweet and yummy fun*
*lick your belly can't you tell he*
*wants you for his one?*

She sat on the bed and cried.

# 97

"Hey dude," says Hook, watching the sweeper from the porch. Eddie Junior's with her, holding a Budweiser. Layla's setting the table. Frank's looking through the window.

Jesus quiets his broom for a second, smiles toward heaven, and goes back to work.

The broom is unlike anything Hook's ever seen. A tall, slender affair with wispy straw woven together using a dozen colors of thread. The handle itself is a gnarly branch of wood with knots and curves that fit the sweeper's hands like it was made for him.

"What's with all the durn sweeping?" yells Hook. "It's Thanksgiving."

Jesus dances a circle round his broom, prompting a long low whistle from Eddie Junior. Hook punches him on the arm and walks to get a closer look at the guy. She's seen him before, but only from a distance. He's her age, though way more worn. His flip-flopped feet carry a hint of blue, his gray-green eyes a hint of sad.

"You wanna eat with us?" says Hook.

"I wouldn't mind," says Jesus.

"What's your name?"

Jesus grinds his eyes with both hands and shakes his head like a dog. He rubs the back of his neck, looking sideways at Hook and grinning.

"Gary."

Thanksgiving dinner unfolds in a thirty-minute frenzy. Eddie Junior gets credit for the turkey and stuffing. Zeke's can of cranberry jelly ties with Frank's bag of potato chips for the most pathetic contribution. Layla's sweet potato pie earns the highest praise because of the burned marshmallows.

During the quick meal, Hook does most of the talking, telling the story of her past few weeks. It goes pretty smooth till she reaches the part about Liz dying. That pushes Frank out to the porch. He doesn't come back for the longest time.

Gary gets up from the table and fills the sink with sudsy water, pulls off his windbreaker, and starts collecting plates.

"You got a nice touch with them dishes," says Layla. "Men don't clean where I come from."

"Thank you," says Gary. He turns to bow and Zeke sees his Jesus shirt.

"I thought I recognized you," says Zeke. He's sprawled in a recliner. "You're that Jesus guy. From Jacksonville." He stabs the air with his finger, but Gary takes it in stride.

"Not me," he says smooth as can be. "I just got his shirt."

"You was with them other two. Sweeping sidewalks."

Gary looks to the turkey for help.

"Leave him alone," says Hook. "Why do you always have to be such a pain in the butt, Zeke?"

"Tell her," says Zeke. "Go on, tell her."

"Sorry man. My name's Gary. Gary Gray." He grabs a curl of burned skin from the turkey platter and crunches it with his teeth. "I know who you're talking about though. He's headed back to Myrtle Beach."

Zeke strains to reason it out. He'd met the boys in a mescaline haze, and the facts are kind of slippery.

"You're lying."

Gary laughs and rests his eyes on Hook.

"I'm no more Jesus than you are, Zeke."

# 98

Faye and Sarah show up at the condo the next day to check on Frank. They'd wanted to come for Thanksgiving, but he said no. It was the first time in ten turkey days they hadn't all been together.

There's no answer when they knock on the door, so Faye uses her own set of keys. They find Frank taking a nap.

"Another place without Liz," whispers Faye. She walks though the condo and looks out toward the ocean, flat and cold under threatening skies. Her sadness surges back.

"Doesn't seem to bother Frank," says Sarah. "He's snoring in there."

"Be nice now. He's depressed."

"So am I." Sarah rifles through the cupboards and finds a dusty bottle of bourbon.

"Make mine a double," says Faye.

It takes an hour before Frank hears their giggles. After a few seconds in the Twilight Zone, he remembers he's at the beach. He remembers Hook is gone. He remembers his wife is dead.

He stretches his mouth to wake up his face. He looks in the mirror and feels a thousand years old.

"Frankly!' Faye pops from her chair when he comes out of the bedroom. She hugs him close and tight, wondering if she's still an in-law now that there's no sister.

"You have to excuse us," announces Sarah. "Faye's drunk."

"I am not," says Faye. "You're the one."

Frank eyes the empty bottle on the counter. "Since you didn't leave enough for me, I think we should all go for a walk."

Out on the beach, Sarah watches Frank through doctor eyes, and he wishes she'd stop. He's handling the sand just fine. Plus he's decided it's time to move on past Lewy Bodies. He might go for cancer again. Or Parkinson's. Or maybe even nothing.

He scans the breakers for finger mullet hanging in the glassy curls.

"You hate walking," says Faye, her cheeks flushed with whiskey and wind.

"Only at high tide," he whispers. "Soft sand hurts my hips." The excuse slips out before he can remember if it's true. A few fat raindrops explode on the beach. He picks up their pace.

"How's Hook doing?" says Sarah.

"She starts housecleaning again on Monday. Holiday season's starting up."

Faye cozies up on his arm. Frank doesn't know if he should notice, and decides not to.

"There she is." He points a hundred yards down the beach. Hook's out, right where she said she'd be.

"Who's that with her?"

Frank squints. "I think it might be Jesus."

Faye pulls him around for some eye-to-eye. "Jesus?"

He pushes her back to walking. "There was this guy at Thanksgiving named Gary. Zeke thinks he's Jesus."

'Zeke?"

"It's a long story," sighs Frank.

"But Jesus?"

"That's what he said."

Frank tries to speed away from more questions. Up ahead, he watches the man who might be Jesus give Hook a hug and hike back over the dunes, leaving her behind.

"Was that Gary?" Frank feels like a father nosing in.

"None a your business." Hook smacks him on the arm. She'd walked down from the dune to meet him by the water's edge. "Yeah, it was him. He was just saying good-bye. He's heading back to Myrtle Beach."

Frank searches the horizon for somebody's shadow. "I thought he made a pretty good Jesus."

Hook laughs and smacks him again.

Faye and Sarah want to catch up on things with Hook, so Frank trudges off to the bathhouse. He's relieved to find the place unlocked. There's even toilet paper on the women's side. He drops his pants and backs up onto the cold black seat. He rests his elbows on his knees and his chin on his hands. He sees a tight swirl of graffiti low on the cinderblock wall. *Do good. Be nice. Have fun. These are the shreds of wife fully killed.*

His heart cracks one more time.

# 99

"You gonna stay here forever?" says Faye. Frank has said he won't go home to Chapel Hill for any reason, so she's come back to the beach for Christmas. They're out on Eddie's Pier, which is deserted except for a few lonely fishermen. It's cold but sunny. Faye's all poofy in her down winter coat. Frank's doing layers these days. Gray sweaters over brown sweaters over khaki shirts over white t-shirts over old man's skin.

"For awhile," he says. "You okay with the house?"

He leans over the railing and spits. Three pelicans glide low across the breakers toward the pier.

With Frank holed up at the beach, Faye has taken up residence in the Chapel Hill home. She'd planned to move in with her sister and brother-in-law for years, but never imagined she'd be there by herself.

"It'd be better if you came home."

"Don't forget to turn off the irrigation," he says. "That pump'll freeze up."

Faye sighs under the weight of chores. Rake the leaves. Inspect the furnace. Change the filters. And now sprinklers.

When the pelicans slide past the end of the pier, Frank closes his eyes and tries to have animal ESP for the hundredth time. The only voice he hears is Faye's.

"You seeing much of Hook?"

"Some."

"Come on, Frank. You have to give me more than one syllable answers."

"O-kay."

She walks away in a snit. He hurries to catch her.

"I got her a laptop for Christmas. Plus high speed Internet for a year."

Faye accepts the apology. She leans and rests her face against his shoulder.

"I have lunch with her every now and then," he says. "She seems happy."

"She's lucky to have a daddy like you."

Frank takes in a salty breath of Faye and fish and fear. He turns his face into the wind, listening for something worth saying.

# 100

Hook: flank got me a rockin new slaptop for xmas. plus hi speed
   cable. woot! he didn't exactly put strings on it but he did say
   i should write more and use better grandma. i might do that
   and i might not. sorry flank.

Grayson: poor flank

Hook: hey gary! you still at moitle breach?

Grayson: i think so

Uncleneddie: grrrrr. ima come in there and eat you

Hook: uncle neddie sounds hungry

Flank: Now children. Do good, be nice, have fun.

Hook: {{{flank}}}

Solitude: chew wood, free lice, bad gun

Justagrl: are you really frank?

Flank: I'd be lying if I said I weren't.

Justagrl: tell us a lie flank

Grayson: sell us a fly crank

Justagrl: are you two living together?

Hook: you two who?

Justagrl: you and uncle neddie

Hook: yeah. except when he pisses me off and i stay with flank

Uncleneddie: you better unlock that door hookster

Hook: whats it worth to you big boy?

Trixiebedlam: take him down hook!

Flank: Time for me to go.

Grayson: shhhh. flank's sleeping

Justagrl: {{{hooks getting laid}}}

Solitude: any body still hear?

Trixiebedlam: jest us

Grayson: us who?
Justagrl: me myself and i?
Solitude: be yourself and fly?
Grayson: see yourself and cry?
Flank: Free yourself and die?
Solitude: sweet screams flank

# FINIS

# JAMES PROTZMAN

James Alexander Protzman had been looking for the meaning of life in all the wrong places – until he found it writing his first novel, *Jesus Swept*. Today he carries that happy knowledge into his work as a blogger and a freelance writer. James graduated from the United States Naval Academy and later earned a masters degree in journalism from the University of North Carolina. He lives in Chapel Hill with his wife and daughter, and is currently working on his next novel.